Mistakenly reported killed by the French in the Peninsular Wars, Edmund, Lord Ashorne, returns home to find that his beautiful fiancée Julia has married his rakish cousin Thomas, heir to the title. Thomas has himself died in Edmund's absence and Julia's younger and quieter sister Anne is now living with her. Anne has always idolised Edmund. To her his return from the dead is nothing short of a miracle. The spoilt Julia, determined to retain her title and her wealth, decides that the simplest course is to marry her ex-fiancé. Must Anne watch them falling in love all over again? Or can she trust her instincts, which tell her that Edmund has undergone a change of heart?

Change of Heart
Margaret Eastvale

MILLS & BOON LIMITED
London · Sydney · Toronto

First published in Great Britain 1981
by Mills & Boon Limited,
15–16 Brook's Mews, London W1A 1DR

© Margaret Eastvale 1981
This edition 1981
Australian copyright 1981
Philippine copyright 1981

ISBN 0 263 73436 6

Set in VIP Baskerville 10 on 10½pt
by Fakenham Press Limited

Made and printed in Great Britain by
Cox & Wyman Ltd., Reading

CHAPTER
ONE

'CHEER up, Julia. The post has come at last!' Anne Wetherly dropped the bulging postbag on to the drawing-room table, not at all anticipating the shock it contained for them both. 'I heard the mail-coach go past this morning and sent a footman along to the Royal Oak directly.'

'Thank heavens!' Julia tossed aside her well-thumbed copy of *La Belle Assemblée*. 'I was beginning to fear that we had lost touch with civilisation for ever.'

She sprang up from the sofa and pounced on the postbag with childlike enthusiasm. Anne retrieved the magazine and, automatically straightening the crumpled pages, watched with amusement as her sister eagerly sorted through the letters. Sometimes it was hard for her to credit that Julia was in her thirties now—nine years older than she was. Often Anne felt immeasurably older than her dainty sister.

Marriage, motherhood—even her husband's death, nearly ten months ago now—had left little mark on Julia's classic beauty. Her sombre mourning garb merely accentuated the frail femininity that made every male hurry to assist her; the black an admirable foil to her ash-blonde hair and flawless complexion. Only the most cruel sunlight betrayed her age, and by now it had become second nature for Julia to sit with her back to the light.

'Isn't it amazing how the bills always seem to thrust themselves to the top of the pile!' Julia complained, casting them aside to investigate the rest. 'Nothing here from that wretched fiancé of yours, my love. I'll give him such a scold when he comes for neglecting us so. We have scarcely set eyes on him all the months we have been penned up here! You haven't been quarrelling with him, have you?'

'Of course not. You know as well as I do that James

appreciates his comfort above anything. You cannot blame him for staying in town while the roads are so bad.'

Julia could—and did.

'If the Mail can get through then so can James. He promised to come three weeks ago. It is too bad of him to let us down. He might guess that it is just as unpleasant for us stuck here in the wilds—at least his coming would relieve the boredom a little. Here's a letter for you from Aunt Mattie.' She tossed it across, riffled through a clutter of invitation cards, then triumphantly dragged out a thick packet addressed to herself in generously flowing script. 'I knew Fanny would not fail me! I don't know how I should endure life here without her letters. They are always bursting with news—all the latest scandals and crim. cons.!'

'It is lucky her husband can give her a frank,' observed Anne, eyeing askance the five sheets her sister was unfolding. 'Otherwise we should be ruined by the post charges.'

'Phoo! It would be worth the expense. To be stuck in this dreary place all winter through is bad enough, but it becomes utterly unbearable when we don't receive a letter for weeks on end!'

'Six days to be precise. You had a three-page epistle from Fanny just before the last snowfall blocked the roads again.'

'Well it feels like six lifetimes!' Julia skimmed eagerly through the first sheet. 'Oh, how I wish we could have been in London this season! Fanny sends the most diverting account of the Grand Duchess Catherine—declares she is at least a hundred and as ugly as sin. She and the Regent loathed each other on sight—well, the meeting must have been an awful shock to them both, to be sure. Fanny says that Prinney is odder than ever—she is convinced that he will end up as mad as his father—and there are the choicest rumours circulating about the Princess of Wales, too delicate for her to specify. Oh it isn't fair! Here we are, cooped up like a pair of crows, missing it all, seeing no one and with nothing to do. And just when I could have been enjoying it most!'

Anne paid little heed to the familiar complaint. The fun-loving Julia had always found it hard even in summer to bear the boredom of country life, but when the London season was in full swing she considered her rural seclusion unendurable;

although even she had to acknowledge that she must observe the proper term of mourning for her late husband. To do anything else would be social suicide, however great the breach that had been between them. But that did not make it any easier for her to accept the tedium.

To make matters worse, this winter had been the most severe Anne remembered, keeping them confined to the house for weeks on end. From London Fanny might write of the delights of the great Frost Fair set up on the frozen Thames, but here in the country deep snowdrifts made even driving to church on Sunday an almost impossible journey, and the few outings that were proper for a widow in mourning out of the question.

Fetching down rusty skates and toboggan from the attics, Anne had thoroughly enjoyed initiating her young nephew into the joys of winter sports. The two of them had spent happy hours swooping across the ice or hurtling into the drifts, but Julia had refused their invitation to join them with incredulous horror. Hunched over the fire with her fashion magazines, she had greeted with disgust their return, rosy cheeked and glowing from the exercise.

Not that a mild winter would have raised Julia's spirits greatly. She scorned such country pastimes as walking, riding or sketching, declaring that she felt truly alive only in the bustle and confusion of balls, routs, theatre visits and all the other excitement of a London season. Anne understood, though she did not share Julia's love of town life. The social scene bored her—perhaps because there she always walked in the shadow of her more beautiful sister. While Julia yearned for London she was perfectly happy attending to the running of the house, amusing Kit, or taking solitary walks with the deerhound who now sat quietly at her side.

'Only ten more weeks and you'll be out of mourning,' she reminded her sister soothingly. 'And it is not fair to say we see no one. I'm sure all the neighbours have been amazingly kind and attentive.'

Indeed, she reflected, every unattached male in the district—and a fair number of the married ones too—came regularly on various ingenious pretexts to offer their services to the beautiful young widow who combined fragile loveliness with a respectable jointure. Came quite unnecessarily, as Julia had a competent steward to attend to her business problems. Although Anne had never liked Weston, she had to admit that he performed his duties efficiently. The estates ran smoothly under his care.

Even so the hopefuls came. Julia's welcome encouraged their frequent return. When Anne protested that this keeping open house would cause gossip, her objections produced only sulks and an accusation that she was jealous—quite unfounded criticism, as she had as little interest in them as they had in her. She doubted whether any of the callers even noticed her presence except as an inconvenient obstacle to the *tête-à-tête* they craved with their idol.

Anne knew that Julia had received at least two eligible offers to change her state, but even in the boredom of this mourning year Julia was too exhilarated by the sense of freedom widowhood gave her to be tempted into another marriage yet. She was impatient to taste its benefits on a wider scale.

'Ten weeks is far too late,' she replied petulantly. 'The season is all but finished then. All the fun will be over. If Thomas had to break his stupid neck, then why couldn't he have chosen a more convenient time to do it?'

Julia's heartlessness on that subject had long ceased to shock her sister. In part, Anne sympathised. Despite its romantic beginning the marriage had been far from happy. Even before his son was born Thomas had been unfaithful, and his *affaires* had soon become more frequent and public. At the time of his death he had been driving hell for leather along the winding country lanes to impress his latest mistress, who had been thrown out of the phaeton with him.

Amazingly, Julia had sought her out and handsomely compensated her for the injuries she had sustained in the accident. Having herself first-hand knowledge of Thomas's single-minded persistence when in pursuit of any object, she declared in answer to all criticism, she did not blame the girl in the slightest. Her only complaint about the entire incident was that she had to observe the customary year of mourning for a man she had long ceased to love or respect. That she bemoaned loud and often. Nothing Anne could say would reconcile her to it.

'Even if you miss this season there will be others,' Anne now reminded her soothingly, but her sister was not to be cheered.

'It is all very well for you to talk so airily. *You* may have plenty of time. *My* years are slipping away too fast for me to squander one. Here I am—twenty-eight already...'

'Thirty-one,' Anne corrected her without thinking. 'I was twenty-two in December and you are nine years older than me, so ...'

'Why must you always be so horridly exact,' complained Julia with an angry pout. 'It is not in the least feminine nor polite to take people up so sharply. Anyway I am only thirty at the moment. I shan't be thirty-one till next month!'

Crossly she returned to reading Fanny's letter. Anne opened her own, ignoring the shriek of horror that Julia let out as she scanned her last sheet. Accustomed by now to Julia's dramatisation of trifles, she presumed Fanny's pug must have fallen sick or an expensive new bonnet been spoiled in the rain. Anne concentrated on trying to puzzle out the crabbed writing that crossed and recrossed the single sheet from their aunt, commenting wryly.

'Perhaps Fanny's extravagance has its merits after all. Aunt Mattie leans too far the other way in her thrift on our behalf. I think she is asking to come and stay with us this summer, but whether this word is 'Julia' or 'July' I cannot determine. It is so mixed up with the other line as to be indecipherable. Do look and see if you can make it out.'

She stopped abruptly as she realised that Julia was still staring in horror-stricken silence at the last page of Fanny's letter, her face as white as the paper she clutched.

'Whatever is the matter, Julia?'

The widow's cornflower blue eyes were wide with shock. 'Edmund!' she whispered. 'Fanny has seen Edmund!'

As Anne stared unbelievingly back at her, she laughed wildly. 'Yes, Edmund Claverdon! Lord Ashorne!'

Anne, conscious of the treacherous lurch her heart still gave at the name, forced herself to remain calm. With only the faintest tremor in her voice she declared, 'Nonsense!

Fanny is just the sort of silly creature to imagine she has seen a ghost.'

'But it wasn't a ghost,' shrieked Julia. 'He's *alive*! He wasn't killed in that wretched battle as we all supposed—only captured by the French and imprisoned.'

'How could he have been alive all this time without anyone knowing?' Anne was still incredulous, not daring to accept so fantastic a tale. It would be too cruel to believe it then have her hopes dashed again. 'Is Fanny quite sure?'

'Positive! She wasn't able to speak to Edmund herself, but she sent her husband to the Home Office to ferret out the details and there is not the least doubt about it. Edmund is alive.'

'But why haven't we heard before?'

'It seems that at first he was too badly injured to give his name to his captors and when he recovered and tried to send word all the messages about him were lost. Fanny's husband says things are so chaotic there that it isn't at all surprising. But whatever the reason, he was freed when our forces advanced and overran his prison camp. As the war is all but over now, he has sold out of the army and has come back to England. Fanny unsealed her letter to be first with the news. Says she *expects I shall be interested in it*, spiteful cat! For all the treacly phrases I can tell how she is revelling in the situation. She was always one to delight in other people's misfortunes, even when we were at school. Whatever shall I do!'

Anne found it hard to concentrate on anything but the irrational thrill of excitement that surged through her at the thought of Edmund being alive after all. Her heart pounded unbearably at the realisation that she would soon see him once more after she had supposed him lost for ever.

Impatiently she told herself that Edmund had never had eyes for anyone but Julia. Anne had known that he would never return the childish passion she had once felt for him herself, doubted if he even knew of it. She was ridiculous to allow herself to give way to her emotions in this silly manner. All that was over and done with years ago. Edmund's reappearance could make little difference to her, but still her heart throbbed painfully.

With an effort she forced herself to think rationally.

'We must make arrangements to leave here as soon as possible, I suppose. Edmund must be longing to return to his home without further delay. He always loved the country more than London.' One of the things they had in common, she remembered wistfully.

Her sister stared blankly back.

'*Leave here?* But why should we?'

'Because if Edmund is really alive then Ashorne is still his home, not yours,' Anne explained patiently.

'But Thomas inherited it and left it to Kit and me.'

'That was all a mistake. If Edmund was only captured, not killed, then the estate must still be his. You can check with your lawyer if you don't believe me, but you will find I am correct. How could it possibly be otherwise?'

'All Edmund's!' Julia's voice rose to a shriek. 'Then what am I supposed to live on?'

'There is the money Papa left you for a start . . .'

'That pittance! It wouldn't keep me in gloves.'

Anne, who found that her own lesser share of their father's wealth amply covered all her needs, ignored that petulant comment and went on smoothly.

'Then there is Thomas's own property. All that he owned before he inherited the Ashorne titles and estates—or rather *supposed* that he inherited them. Melthorpe Hall will still be yours, and all its lands. You will have to live there again.'

'Go back to that poky little hovel after living in this beautiful house?' shrilled Julia, scarlet with fury. 'I couldn't bear it. I should be stifled.'

Anne thought fleetingly of all the times Julia had complained of the inconvenience of traipsing the endless corridors of what she then termed '*a gloomy barn of a place*'; of her regular annoyance when the dishes arrived at the table lukewarm after their long journey from the kitchens to the dining-room. But she knew it was useless to remind Julia of these faults now. Instead she contented herself with observing,

'You liked Melthorpe Hall well enough when you were first married. I am sure you will soon get used to it again. It is fortunate that you never got round to letting it as you intended. Perhaps it may need some attention after lying empty for so long, but we can put the work in hand immediately. It shouldn't take too long. Does Fanny say when we may expect Edmund?'

'No.'

'I expect it will be a while yet. Edmund is bound to have business to attend to in town; his reappearance must cause many problems that will take time to unravel. On the other hand Fanny's letter may have been delayed by the bad weather.'

Julia glanced anxiously at it.

'Lord, yes!' she wailed. 'It is dated a week ago and the postscript concerning Edmund only one day later, so he may arrive at any time to cast us out into the snow!' Seeing her sister's involuntary smile, she amended this irritably. 'Don't tell me! The snow has all melted now—out into the floods, then. That is equally nasty.'

'I can hardly believe Edmund will have changed so greatly as to do that. He may have been impatient at times, but never heartless. I am sure he will guess how difficult it will be for you to revert to being plain Mrs Claverdon again without expecting you to leave, all in a minute, what has been your home for nearly five years.'

'Plain Mrs Claverdon!' echoed Julia indignantly. 'I will *not* be anything of the kind. I shall insist on being addressed as Lady Ashorne still. Surely no one could expect me to give up my title as well as all the rest. It would be too cruel!'

Fervently Anne wished that she had not raised the subject, but the truth had to be faced sooner or later, unpleasant though Julia might find it. Perhaps it was as well to get all the shocks over in one.

'I fear that they will. That title is reserved for Edmund's wife. Unless in the peculiar circumstances they allowed you to call yourself the Dowager Lady Ashorne, but you would hardly enjoy that, would you?'

'Lord, no!' Julia shuddered dramatically. 'I could not endure it. *Dowager* is such a horribly ageing expression. Poor Sally Painswick put on twenty years when her son took a wife and everyone made such a point of the Dowager whenever they spoke of her. I'm convinced that to be rid of it was the sole reason for her second marriage to that insipid baronet.' Her face cleared miraculously. 'How stupid of me! Of course, that is the solution. I must marry Edmund. After all, we were engaged before he went to Spain. I expect he has returned with every intention of honouring his promise.'

For a moment this airy suggestion took Anne's breath away. Recovering, she ventured, 'Don't you feel that he might consider your eloping with Thomas broke the engagement?'

Reproachful blue eyes chided her as Julia replied soulfully, 'One cannot mourn for ever! Edmund will not condemn me for trying to grasp a little happiness when I supposed him lost to me for ever.'

'Perhaps not but if I remember rightly you married Thomas a full month before Edmund was reported missing.'

'There you go again!' complained Julia bitterly. 'Always so aggravatingly precise about details. Sometimes I think you are more of an old maid than Aunt Mattie! You may be too cold-blooded to understand how one can be carried away by one's emotions, but I am sure that Edmund will be more sympathetic. I was so lonely and upset about his being torn from me that I didn't know what I was doing!'

Anne could not imagine anyone, even her sister, marrying the wrong man in a fit of mental abstraction, but knowing that it was useless to argue with Julia in this mood she remained silent. Julia went on hopefully:

'And perhaps Edmund will not have heard about my marriage. After all, he never received the letter I wrote explaining it to him. That was returned to me unopened after he was presumed dead. Could we not keep the whole thing secret?'

'And how, in that case, would you explain away Kit?' enquired Anne drily.

'We could say he was *your* son. No!' she decided regretfully before Anne had recovered sufficiently to express her opinion of this preposterous suggestion. 'We'd never get away with that. Too many people know the truth. We couldn't hope to bribe them all to be silent. And it wouldn't explain how we came to be living here at Ashorne. Oh, why was I so stupid as to marry Thomas!'

Anne had often wondered the same thing. She remembered their aunt's despair as Julia had flirted her way through five successive seasons without showing any sign of especially favouring any of her suitors. She had turned down any number of eligible offers till at last, when Aunt Harriet was ready to wash her hands of her, Julia had attracted the attention of Edmund Claverdon, shortly after he had inherited the Ashorne title and fortune.

The young cavalry officer, allowed home from duty in Canada to deal with the legal formalities of his inheritance, had fallen head over heels in love with Julia and she had seemed equally enchanted with him. After a whirlwind courtship they had become engaged. Anne had not really been envious then. Deep in the throes of calf-love, she had been content to adore her idol from a distance. She considered it perfectly natural that he should want to marry the sister she admired almost as fervently.

With the wedding date fixed for early October Edmund was unexpectedly posted to the Peninsula, upsetting all Julia's plans. That then, after she had been fortunate enough to attract someone, who in her sixteen-year-old sister's eyes had seemed the embodiment of all the story-book heroes rolled into one, Julia should throw all consideration to the winds and run off with Edmund's middle-aged cousin, had been difficult for Anne to understand—then or now.

True, Julia had been furious at Edmund's refusal to abandon his military career for her sake. When he had begged for an early wedding before he sailed, she had turned a deaf ear to the plea, obstinately clinging to her plans for a huge society celebration. Which only made it the more amazing that she should elope a few weeks later with Thomas, who was nowhere near as eligible or attractive a match.

Perhaps something of this showed in Anne's face now because Julia added defensively,

'I know you have always thought it odd of me, but I was so horribly depressed at the time that I didn't know what I was doing. It was all very fine for Edmund! He was full of heroic fervour and got all the glory of dashing off to fight for his country. No one considered how dull it was for me, left behind to wait for him. I was so dreadfully bored, and

Thomas could be enormous fun when he wanted. He hadn't let me see the other side of him then. Somehow he persuaded me to run off with him. It all seemed that it had been for the best when Edmund was reported dead, so soon afterwards and I became Lady Ashorne after all. But now it turns out it was all a take-in! It is too provoking. Who would have dreamed that Thomas, safe at home, would be the one to die and Edmund, out in the thick of battle, would come home to wrench his title away from my darling Kit?'

'Losing his title will scarcely bother Kit,' observed Anne, thinking it safer to ignore the rest. In a passion Julia often said more than she meant. 'His sympathies are totally radical at present. His keenest ambition is to become a postillion.'

'That is what comes of letting him spend every spare minute with the stable boys,' retorted Julia. 'I wish you would not encourage him to waste his time with them. Whatever he may feel on the subject now, later on he will realise the value of the position he has lost.'

'I doubt if he will repine even then. He is a most resilient child. Anyway, there is no immediate cause for gloom. At the moment Kit is heir to the title. Unless Edmund has a son of his own Kit will still inherit.'

'That's true,' Julia's face brightened, 'and when we are married I shall take good care there are no children. I'm not such an innocent as I was six years ago. I don't intend to go through that lowering process again. It utterly ruined a whole season for me—quite as bad as being in mourning! I am sure Edmund will not expect it of me. I am sure my little Kit will be proud to inherit Ashorne when Edmund passes away.'

'At the moment,' Anne reminded her tartly, impatient of Julia's selfish scheming, 'we should be planning for Edmund's arrival, not his departure. How awkward it is all going to be! Do you wish me to explain matters to the servants and arrange for Melthorpe Hall to be set to rights, or would you rather do it all yourself?'

'No, don't do anything yet,' exclaimed Julia quickly. 'Let us leave everything of that sort until Edmund gets in touch with us, himself; wait until we know what he intends to do first.'

'But we must make some plans. He'll think it is so odd if we do nothing,' protested Anne.

'Why should he? Who is to know we have heard of his return?' demanded Julia.

'Fanny, for a start.'

'She won't say anything if I ask her not to. I know too much about her goings-on with that hussar for her to dare.' Julia rummaged through the rest of the mail. 'There is nothing here from Edmund. Not that I expected it. He never enjoyed writing letters—even when he first went to the war I got only one measly sheet a week from him. We'll pretend we have heard nothing when he arrives. Let him make the first move. There is more chance of his remembering the affection he and I used to have for each other if he finds us settled here when he arrives. Out of sight, out of mind, they say.'

Anne was silent. That had certainly proved the case with Julia, but she doubted whether Edmund had been equally fickle. From what she remembered of him six years ago his nature was more steadfast. He would not have forgotten as easily as Julia—unless, she thought, suddenly doubtful, she had idealised his character in her daydreams.

In the intensity of an adolescent passion, had she endowed her idol with virtues he had never really possessed? That would have been easy enough to do when Edmund was dead and unable to return to shatter the image she had built up of him; gradually adapting her memories to fit the dream personality she had wanted to dwell upon. Would she be disappointed in him now he had come back?

It was an uncomfortable idea. In an odd way Anne felt cheated by this unexpected return. After Julia's marriage, the Edmund of her secret fantasies had seemed to belong to her alone. Now, Anne realised with a stab of regret that his homecoming must take him away from her.

His memory had been exclusively her concern for so long that it was hard to accept that once he was back with them his interest would be in Julia again as before—though whether his affection, if it had lasted, would survive the shock of the news of her marriage was another question. Julia's betrayal might cost her dear.

'When Edmund does turn up you'll have to see him for me

first,' Julia continued, clearly untroubled by any such doubts. 'You can explain how it came about that I married Thomas. Tell him I was so distraught—so young that—so... Oh I don't know what, but I'm sure you can think of something. You've always been far cleverer than me.'

'I will do nothing of the kind!' snapped Anne. To her annoyance she felt her eyes fill with angry tears. 'I'll have no hand in deceiving him. Tell your own lies if you must!'

After one astounded gasp Julia was overcome with remorse.

'To think that I had forgotten! You were madly in love with Edmund yourself before he left, weren't you? I remember now how we used to laugh at the way you mooned after him. Like a love-sick calf he said. How could I have been so forgetful? I'm sure you cried more when they said he was dead than I did myself. I had supposed you recovered from that foolishness years ago, but of course it must be you who has been putting the flowers on that ridiculous stone Thomas insisted on setting up in Edmund's memory in the churchyard. Downright hypocritical, when Thomas never liked him and rarely lost a chance to serve him an ill turn. I told him it was pointless when we had no body to bury under it, but Thomas was always obstinate. Now it turns out Edmund was alive all the time it makes the whole thing ludicrous, doesn't it? But surely, my love, it isn't on Edmund's account you have been wearing the willow all these years, is it?'

'Of course not. That was just a childish infatuation—over long ago!' protested Anne, appalled at the casual reference to the secret she had cherished so long, imagining it unsuspected by anyone. It had become a pleasant ritual to put out the flowers, but she had not realised Julia had noticed.

It was certainly untrue to say that she had allowed Edmund's memory to prevent her from forming an attachment to any other man. She was not that foolish. No other man she had met had measured up to her remembrance of Edmund but she had always thought of him as an ideal not a possible lover—a standard against which to measure her suitors. Not that many of those had remained interested in her after they met Julia, she reflected ruefully.

To be fair, Julia had had no intention of stealing her sister's admirers. It was just that after they saw the two of them together, no one could help noticing that, attractive though she was, Anne's hair was a little less delicately golden than Julia's, her figure less dainty, her complexion browned by careless exposure to wind and sun. Few considered Anne's greater intelligence and keen sense of humour an advantage. Only youth was on Anne's side, and her age was scarcely a handicap to Julia yet.

'I am relieved to hear you aren't still nursing that absurd passion, because it was always me Edmund was crazy about,' Julia went on, blithely rubbing salt in the wounds. 'He considered you a silly child. Don't get any false hopes about his return! I wouldn't want to see you hurt, but I won't brook any interference. I am determined to have him. Just you wait and see, he'll be eating out of my hand by mid-summer.'

'You are welcome to him,' snapped Anne. 'I think you are forgetting that I have been engaged to James for over a year now!'

'Engaged, but not married yet. Oh I know you put the wedding off on my account,' she added, anticipating Anne's protest. 'Don't think I'm not grateful. I don't know what I should have done without you, but if you have been as wildly in love with James as I was with Thomas you'd have let nothing prevent your marrying him immediately.'

'Then perhaps if our affection is more temperate it may last longer!' retorted Anne crossly. The amazing news Fanny had sent must have upset her more than she imagined, she reflected wryly, to make her snap at Julia's foolishness like this. Or was it her knowledge that Julia was right for once, in assuming that by accepting James she was accepting second-best, which was disconcerting her?

She had never pretended any violent feeling for James, and he in turn had appeared well content with the genuine affection they felt for each other, not asking for anything stronger. James had been part of her life for years now, seeming to change little through the whole time she had known him.

Sixteen years older than Anne, she had viewed him as a sort
of extra uncle during her childhood. Then in the bitter
months after her father died he had been a great comfort.
Indolent and pleasure loving though he was, James had
rallied round the daughters of his old friend. Julia, securely
settled then with husband and child, had not needed his
support so badly but Anne accepted it gratefully. She did not
realise at first how close it drew them.

She had been surprised, even shocked when he proposed,
and had refused him. Later she let him persuade her to alter
her decision. Even so, although she had warned him then
that she felt only affection not love for him, she had supposed
his feelings to be warmer towards her, and it had rankled a
little when he agreed so readily to her plan of postponing
their wedding after Julia was widowed. It would have been
more flattering if he had protested, even given a grudging
consent instead of urging her to wait as long as she deemed
necessary, to stay with her sister until Julia was totally
recovered from her loss.

'You do well to scold me. Such a transient flame mine
proved to be!' Julia declared soulfully. 'Perhaps after all, my
heart was true to its first love.'

Which was not Edmund, Anne told herself tartly. Julia's
first love was, and always had been, Julia. Fond though Anne
was of her attractive sister, she had always recognised the
basic selfishness of Julia's nature.

'Don't build your hopes too high,' she warned her, 'six
years is a long time.'

'I can make Edmund forget them,' Julia told her
confidently.

Beside Anne the dog shifted and growled in her throat as
footsteps sounded in the hall.

'That must be Weston. I asked him to call this morning,'
Julia exclaimed, clearly relieved at the interruption. 'Not a
word to him about all this, mind! Let everyone think
Edmund's arrival, when it occurs, as great a shock to us as to
them.'

Anne was not happy at the deception, but on the other
hand she did not wish to help Weston. She preferred to have
no more dealing with him than was absolutely essential. She

had never liked the steward. It was probably her antagonism transmitting itself to the dog that made the normally placid animal uneasy and aggressive whenever he approached.

She had to hold Bess's leash firmly as Weston came in, beaming the overfamiliar smile she resented and hurrying to grasp Julia's hand a shade too enthusiastically. Not that Julia appeared to think so. She fluttered her long lashes and greeted him with a delighted, 'Phillip! Just the person I most wanted to see!'

'I am flattered, my dear Lady Ashorne. How may I serve you?'

As he bent to kiss Julia's outstretched hand, Anne saw his glance slide across to note her own reaction to the extravagant gesture.

'I *must* have some more money, Phillip! My sister has just reminded me that I shall be out of mourning shortly, and I will need a new wardrobe then. Everything I used to wear must be horribly out of fashion by now. I don't want people to think me a dowdy!'

She cast a mischievous warning glance at Anne. So that was it! Julia meant to milk the estate of all she could before it was taken from her. Anne almost intervened in protest, then weakly decided against it, unwilling to argue with her sister in front of the steward.

Weston laughed as incredulously as he had been intended to.

'A dowdy! You, Lady Ashorne! I could not imagine it. But you are right to demand the best. The perfect jewel deserves the most precious setting! I am sure we can manage something. We cannot have you outshone by any of those other London belles—not that any of them could hold a candle to you whatever you wore!'

As ever, his manner grated on Anne. It was always that shade more familiar than she deemed necessary. There was rarely anything in his conversation she could positively object to, but always behind the words lay that hint of impudence.

Perhaps the fault was as much Julia's as his. She certainly made more of the handsome young steward than Anne felt proper, and presumably he hoped to profit by her partiality and played up to it. It was fortunate that Julia was too hard-headed to be seriously affected by his attentions.

Cynically Anne reflected that the problem might solve itself when he discovered that Julia's prospects were so radically altered by Edmund's reappearance, but she would not provoke Julia's wrath by telling him of it now.

'Don't you agree with me, Miss Wetherly?' Weston continued blithely. 'We must have your sister looking her best when she returns to grace the social scene once more.'

Bess growled again as Anne replied curtly, and she made the animal's restiveness her excuse to leave them to their business. Julia evidently had no need of her, and Anne wanted solitude to sort out her troubled thoughts. What would be the outcome of Edmund's unlooked-for return? Was his love for Julia strong enough to last the years of separation and the shock of her marriage?

For her part Anne longed to see him once more, yet dreaded it too. After six years of building up an idealised memory in secret she did not want to run the risk of finding that her idol had feet of clay. Nor would it be easy to watch him being enmeshed in Julia's toils once more. Julia's casual reference to their laughing together over her childish devotion had hurt her bitterly. She would never let them guess how long the foolishness had persisted.

Of one thing she was quite adamant. She would *not* be the one to tell Edmund of Julia's marriage—the one to make Julia's excuses for her. She could not bear to see the hurt that disclosure must surely cause him. Nor would she willingly live here with them, to see Julia worm her way back into his affections. She had to remain a while—it would be impossible to leave them alone here, unchaperoned—but she was determined to make arrangements immediately for an alternative home for her sister and herself.

Melthorpe Hall was the obvious choice. Despite Julia's scorn it was a beautiful mansion, dating from Queen Anne's reign. Not as large as this, but surely that only made it more suitable for a widow with one child than this huge manor? Anne loved Ashorne, but that did not make her blind to its disadvantages. It needed the fun and bustle of a large family to animate its echoing rooms.

Whatever Julia might say Anne intended to go across at once to Melthorpe Hall and discover the state of affairs there. It was within easy reach. From time to time Julia had spoken vaguely of getting a tenant for it, but nothing had ever been done. Anne would make that intention the excuse for her interest. She would ride over now, this very day, to inspect the house and set any necessary repairs in progress.

Resolutely she turned back to the drawing-room to demand the keys. Julia dare not raise any objection in front of Weston. Her hand on the doorknob she hesitated as Weston's voice came from within low with fury: 'Be damned to the money, Julia! Listen to what I am saying. We can't go on this way! You must tell her!'

Julia's silvery laugh tinkled out.

'Now, Phillip, don't be tedious,' she replied lightly, 'I've told you we must wait a little longer.'

'Don't try my patience too far!' The menace in his voice made Anne shiver. 'Or I might be tempted to reveal a few more secrets that you would prefer to keep hidden.'

CHAPTER
TWO

'THERE it is at last, Jonas, Ashorne! Isn't it as beautiful as I've always told you?'

Edmund reined in his black horse at the top of the hill and proudly pointed out to his groom the green valley spread below, at its head an extensive mansion of mellowed brick. Originally the retirement home of an Elizabethan mariner, rich from exploits in the Spanish trade routes into which his descendants preferred not to enquire too closely, the manor had been added to by successive generations in a clutter of styles that nevertheless blended into a harmonious whole.

Perhaps it might not appeal to the classical purist, but it was very attractive to Edmund's eyes and very dear too. Doubly so as in the past six years there had been many times when he had despaired of ever seeing it again.

'Fairish place,' conceded Jonas with Northern caution. 'Tidy bit of farmland too. Graze a goodish number of beasts, I'll warrant.'

'The best in England!'

'Bar Yorkshire,' declared his groom, automatically but without much conviction.

Edmund grinned broadly back at him. 'I've already told you that you may return home if you can't bear to settle in the south here.'

'Nay, sir, what's the use? My folks are all dead and gone now. There's nowt to go back for. I've looked after you for nigh on six year and I'll not desert you now. This'll do me. It may not be Yorkshire, but it's a sight better than those rubbishing Frenchy lands we're just come from!'

Edmund nodded sober agreement.

'Don't mention them in the same breath. It's good to be home at last.'

He gazed round in contentment at the green buds bursting

free from the spiky hawthorn hedges. Already the birds were busy gathering stuff for their nests. The first primroses were thrusting their yellow heads into the bright spring sunshine. All around everything seemed to be burgeoning into new life as if to celebrate his return. Only a gleaming sheet of water across the meadows on either side of the stream below, reminded him of the snow that had so lately covered the landscape. He spurred his horse on in a sudden fever to reach his destination.

'Come, Jonas, no dawdling now we are so near. We take the path down and across the stream. That willow on the far bank is where I used to fish when I was a boy and could manage to get away from the schoolroom. Many's the trout I've landed there.'

'Aye, I reckon we'd best press on, Major. There's a nasty cloud coming up behind us that threatens a downpour. I told you we ought to have come in the carriage.'

'And been shut up inside it for hours on end! I'd rather be soaked a dozen times. Haven't you had your fill of being caged in, Jonas?'

'Sorry, Major, I was forgetting. Being a prisoner was harder for the likes of you than for me. I got pushed into a factory when I was a nipper for twelve hours a day. Not much light or air for us there. Th'army was a rest cure after that, and even the Frenchy prison not too bad. It didn't chafe me to be locked up like it did you.'

'I think it was only the thought of all this waiting for me that kept me sane for all those years,' admitted Edmund soberly.

Of Ashorne and Julia, he added inwardly—but he must not think of Julia now; must not waste time hoping that, against all reason, she had remained true to him.

As so many times before, he put a hand to his pocket to touch the miniature that had been his consolation throughout his captivity. His captors had seized its jewelled frame, but with Gallic sympathy for romance had allowed him to keep the portrait it contained, which in his eyes had been infinitely more valuable.

Throughout his long incarceration Julia's dancing blue eyes and teasing smile had cheered his cell. For six years he had pored over her picture, using up the endless hours in day-dreaming, planning their future in a thousand different ways. It had been difficult to remember in that dreary period that time was not standing still for Julia too.

It was only on his return to England that doubts began to torment him. It had been frustrating not to be able to seek her out at once to set his mind at rest, but his own affairs must wait a little longer. Before he sought Julia out he must settle matters with the poor woman who dwelt in the house below, unaware of the blow fate had dealt her—Thomas's widow. It would be too cruel to let her hear of this extraordinary tangle only from rumour while he was busy with his own concerns. Much as it irked him, he had to deal with her first.

Edmund had often wondered in those long-drawn-out years how things were going at Ashorne in his absence. He had fretted helplessly over what confusion might ensue, but never in his wildest imaginings had he envisaged a state of affairs such as met him on his return to England. How could he have supposed that everyone might think him dead?

When, before that fateful battle, he had lent his spare tunic to Harry Ashburton, whose own kit had been lost somewhere on the long march across country, neither of them could have foreseen what confusion the simple action could cause. It had not even been a major engagement that day—just one of the minor skirmishes. Yet after it Ashburton lay dead, his corpse so mutilated that only the papers in his pocket identified him—Edmund's papers—while Edmund himself had been taken prisoner, suffering from a head wound that made remembrance of those early days hazy.

If it had not been for the efforts of Jonas, captured at the same time, he might never have survived, and the mistake would never have been discovered. But he had recovered and returned home at last to find himself officially dead; to discover that Thomas had, nearly six years ago, succeeded to his title and lands.

Which, he reflected, must have delighted Thomas who had always been envious of everything his cousin owned. Edmund would not have minded upsetting Thomas by his return but to dispossess his widow was a different matter. It appeared there was a child too though fortunately, from what the lawyers said, he was too young yet to understand what he was losing.

The lawyers had offered to write on Edmund's behalf to explain the tangle to the supposed Lady Ashorne but he had refused, feeling that this was something he must sort out himself and do it face to face, not by an impersonal letter.

It had seemed simple enough in London, he thought ruefully, to decide that by seeing Thomas's widow himself he could break the news more gently, could set at rest any fears that she might be left destitute. Now as he neared the Manor it seemed less straightforward as, for the first time, he wondered how he was going to set about the task.

Men he knew and understood after his years in the army but he had little experience of dealing with women. Suppose the poor creature had hysterics? He still had an uncomfortable memory of his helplessness in face of Julia's terrifying outburst of sobbing and screaming when he first told her of his posting abroad—innocently expecting her pride and delight to be as great as his own. Not that he blamed her—women looked at these things very differently. It had been foolish of him to break the news so baldly. All the same he had been heartily glad of her young sister's intervention to calm Julia down. But for Anne's help he did not know how he would have coped.

Julia had begged his pardon later and he had readily forgiven her but he could not forget the incident nor his inability to deal with it. Would there be anyone at the Manor to help him cope with the distress Thomas's widow was bound to feel. Already bereft of her husband she must find the loss of her home and lands a stunning blow. Small wonder if it precipitated an even more violent reaction than Julia's had been.

For a moment his courage failed. He checked but immediately urged his horse on again. Now that he had come this far he must not give up. With Ashorne so close he could not bear to turn back without seeing it once again; and more than that, he knew it his duty to go on. The confusion they were now in was none of the widow's making. He had to ensure that she understood that although he took his estates back from her, she would not be left wanting. Poor woman! She had suffered enough in being left widowed with a young child after so short a marriage. He must treat her as generously as he hoped anyone else might deal with Julia were she in the same plight. Only then would he feel free to pursue his own interests.

In front of the familiar porch he dismounted and gave his reins to Jonas.

'The stables are through that archway. There is bound to be someone about to help you deal with the horses, but mind what you say. Let them think us ordinary callers as yet. I don't want any wild rumours circulating before this poor woman has had time to recover from the shock of my news.'

The dour north-countryman sniffed his contempt of the injunction.

'I hope I know by now how to keep a still tongue in my head. Shall you be wanting the beasts again today?'

'Yes, I imagine so. We'll need to ride down to the village later and rack up at the inn there for a while. We must give the widow time to arrange her affairs, and I cannot expect a stranger to take us into her home without warning.'

He stood for a moment in the porch running an affectionate hand over the great lion's-head knocker that had hung there as long as he could remember. Nostalgia overwhelmed him. Behind him towered the great beech tree he had scaled so often as a boy. Just the faintest tracery of leaves clothed the huge branches that would be hidden in foliage in a few weeks. Nothing had changed here!

Then, chiding himself for dawdling to put off the evil moment, he took a deep breath and knocked loudly.

The echoes rang round the great hall inside. Soon Edmund heard the thud of the butler's footsteps as he walked slowly to answer the summons. When the door opened Edmund, set to greet Wickford, saw with a shock that it was a stranger confronting him. Wryly he reflected that although things might remain static, people continually reminded him of the passage of those six lost years.

Of course Wickford had been well into his sixties when Edmund left home, and already was ponderously slow. Thomas, with little time for sentiment, would have had no compunction about replacing him. He must seek out the old man and make certain he had been given an adequate pension for his years of service.

Suddenly he realised that Wickford's successor was still holding the door open, impassively awaiting his instructions. Resolutely he stepped inside and asked for Lady Ashorne.

'I fear that her ladyship is out at present, sir.'

Edmund stopped in dismay, not having anticipated this setback. His concern must have shown in his face for the butler went on smoothly, 'I believe, however, that Miss Wetherly is at home if you wish to speak to her instead, sir.'

Julia! The relief that flooded through him was so tremendous that he did not stop to wonder what she was doing here at Ashorne. Julia would be able to solve his problem of explaining matters to the widow, quite apart from the fact that her presence here would save him more weeks of agitation while he sought her out. He had dared make no enquiries before, lest his resolution to deal with Lady Ashorne's affairs first weakened. Thankfully he exclaimed,

'That would be even better. Please ask Miss Wetherly if she will be so kind as to spare me a few minutes.'

Miss Wetherly! His heart sang the name over again. So, after all, Julia had remained unmarried as he had scarcely dared to hope. In a few moments he would see her once more. His pulses quickened at the thought. Exasperated, he saw the butler was still lingering.

'Who shall I say wishes to speak to her, sir?'

Edmund hesitated, knowing how swiftly gossip would spread through the servants' hall into the countryside around if he gave his correct title. To delay its start, spare Thomas's widow, cushion Julia's shock, he temporised.

'Tell her that it is Major Claverdon—a relation of the late Lord Ashorne.' Which was true enough, though not quite as the man might suppose.

'Very good, sir. Will you wait in the library?'

Impatiently Edmund followed him. He seethed while the portly butler stalked away with maddening slowness. Why could he not hurry, this red-faced stranger who had taken Wickford's place? Had not sufficient time been wasted since he saw Julia last? Edmund listened tensely as the footsteps plodded down the hall, bracing himself to meet Julia once more. What would she say? How would she react to his sudden reappearance? Could it be possible that her love had remained as unchanged as his?

Unable to keep still, he paced the room. Even in his agitation he noted the alteration there. Foolish to resent the fact that a thick red carpet now covered the oak floorboards, or that rich velvet curtains took one's eye away from the leatherclad books, but he could not help regretting it. After feeding on his memories of Ashorne for so long it was disconcerting to find the reality changed, even in such minor ways. What alteration, he thought in sudden panic, would he find in Julia?

Anne had taken advantage of her sister's visit to the local dressmaker to make a thorough onslaught upon the linen stores. She was determined, whatever Julia might say, to have everything in perfect order for Edmund's return. It would be difficult enough to arrange matters and make a fair division of the household goods, without finding everything higgledy-piggledy and in need of repair.

So for the past week a startled housekeeper had found herself embarked on the earliest and most thorough bout of spring-cleaning she had undertaken for years. Already Anne had whisked her through the kitchens and china store, sorting and cleaning things that had lain untouched for years. Now they had turned their attention to the upstairs rooms.

Here were the same signs of lack of a proper care. Everything was clean and neat enough, but clearly there had been no overall system in the management of the stocks. Julia paid little heed to her household duties, and her careless attitude had in turn made the servants slapdash in their approach; knowing that their mistress had interest only in those parts of the manor she used herself, they neglected the rest. Anne was unfolding some sets of linen that she judged from their yellowed creases to have been part of Edmund's mother's trousseau when the butler interrupted her.

Her heart thumped so wildly as she listened to his message that she thought he must hear it. She knew this Major Claverdon must be Edmund. So he had come at last!

'I told him that her ladyship was out so he asked to speak with you, miss.'

For a brief panic-stricken moment Anne was tempted to deny herself but she realised what a strange impression that would give—enough to cause the sort of comment she most wanted to avoid. After all, she had to meet Edmund some time. Perhaps it was better to get it over at once. With an outward calm masking her inner ferment, she replied,

'Thank you, Stone, I will come down directly. Have the maids wash these sheets, Mrs Norwich, and put them into use in the guest rooms immediately. It is criminal to see them lie here going to rack and ruin.'

Only a faintly heightened colour betrayed her agitation as she smoothed down her gown and hurried downstairs. After all those romantic fantasies long ago of greeting Edmund's return in a breathtaking ball gown, she was in her oldest work dress now as she went to welcome him. Her hair was dusty and she strongly suspected that there was a smut on one cheek. She rubbed anxiously at it then stopped shyly in the library doorway, gazing at the tall figure awaiting her there.

It had grown more difficult over the years to recall Edmund's features, but now that he stood before her she could recognise the slight alterations. His dark hair was as thick as always, his eyes as keen. Though thinner after years of deprivation, he held himself as erect as ever he used. With a rush of pity she saw that those six years had etched lines on his handsome face, making it sterner, less carefree. But despite the differences there was enough resemblance to her childhood hero to make her pulses throb, however calm she had determined to remain.

'Edmund?' she faltered.

He moved eagerly towards her, hands outstretched to grasp hers. Then, in a daze, she saw his expression alter and, as in those foolish day-dreams of so long ago, she watched his eyes light with passion, felt his arms close about her. He bent to kiss her with all the pent-up longing of six lonely years.

His touch was more thrilling than she had ever dreamed. Anne felt the delight flood through her as for one heart-stopping second she responded with an eagerness that equalled his.

Then as sanity returned she tried to pull away. Even before he raised his head to murmur, 'Julia, it has been so long!' she had realised his mistake.

Scarlet with shame at her stupidity, she struggled free, exclaiming in panic, 'No, you must not!'

'Forgive me, Julia,' contritely he released her. 'My coming has been too great a shock for you. I should not have been so sudden.'

'You certainly should not!' she retorted fiercely. 'You ought first to have made sure of your facts. I am not Julia!'

'Not Julia? Oh my God! But who...?'

His dismay was even more infuriating than the error.

'I am Anne Wetherly, of course!' she snapped quivering with mortification.

'Anne? But Anne was only a child when I left.'

'That was six years ago, Edmund. Things change.'

'Not things—it is only people who change,' he said regretfully. 'I beg your pardon, Anne, but you looked so like Julia standing there that I lost my head. I can see now that you are not she. Forgive me! I hadn't meant ... But the butler said *Miss Wetherly* not Miss Anne, so I naturally assumed it was Julia he spoke of.'

'Obviously! But I am Miss Wetherly now, and have been so ever since Julia married.'

'Married?' he echoed dully.

The pain in his eyes at this blunt announcement hurt Anne. Illogically it made her lash out at him.

'Yes, married! Did you imagine that Julia would remain single all this time? Are you so arrogant that you expected her to mew herself up like a nun when for six years we have supposed you dead?'

'Of course not,' he protested, but knew this was not entirely the truth. Although in countless nightmares he had watched Julia walk down the aisle to meet some shadowy stranger, in his waking hours some small part of his being stayed confident that she would wait for him. Common sense had warned him that Julia would be exposed to more temptation than he was—there was little scope for unfaithfulness in his prison cell—but, poring over the miniature that smiled so warmly back, he had assured himself that she would remain true.

Even when he discovered that everyone believed him dead, a spark of optimism had lingered. It was hard to have it finally extinguished. Bleakly he went on, 'Don't let us quarrel, Anne. I am sorry I treated you so unmannerly. Please forgive me.' He smiled briefly. 'I am sure you will not hold one kiss against me! If I remember rightly you used to have some fondness for me once.'

Furious at the reminder, Anne hardened her heart. She might have been betrayed into foolishness once, but she would not be so weak again. Remembering Julia's tale of their laughing together over her folly, she retorted icily, 'You need not suppose I am so silly now. That was when I was younger and less discriminating, more . . .'

'Polite?' he suggested as she searched for a word.

With a gasp of fury at the forthright comment that she secretly had to admit was justified, Anne exclaimed, 'I did not have a very good example shown me in that respect, did I? Was it polite of you to liken me to *a lovesick calf*? You need have no fear that I will moon after you now in the manner that so embarrassed you then.'

'Is that what rankles? You are putting the blame on the wrong shoulders. That phrase was Thomas's, not mine. I valued your affection too much to mock it. But come, Anne, we cannot fall out over what happened six years ago. You say your sister is married. Whom did she . . .?' Anne's heart sank as he broke off and she saw realisation dawn in his face. 'Of course, it is Julia who is Thomas's widow. It is she I have come to see on this unhappy errand.'

Anne nodded unable to speak. Wryly she reflected that fury had lead her to do all that Julia had wished. Without stopping to consider, she had given the impression that it was Edmund's death that had caused her sister's lack of faith. How long would it be before he learned the truth?

'My God! What a coil!' groaned Edmund. 'I came here expecting to deal with some middle-aged stranger. That seemed a harrowing enough prospect, but this is far worse. How can I face Julia? I knew that Thomas was always jealous of my good fortune, but *Julia*! How could she have married him—and so soon after I was captured? The lawyers told me the child is no longer a baby. How old is he?'

'Four,' Anne admitted. 'He will be five this year.' She coloured as she saw him realise the implications of that. Now that the truth was out she wished that she had been less bitter.

'So she was married even sooner than I supposed. I could barely have been reported missing then. And to Thomas of all people!'

Even then Anne could not bring herself to tell him the whole truth. How long it would be before he discovered it, she could not tell, but she would not be the one to shatter his last illusions. It would be too unkind.

'After all her promises I would have thought she might have waited a little longer,' Edmund murmured brokenly, then with an effort checked himself. 'Yet who am I to guess how shock will affect other people? Julia was never strong enough to live alone.'

Again his words pricked at Anne's conscience. Was she wrong to let him go on in this mistaken belief? Unaware of her silence Edmund went on: 'And how will she bear this new shock? Perhaps after all it is a·blessing that I met you first, Anne. You must break the news to her.'

Despite all her objections Anne found herself weakly agreeing, unable to withstand the appeal in his eyes. She knew it was foolish to go on deceiving him, but now she had gone this far there seemed no way of extricating herself from the tangle of half-truths. She must go on with the charade.

Perhaps fortunately, her sister saved her from this new problem. Exquisite in her most becoming black silk gown—which she had certainly not been wearing earlier on—Julia hurried in looking fragile and lovely.

'What is this Stone tells me of one of Thomas's relations enquiring for me, Anne?' she exclaimed anxiously, then stopped abruptly as he swung to face her, breathed, '*Edmund!*' in a husky whisper, swayed and fell gracefully towards him, clutching at his arms.

Even Anne would have thought the swoon natural had she not noted the adroit manner in which Julia contrived to twist herself round as she fell so that the light shone safely over one shoulder, not directly on to her face.

Edmund was completely taken in. Clutching Julia's limp form in his arms, he looked helplessly at Anne. She was sorely tempted to leave him to cope alone, but his distress touched her unwillingly. As, yet again, his eyes implored her assistance over Julia's drooping head, she indicated the sofa.

'Put her down there, Edmund.'

While he endeavoured to lower her gently Anne glanced round. A jug of water standing on a side table suggested an excellent chance of revenge. She handed it to Edmund, advising him blandly, 'I think if you pour some of this over her it should revive her.'

That would teach Julia to play her silly tricks! Edmund was uncertain. 'I don't think I ought . . .'

'Nonsense,' Anne declared briskly, considering it just what Julia deserved. 'It is the ideal treatment for the vapours. Move away, if you won't do it, and let me.'

As she anticipated, her sister's eyes fluttered open before she could carry out her threat.

'Edmund, is it truly you?' Julia faltered.

'Of course it is. Forgive me for not warning you, Julia. I had not realised that you were the Lady Ashorne I had come to meet, or I would have taken more pains to prepare you for the shock. I had expected to see a stranger.'

The ardour with which he had mistakenly greeted Anne earlier was gone. His voice was expressionless now, his face unreadable. Anne watched uncomfortably. Poor Julia! Pray heaven she never learned of the error Edmund has made; she would never forgive her sister. If it had been Julia clasped in his arms a few minutes ago, everything might have turned out as she intended. Julia would have known how to turn his weakness to her advantage.

But there was no hope of a return to that mood at present. Shock had driven all thought of romance from Edmund's head. Now the knowledge of Julia's marriage and all its implications lay between them.

Anne could not determine whether she was glad or sorry at the turn events had taken. She was truly unhappy to see Edmund so bewildered, yet at the same time could not deny a

secret satisfaction that this time Julia's wiles had not succeeded, that for once she had been unable to make a suitor
dance to her tune.

Anne's own feelings were still chaotic. That kiss had stirred her more than she liked, rousing longings she knew could
never be fulfilled. Julia would make sure of that. From the
sofa Julia frowned at her and jerked her head meaningfully at
the door. Anne heartily wished that Edmund had not come
back to confuse her so cruelly. She was about to make an
excuse and leave him alone with Julia, as her sister clearly
wished, when Kit burst into the room.

'Mamma! Did you fetch the toy soldiers as you promised? I
need them for . . .' He broke off as he saw the tall stranger
beside the sofa. 'Who is that, Anne, and what is the matter
with Mamma this time?'

'Hush, love, she has had a shock. A pleasant one but still
upsetting.' Anne tried to explain simply. 'This gentleman is
Lord Ashorne—your papa's cousin. We thought that he had
died in the Peninsular war, but we were wrong.'

Kit considered this information for a moment then
pounced on the salient point.

'How can he be Lord Ashorne, when Mamma said I was
after Papa died.'

'I am afraid that we were all mistaken. It is difficult to
explain, but . . .'

'You mean that I am not a lord any more?'

'I'm afraid not, love.'

'Good!'

Anne was too startled by the satisfaction in his voice to
comment but Julia sat up furiously, demanding, 'Whatever
do you mean, Kit? Don't you want to be Lord Ashorne?'

'Of course not! I don't want to have my head chopped off!'

'Whatever is the wretched child talking about?' exclaimed
his mother fretfully.

'When the Revolution comes here like in France, they'll
cut off all the lords' heads,' explained Kit. 'I didn't think it
was fair. After all I never asked to be a lord, but now it'll be
his head, not mine.'

'I don't think either of you needs to worry, love.' Anne's
amused glance met Edmund's over the child's head. 'I fear

that some of Kit's stable friends are a trifle radical in their sympathies.'

'It wasn't the stable boys who told me that,' Kit objected indignantly. 'It was Weston.'

'The steward,' said Anne in reply to Edmund's unspoken query.

'Then he should know better. He had no right to frighten the child with such tales. Shall I dismiss him?'

'No!' exclaimed Julia sharply. 'It was a joke. Nothing more!'

Her voice was shrill with panic, and uneasily Anne remembered the conversation she had overheard. Weakly she had put it out of her mind to concentrate on the preparations for Edmund's homecoming. Now she wondered whether she ought to have investigated further—tried to discover what hold Weston had over her sister. She was beginning to suspect it was stronger than she had supposed.

Misunderstanding Julia's distress, Edmund flushed with embarrassment.

'I beg your pardon,' he apologised in stilted tones. 'I had not meant to remind you of your awkward position in that unmannerly way, Julia. Please forget what I said. I will leave you now and return when you have had time to recover from the shock of my reappearance.'

'But you cannot mean to go already,' exclaimed Julia. 'Not when I am just growing accustomed to the idea you are alive again. Tell him he must stay, Anne!'

'Indeed he must. After all, this is his house, not ours.'

'But I cannot thrust myself upon you in this way. I fully intended to put up at the inn till everything could be settled. I will go there now.'

'That will not be necessary,' Anne told him. 'We have a room ready prepared.'

'For Anne's fiancé,' Julia put in quickly. 'He was due to arrive some time ago, but he has been delayed by the bad weather.'

'Or the good company in town,' said Anne with a smile.

'But won't he be annoyed to find me taking his place when he gets here?' protested Edmund.

'Of course not. You have a far better right to any room here than James. This is your home. If anyone moves out it should be us. I'm sure Julia agrees with me.'

'Naturally I expect you to stay here as long as you need,' Edmund told them awkwardly.

'Always so generous!' murmured Julia. She frowned warningly at her sister as Anne declared,

'We will not need to trespass on your hospitality for very long. In a few weeks Melthorpe Hall will be fit for us to move into. It is being made ready now.'

She had forgotten Edmund's quick brain, his ability to draw accurate conclusions from the slenderest clues. Apprehensively she met his suspicious glare as he demanded,

'How is it that you are so well prepared? Did you know that I was coming, after all?'

CHAPTER
THREE

ANNE could only stare back speechlessly, horribly conscious of the piercing scrutiny that seemed to bore straight through to her brain. Six years dwelling on Edmund's virtues had allowed her to forget the less comfortable aspects of his make-up—of which this disquieting ability to ignore the details, and pounce on the underlying truth which one least wished him to see, was the most disconcerting. It had effectively demolished many an attempt at evasion in the past.

How should she reply? She could not lie to him; nor could she tell the truth and show up her sister's foolish sham. Julia would never forgive such treachery, and Anne feared she had already unwittingly done enough harm to her sister's cause. Why had she let Julia thrust her into such a position?

From the sofa Julia glared at her, hastening to retrieve the situation herself. 'Of course we did not know!' Her conscience was less tender. 'How could we learn of it when we have been snowed up here in this wilderness for a month or more?'

Edmund still looked far from satisfied, and Anne tried to pull her scattered wits together. Hastily she contrived an explanation which was accurate if not the entire truth.

'You startled me taking me up so fiercely, Edmund! I suppose that I thought of the Hall so readily because I have been busy there for some time now. Julia wanted to have it renovated so that it could be let, but I have been making all the arrangements on her behalf. We had not got as far as advertising for a tenant yet, so to move there ourselves seemed to me to be the ideal solution to this problem. I have often thought that Melthorpe Hall would be a more suitable home for the three of us than this great mansion, and now it seems events have made it a necessity. The repairs are going well and I think ...'

'It seemed wicked to allow such a lovely old place to go to rack and ruin!' interrupted Julia, casting a look of burning reproach at her sister. 'I felt that despite all the difficulties we must endeavour to make it habitable once more. Not that I dreamed I should be forced to return there myself. Living here we have grown accustomed to much more comfortable surroundings, and the Hall has been left derelict for so long . . .' Her voice tailed off despairingly.

'Naturally,' Edmund hastened to reassure her, 'I shall expect you to remain here until everything is made perfectly ready at Melthorpe Hall or wherever you decide to settle, however long it may take, I don't mean you to suffer from this damnable muddle.'

Julia darted a look of triumph at her sister then, turning back to Edmund with a brave smile, risked a show of reluctance.

'You are too generous, Edmund. We should not want to intrude on your privacy here.'

'There is no question of intrusion. I shall be delighted to have your company—or if you prefer I will go back to London until . . .'

'No!' protested Julia sharply. 'You must stay!' Her voice softened again to a caressing murmur, 'We will be more than happy to share your home with you if you are sure that we will not be a burden.'

'How could you ever think that?' One lingering glance took in her exquisite face, raised trustfully to his, then he turned briskly away. 'Now that is all settled, if you will excuse me I must go and see that my horses are stabled. I told my man to have them ready to ride to the inn later, so must tell him our plans are altered.'

'Shall I show you the way?' offered Kit eagerly.

Edmund smiled down at him.

'I think I know my way well enough even after six years' absence, but you may come to introduce me to your friends in the stables if you wish. Some of them are bound to have changed even if the buildings have not.'

Kit led him proudly away, chattering excitedly. Immediately they were out of earshot Julia rounded furiously on her sister.

'What were you trying to do, Anne? Ruin my chances? I thought you'd really let the cat out of the bag with your cut and dried plans to move to Melthorpe. Then when Edmund grew suspicious you stand and gape at him like a ninny. Are you mad—or merely malicious?'

'I'm sorry. I know we were expecting him, but when he turned up so suddenly I was disconcerted.'

'So I noticed! What had been going on between you and Edmund before I got back?'

'Nothing,' lied Anne, but as she remembered that kiss and her instinctive response to it, her cheek burned with shame. Edmund had said nothing, but surely he was bound to have noticed her eager acceptance of his embrace. What must he have thought of her? She dare not let that momentary madness overtake her again.

'There must have been something,' Julia persisted. 'I could feel the tension in the room when I came in!' She eyed her sister's heightened colour with suspicion. 'You haven't any foolish ideas of stealing Edmund from me, have you?'

'Of course not!'

'I hope that is true. I'll brook no interference with my plans.'

'And I intend none. I've told you before, that childish infatuation was over long ago.'

'I suppose I must believe you. Not that I could credit that you'd be trying anything in that dreadful rigout! What have you been doing in it? Sweeping the chimneys?'

Anne looked down at the shabby gown, doubting whether Edmund had even noticed it.

'Only turning out the linen-room. You cannot imagine what a muddle it was in! There were great piles of things years old and quite untouched. I've told Norwich to put some into use at once. There's enough there to furnish ten houses, not two, but it still has to be sorted through to determine what is yours and what Edmund's.'

'You can forget all those silly details,' Julia told her impatiently. 'The question of division won't arise. I've already told you that I intend to marry Edmund.'

'Is he to have no say in the matter?'

'He won't raise any objections,' said Julia confidently.

'Didn't you see how agitated he was at meeting me once again? He hasn't forgotten what we used to be to each other. It won't take long for me to persuade him that our marriage is the obvious solution to the whole problem. I won't let you or anyone else stand in my way.'

'What about Weston?' Anne was stung into retorting. 'What will he think of this plan? He appears to be adopting a very dictatorial attitude to you lately.'

Her sister paled.

'Good lord! I was forgetting. Weston won't have heard the news yet. I must send word at once to warn him of Edmund's arrival.'

'Why?' demanded Anne. 'He'll hear of it soon enough. If anything isn't in order then that is his own fault. Why should you worry about Weston?'

'You don't understand!'

'I think I am beginning to, Julia. There is something odd going on between Weston and you, isn't there? What is it? You aren't in any kind of trouble?'

'Trouble? Gracious, no!' Julia laughed scornfully. 'What do you take me for? Some silly little servant girl who has been seduced by the footman?'

'Not that sort of trouble. It is just that when I accidentally overheard you talking the other day, I imagined that Weston was in some way threatening you.'

'Then stop imagining things. There's no need for any more eavesdropping. I can deal with Phillip Weston.'

Julia sounded confident enough, but Anne was not satisfied. Remembering the angry exchange she had unwittingly overheard, she knew there was something afoot between her sister and the steward. She was not as sure that Julia could cope alone as the other seemed to be. Weston's manner then had been horribly menacing. Although Julia might be unwilling to accept help or advice at present, Anne determined to watch how the situation developed. Things should not go all Weston's way if she could prevent it.

It might be interesting to see the steward's reaction to Edmund's arrival. It was unlikely that even Weston would have the impudence to come to the house today, but they were bound to meet him at church tomorrow. Julia had been in the habit of inviting him back to dine with them after the service. Her sister disapproved of the arrangement and the familiarity it encouraged, but Julia had never consulted her feelings so she had to accept it. Weston had begun to expect the invitation as his right; presumably he would be waiting for it tomorrow. Would Julia extend it?

Anne was not looking forward to the ordeal of encountering all the friends and neighbours who were bound by then to have heard of the upset at the Manor. Julia had no such qualms. Despite her sister's protests, she blossomed out in one of the newly purchased gowns for the occasion, a blue silk gown trimmed with deeper blue lace. It suited Julia's dainty figure to perfection. Though the bodice was too tightly fitted for Anne's taste, a matching silk redingote concealed that for the present. Blue kid gloves, a fur trimmed bonnet and enormous fur muff completed the outfit. Anne felt positively dowdy beside her in last season's muslin and a sensible dark cape.

'If they are going to talk about me I might as well give them something worth talking about,' Julia declared airily, when Anne had questioned the wisdom of choosing this occasion to cast off her blacks.

'But won't they think it odd? Half-mourning might have been wiser. It isn't quite a year yet.'

'Phoo! What do I care for the opinions of a parcel of country bumpkins? I'm tired of that dreary black and they all know Thomas didn't care a fig for me, nor I for him!'

'They'll say that you are setting your cap at Edmund.'

'Let them! They won't say it to his face, so what's the harm?'

Julia totally ignored the ripple of curiosity that ran through the church as they entered, though Anne was uncomfortably aware of it. While she sat embarrassed in the high-back pew feeling that all eyes were boring through to them, speculating the consequences of Edmund's unlooked-for return, Julia beside her appeared perfectly at ease. At the far end Edmund looked equally unconcerned.

The service ended at last, and again they ran the gauntlet of curious onlookers. Once in the churchyard, many people came over to congratulate Edmund on his safe return. While they stood waiting for him Weston hastened across to greet them. Julia acknowledged his bow coolly and turned to present him to Edmund, who surveyed him with some astonishment.

Weston had, as ever, taken pains with his appearance. His fair hair was combed into the latest style; his white-topped boots gleamed spotlessly. His pale primrose pantaloons and elaborately knotted neckcloth were far finer than was usual for a steward to wear. But despite the care he had taken to present a gentlemanly appearance, to Anne's critical eye, Weston's coat with its nipped-in waist and exaggerated collar looked fussy beside the military elegance of Edmund's more soberly cut but perfectly fitting one.

If Weston's dress was suspect, however, his manners could scarcely be faulted. He was careful not to betray the over-familiarity he normally used towards Julia. If there was any censure Anne could level, it was of a faint obsequiousness that was perhaps excusable in one anxious not to offend his new master.

'You appear very young to be in so responsible a job, Weston,' Edmund observed with a slight frown. 'Stoneleigh was the steward when I left. What happened to him?'

'Oh he grew too senile to be borne!' declared Julia. 'He would not agree to a thing I asked. It was most provoking. So after Thomas was killed I asked Weston to take complete charge of both estates. After all, he had been doing the lion's share of the work for years. I knew him capable, as his father had always handled Thomas's Melthorpe estates and had trained Phillip to follow him.'

'I trust, my lord, that you will be gracious enough to allow me to continue to serve you in the same capacity. I feel sure that her ladyship will vouch . . .' began Weston, but Edmund cut him off brusquely.

'This is neither the time nor the place to discuss business. Come to see me tomorrow at ten and we can go through the accounts and discuss your position then. Good day.'

He turned back to Julia and so missed the furious scowl that darkened Weston's face at this summary dismissal, but Anne noted it. So, she suspected from her sister's heightened colour, did Julia. Weston lingered a few moments longer, clearly expecting Julia to extend the customary invitation to dine with them. Instead, tucking her arm in Edmund's, she began an animated conversation with him, totally ignoring the steward. Weston was forced to turn on his heel and walk away under the amused gaze of the other parishioners, amongst whom his supercilious manners had never been popular.

Anne hoped that Julia knew what she was doing. Weston's pride had been wounded and she fancied that he would make a bad enemy. It might be unwise to drop him so haughtily after indulging his pretensions so long.

She turned back to find that Kit, who had been fidgeting impatiently at all the delays, was tugging at Edmund's sleeve and trying to persuade him to follow across the churchyard.

'Do come and see this!'

'No, Kit! Don't tease Lord Ashorne!' she protested sharply, guessing his intention, but she was too late. Kit was already laughingly dragging Edmund over to the tall stone column that stood beside the lych gate, a bunch of withered snowdrops at its base.

'See! It says *Sacred to the memory of Edmund, Lord Ashorne.*' Kit pointed out triumphantly. 'That's you, isn't it?'

'It is indeed.' Edmund bent to read the rest of the adulatory inscription then straightened with an amused smile. 'I had not realised what a worthy fellow I was! Thank you for showing it to me, Kit. It was most illuminating. Not many people have the pleasure of discovering what their friends think of them after they are dead.'

'Surely you don't expect to find *that* on a tombstone,' Anne exclaimed. 'Whatever one may think is quite a different matter from what one *says*. No one speaks ill of the dead.'

'Perhaps you are right, but if I have to admit that the sentiments are exaggerated, it is at least pleasant to learn that someone remembered me with affection even after six years.' He smiled tenderly down at Julia. 'You did not forget that snowdrops were my favourite flowers, did you, Julia?'

'Snowdrops . . .?' she faltered, at a loss, then following his glance saw the bunch of fading blooms. 'Oh those! Days old,

I fear. I little thought when I gathered that poor tribute that I should be seeing you again so soon.'

'But it wasn't ...' began Kit indignantly before Anne could prevent him. He had often accompanied her when she left her tributes, and had helped pick these. How, she wondered wildly, could she prevent his betraying her?

'Now, Kit, that is quite enough talk of tombstones and suchlike.' Julia was prompter to interrupt him. 'Don't let us ruin such a lovely day with such gloomy subjects. I am too happy to have Edmund back with us, safe and well, to bother about such matters, and I am sure he doesn't want to be reminded of them either.'

'I am certainly ready to forget a monument that will not, I trust, be appropriate for many years yet,' agreed Edmund laughing. 'I'd far rather look at the delightful picture you present in that charming outfit, Julia. Dare I suppose it was put on in my honour?'

'Do you really like it?' Julia preened herself happily. 'I wanted to wear something a little special to celebrate your return. Black is so lowering, and I cannot be expected to mourn when you are restored to us, can I?'

Anne let out the breath she had been holding and relaxed. Another awkward moment had passed safely. Had she imagined the intent look Edmund had given her crimson countenance when she had feared Kit would blurt out that the flowers had been left by her not Julia? She hoped so, but he was so quick to see through evasion that she could not be sure.

How many more petty lies would they be forced into? she wondered despairingly. She had not realised when she reluctantly embarked on this deception how difficult it would prove—how many silly little details there would be to trap them or how far Julia was prepared to dissemble to gain her ends. Anne was not the stuff of which conspirators were made. Her only hope was to keep as much out of Edmund's company as she could. Those clear grey eyes were too penetrating for her peace of mind. If she did not take immense care then sooner or later she would betray herself—and Julia.

It was not difficult to avoid Edmund for the rest of the day.

Julia was only too glad to entertain him unaided. Anne watched them walking together in the grounds and heard Julia's silvery laugh ring out. She seemed to have no qualms about their deception.

Dressing for dinner took little time but she sat waiting in her room until she heard her sister go downstairs not wanting to run the risk of an uncomfortable *tête-à-tête* with Edmund. She knew she could not handle the situation as light-heartedly as Julia did.

Downstairs she was grateful to let Julia monopolise the conversation. Then, just as dinner was about to be announced, they heard the rumble of a post-chaise drawing up outside.

'Who in the world can that be, calling at this hour?' fretted Julia. 'How vexing! Don't they know that dinner will be on the table in minutes?'

'Perhaps it is Anne's fiancé,' suggested Edmund. 'You said that you were expecting him.'

'On a Sunday! No, it couldn't be James,' Julia dismissed the idea scornfully. 'Not possibly. James is far too correct to contemplate travelling on the Sabbath.'

But Anne, who had quietly slipped out to investigate, soon discovered that her sister was mistaken. As Stone opened the door she saw James, plump cheeks aquiver, panting up the steps towards her, feverishly clutching the shallow hat he had not given himself time to put on.

'Dreadful news!' he gasped, forgetful of the listening servants. 'Must warn Julia without delay. There's a rumour going round town that Ashorne is alive after all. What shall we do?'

'Calm down, James,' advised Anne, drawing him out of earshot into the library. 'Have you rushed all the way here on a Sunday just to tell us that?'

'You don't understand!' James was pacing up and down the room in his agitation. 'It's the soldier chappie I mean. If it is true he is alive, Julia will lose everything. Home, title, lands, the lot! It is enough to kill such a delicate creature. I came immediately I heard to break it to her gently.'

'I fear that even so you are too late. Edmund has beaten you here. He arrived unexpectedly, yesterday.'

'Here already?' James's plump jaw sagged as far as the elaborate neckcloth and high collar would permit. 'But—how did he manage it? They told me at the turnpike that the Mail did not get through till a few days ago, and that mine was the first private carriage for nearly a month.'

'I believe that Edmund rode across country.'

'Rode! Not at all the thing. Makes him appear far too eager to turf you out,' declared James censoriously. 'You are sure that this *is* Ashorne and not some impostor?' he added hopefully.

'Don't be so foolish, James. Of course we know Edmund!'

'I was afraid it wouldn't be a mistake. Why does he have to turn up, upsetting everything when we thought him decently dead and buried!'

'Keep your voice down!' Anne warned impatiently. 'He is in the drawing-room. You surely cannot blame him for being captured alive instead of dying.'

'I suppose not,' James admitted grudgingly. 'But why did he go about it in such a peculiar fashion? Why skulk in prison for six years without telling anyone where he is? I'd have thought a dashing young fellow like that would have tried to escape, too, not waited tamely till someone came along to rescue him.'

'You have been totally misinformed if you imagine that is what he did,' Anne exclaimed indignantly. 'Edmund grasped at every opportunity to escape once his wounds were sufficiently healed, but it is less simple than you suppose. On one occasion he was free for five days, but the French recaptured him.'

'So he has been puffing off his exploits, has he?'

At the hint of scorn in his voice Anne fired up.

'Not in the least. Edmund will speak very little about that time, but his servant told the grooms about it and you know how these stories travel. The groom told the footman and he passed it on to the maid who told us.'

'With the tale growing more far-fetched at every telling, I'll warrant.'

'Now, James, be fair,' Anne could not help smiling at his aggrieved tone. 'Anyone would think you were jealous to hear you.'

'Of course I am not,' James protested sulkily. 'But I am surprised to see you making so much of the fellow. Inviting him to stay here and everything.'

'You are forgetting that this is Edmund's home, not ours. He has been generous enough to allow us to remain until we can make other arrangements.'

'How could he do anything less? Even the most arrant blackguard must be affected by your sister's plight. But all this upset cannot be pleasant for her, poor Julia! When she has barely had time to recover from her husband's tragic death too. This must be the last place she wants to be. Why don't you both leave and come to stay with me at Torrington?'

'I don't think Julia would agree to that. Think how odd it would appear. She has no more right to expect your help than Edmund's—less in fact, for after all he is a relation by marriage.'

James's anxious face cleared.

'Well if that is the only problem it is soon solved. We can be married as soon as you wish, then my claim is as valid as his. With a special licence we could have the whole thing settled in a trice. I'll send off to town immediately.'

'No!' interrupted Anne firmly. 'That won't be necessary. I have already told you that I don't intend to start my married life with my sister living with us. It will be far simpler to leave things as they stand. Melthorpe Hall is Julia's still, and we intend to move there as soon as it can be made habitable once more. When Julia and Kit are comfortably settled there, will be the time to start to think of our wedding. A few more months can make little difference. In the meantime it is much more convenient for us to accept Edmund's hospitality. There are a great many details to be worked out yet. Although the estate reverts to Edmund, much of the furnishings and equipment were brought across from Melthorpe and remain Julia's. We have to sort out all that kind of thing, and it is far more easily settled on the spot.'

'Then I will remain too, and make sure that Julia is not cheated of her rights. Poor little woman! She needs someone to protect her interests.'

'I am perfectly capable of looking after my sister's affairs, thank you,' Anne retorted. 'Not that she is in any need of protection. Edmund is scrupulously fair.' Indeed, she reflected, remembering Julia's recent bout of lavish spending and the plans she had already disclosed, it was Edmund who most needed protection from her rapacity.

'You are only a female,' James could be infuriatingly condescending when he chose, 'so wouldn't understand these matters. Let the fellow realise he has a man to deal with and it will be a different story. I shall not abandon Julia to his clutches.'

Knowing that once his mind was made up no argument would budge him, Anne grudgingly capitulated.

'I suppose you must remain if you insist, but in that case you will have to put up at the inn. We cannot expect Edmund to house all our friends as well as us. And don't blame me if he finds your interference unnecessary and insulting!'

'I hardly think Lord Ashorne will make any objection when he understands that I am acting solely out of concern for poor Julia.'

'If you are so worried about Julia,' snapped Anne, goaded beyond endurance by his lofty air of condescending to an infant, 'why didn't you ask her to marry you instead of me?'

'She wouldn't have me,' he replied simply.

Anne's mouth gaped wide in astonishment.

'You mean you have asked her?'

'Oh, not recently!' he hastened to reassure her. 'Popped the question years ago—before she became engaged to Ashorne even, but she wasn't interested. I wasn't surprised—too far above my touch.'

After all the upheaval of the past few days this was too much for Anne to endure.

'So you decided that I would be the next best thing?' she demanded with bleak sarcasm.

'Not like that at all,' he muttered uncomfortably. 'Very fond of you too, though not the same way as Julia. She's—well—special!' Recovering a little, he went on in an aggrieved tone, 'I thought you'd understand. You said when you agreed to marry me that you weren't in love with me. I thought you'd sympathise, not get in a miff about it.'

'Of course I understand,' Anne replied quickly but she

could not disguise the hurt at this fresh blow to her pride. Bitterly she reflected that she ought to have guessed that Julia had his preference, but foolishly she had not even suspected it, although his reaction after Julia was widowed should have warned her. The greatest part of James's appeal had lain in the fact that he was one of the few men who had appeared to prefer her to Julia. Where other suitors had neglected her to flirt with her married sister, James had concentrated on trying to please Anne. She had never realised that he was wooing her as a substitute—a pale imitation of the unattainable Julia. It was a shattering blow to her self-esteem.

Anne had not taken his suit seriously at first. It was only in the period of grief after her father's death that she had succumbed to the temptation of letting someone else deal with her problems. James had been a friend for years and in those first unhappy weeks he had to some extent filled her father's empty place. She enjoyed his friendship and was flattered by what she had supposed was his genuine affection and admiration. Although she knew that she could never experience the same poignant emotion for him that she had once felt for Edmund, she had despaired of ever finding anyone else who would rouse such a passion in her. When she decided that she must marry or degenerate into a lonely old maid like Aunt Mattie, then James had seemed the obvious choice. Though not in love with him, she had had a warm affection for him and had supposed that he loved her.

It was a shock to discover that his love for Julia had always been stronger than any feeling for herself. No wonder he had agreed so readily to the postponement of their marriage after Thomas died. Was he still, despite his protests, hopeful of winning Julia, sorry that he had been so foolish as to offer for Anne instead just before Julia became free?

'If you wish to marry my sister, please don't allow our engagement stand in the way,' she told him stiffly. 'I am perfectly willing to release you from your promise whenever you wish.'

James shook his head.

'No point. She'd never have me. Too good for an ordinary chap like me.'

Anne clenched her fists to bottle in the anger that shook her at his matter-of-fact tone, bitterly resentful of his airy assumption that she was eager to take up her sister's leavings. She was strongly tempted to throw his ring back in his face and storm away.

She managed to restrain herself, but only the realisation that everyone would suppose her decision had been prompted by Edmund's return, stopped her from ending the engagement immediately. Julia did not believe that her childhood passion for Edmund was over and done with now; that for Anne his coming had only spoiled a memory not kindled new hopes. If she broke her engagement as soon as he came home that would convince Julia that her suspicions were justified. She would never accept that the link between the two events was so slight.

Anne could imagine the derisive laugh with which she would share the jest with Edmund, and flinched at the thought. She would do nothing to court their mockery once more. There could be no harm in keeping up the engagement a little longer to salve her pride.

While she was still hesitating, a dramatic voice from the doorway thrilled, 'James! It is you! I could not credit it. How wonderful to see you, my dear. Edmund, you remember Sir James Shrivenham, don't you?'

'Of course. I am pleased to see you once more, Sir James.'

The baronet barely acknowledged his greeting with a stiff nod before turning to grasp Julia's hands in his.

'My poor Julia! I had to come immediately I heard the news. What a terrible shock for you this must have been.'

'Dear James, you are too kind!' Julia pressed his hands affectionately.

Anne's nails dug into her palms in fury as she watched him wriggle like an overweight puppy basking in its mistress's approval. She wondered how she had ever been so blind as not to guess at his true feeling for Julia. Had his adoration always been this obvious? Sensing Edmund's astonished recognition of it, she was doubly resentful.

'How fortunate Anne will be to have so thoughtful a husband. We are not all so lucky,' Julia sighed. 'Have you come to help us over this difficult time, James?'

'I will do anything I can, my dear,' he beamed fatuously. 'Could you doubt it?'

'So generous of you! But why aren't they bringing in your things?' demanded Julia. 'Surely you mean to stay after travelling so far? Or did you set out so quickly that you had no time to pack anything?'

'Gracious, no!' James looked horrified at the idea. 'It is just that Anne had the notion it was not the thing as matters stand...'

'I have been telling him that with things so altered here he must put up at the inn if he means to remain,' Anne explained.

'There is no need for that,' put in Edmund. 'I appreciate that I have taken the room you had ready for Sir James, but surely there are plenty of others. I feel sure that one can be made up for him without any difficulty.'

'Very kind,' James glanced triumphantly at Anne.

There was little she wanted less than to have James under the same roof at this time but there was no way she could refuse without downright rudeness. 'Very well. I will go and see that everything is made ready...'

'Let Norwich arrange all that,' Julia interrupted. 'That is what she is paid for. Dinner was ready ten minutes ago. You don't want to change or anything, do you, James?' As he hesitated she added plaintively, 'It is dreadfully late already and I am famished.'

'In that case,' James hurried to placate her, 'I will sit down to it as I am—if you are sure you have no objection to my appearing in all my dirt.' He looked anxiously down at his spotless travelling clothes, clearly torn between his desire to please her and his private conviction that it was quite unacceptable to dine in such a garb.

'We don't mind, not in the slightest! Now come straight into the dining-room and tell us all the news from town. I get only snippets in the few letters that arrive to relieve the tedium here. Confess that you have been horribly remiss in that respect yourself. You have forgotten all about us poor exiles.'

'Never! But I was always a poor hand with a pen.'

'Excuses! Still I suppose we must forgive you this time. But don't keep us in suspense any longer. Tell me everything! What is this tale of a marvellous new actor at Drury Lane? Fanny was in raptures over him in her last letter. Have you seen him yet?'

'Kean? Only once. I thought him very overrated. A miserable little fellow,' the plump James dismissed him contemptuously. Edmund glanced laughingly at Anne to share the jest, and despite her indignation she had to smile back.

Julia, totally oblivious of anything amusing in James's attitude, went on eagerly, 'And is it true that the waltz is danced everywhere now?'

'Not quite everywhere, but only the most prim frown on it. I heard a whisper that even the Patronesses at Almack's may soon relent and you know how strait-laced they are!'

'Oh quite Gothic, poor creatures! But don't say I told you so—one has to keep in their good books. Their assemblies may be sadly dismal affairs, but one has to attend to be in the swim. Still, the waltz should liven them up considerably. How I long to try it myself! Anne and I have practised, of course, but never in public, and to dance with a gentleman must be vastly different. You must try the steps with me after dinner, James. Anne will play for us. But come along! Dinner is spoiling while we stand gossiping.'

She led him off chattering with more animation than Anne had seen her display for months. Edmund followed, forgotten for the moment.

Anne stopped in the hall to give detailed instructions to the anxiously hovering housekeeper. It was all very fine for Julia to talk airily of leaving everything in Norwich's hands, but even the best of servants needed some guidance and Julia's household was far from the best. Since Anne had taken over the reins things had improved greatly, but the staff were still far from able to cope unaided.

'The Blue Room, miss? Very well. I'll get the fire lit at once, so it'll be cosy for the gentleman when he goes up.' Norwich hesitated a moment then went on in a rush, 'There's that Mr Weston out in the back, miss. Says he must see her ladyship. I tried to tell her about it just now, but she wouldn't listen to me.'

'Then Weston must do without seeing her. Tell him to come back tomorrow.'

'He won't like that, miss. Very nasty he can be when he's crossed. Couldn't you ask her ladyship?'

'Certainly not!' Anne retorted sharply. 'You may tell Weston that Lady Ashorne is far too busy with her guests to deal with business matters tonight. Whatever it is must wait till tomorrow.'

Norwich hurried away, clearly unhappy with the message. Anne walked crossly upstairs to check that everything in the room was satisfactory, thinking that it was typical of Weston's insolence that he should expect Julia's attention whenever he desired it. What impudence to send his demands by the servants! Well, for once he would be disappointed.

The others were on the second course when she joined them in the dining-room.

'There you are at last, Anne! I thought you'd never come,' exclaimed her sister. 'We knew you wouldn't want us to wait for you. James was ravenous after his long journey, poor lamb, and I couldn't let him starve. I'm so grateful to him for bringing me all the latest news. Just fancy! He tells me that it is rumoured we shall be able to visit France again within a few weeks! Isn't that marvellous! To think of being able to buy really modish clothes again at last. The English have no flair for fashion. I've hated the dowdy gowns I've had to put up with for years.' She put up an imperious hand as James began an anxious denial. 'There's no point in trying to be polite, James. I know how inferior they are to the French styles. What bliss it will be to shop there again! Don't you yearn to be in Paris, once more, Anne?'

'You forget that I have never been there,' Anne responded flatly. 'I was too young to come when you went with Papa.'

'Of course you were. How silly of me to forget! I was a mere babe myself then but I remember how marvellous it all was—how romantic all those Frenchmen were, and so charming to me!'

'How could they help but be enchanted by you? You must outshine all their belles, however fashionably clad.' James raised his glass in ponderous tribute to her.

Julia clapped her hands in delight. 'See! Even the thought of Paris is making James gallant! What about you, Edmund? Aren't you wild to visit *La Belle France* once more?'

'Not in the least. I have had enough of the French in the past six years to last me a lifetime.'

'Don't be such an old sobersides!' Julia laughed disbelievingly. 'Things will be quite different in peacetime. You cannot blame the ordinary French people for what that monster Napoleon made them do. James is more forgiving, aren't you, James? He'll be off across the Channel as soon as may be. Just think, James; you can take Anne on a tour of Europe for her honeymoon, now. Oh, how I envy you!'

'I am sure that your sister would be delighted to have your company if we decide to do so,' suggested James with as little accuracy as tact. Anne quivered with fury as Julia clasped her hands together rapturously.

'If only I could! But no, I must not be tempted. You will want no unwelcome third at such a time.'

'Nonsense! It is an excellent notion. Anne will be overjoyed to have a companion,' James assured her, oblivious of Anne's frown.

It galled Anne most to see Edmund's startled reaction to the fervent offer. Before she could utter the angry retort that trembled on her tongue, a servant interrupted them, bringing a note for Julia. She unfolded it, read it through, then crumpled it crossly in her hand, her face flushed with fury. Though she recovered quickly and returned to her spirited exchange with James and Edmund, her gaiety seemed a little strained. When, at last, the ladies withdrew to the drawing-room Anne tackled her.

'Is anything wrong, Julia? That note was from Weston, wasn't it? I wonder he had the impudence to bother you. Norwich said that he wished to speak to you, but I told her to send him away.'

'You had no right to do so. The matter might have been urgent.'

'I presumed that you were too engrossed with your guests to trouble with him tonight. What crisis has arisen so vital that it cannot wait till morning? Anyhow, if it is to do with the estate it is Edmund's affair now, not yours.'

'Phillip does not wish to consult me on estate business—just a private matter.'

'But one which has upset you. Don't let him browbeat you, Julia.'

'He doesn't. I've told you before that I know how to deal with Phillip Weston.'

'It hardly appears that way to me. The man presumes too much on your friendship. Let Edmund deal with him for you. He will stand no nonsense.'

'Don't fuss so!' Julia burst out. 'You have no call to interfere in my affairs.'

Sitting at the piano she crashed out a tune, playing so loudly that it was impossible for her sister to say any more. Anne watched her uneasily, all her doubts returning. Recalling that overheard conversation, she wondered what the secrets could be which Weston had threatened to reveal. Were they really important enough to give him a hold over Julia, or had anger made him bluster?

Clearly something was upsetting Julia, but it was useless to try and force a confidence. Opposition only made Julia more obstinate. She would have to wait until Julia was ready to confide in her, and hope that matters had not gone beyond aid by then.

Ignoring her sister, Julia went on playing *fortissimo* until the gentlemen joined them. Then she switched to a softer melody and set out to be charming once more. Clearly aware of the attractive picture she presented in another of the new gowns—a soft lavender this time, cut very low, with a heart-shaped locket accentuating rather than filling the bare expanse—she turned and patted the stool beside her invitingly.

'Come and sit here, Edmund. I've been looking through all my old music. Do you remember this song we used to sing together?'

Carefully placed candles shone on her fair curls, lending them a golden gleam. As she began softly to play, Edmund took his place beside her smiling reminiscently.

'How could I forget it? You made me sing it that last evening before I left.'

'Sing it again now,' she urged.

His protests were soon overcome. Their voices blended harmoniously, Julia smiling happily into Edmund's eyes as they sang the sentimental words. His face was less revealing, but with a pang of envy Anne thought she could see affection in the gaze fixed upon her sister's exquisite face.

James hovered jealously beside them. Face flushed with the wine he had drunk so avidly throughout the meal, he glowered impotently at his rival. He might claim to have given up any hope of winning Julia, thought Anne, but clearly he did not want to see her find happiness with anyone else. She watched his dog-in-the-manger scowl grow blacker from her corner, forgotten by them all.

If she had not been so closely involved it might have been amusing to see them act so foolishly, but the scene brought back unhappy memories of the past when she had nursed an envy as unwarranted as that now displayed by James. She writhed inwardly at the realisation that her doting passion for Edmund must have made her behave as foolishly as he was doing now. No wonder Edmund and Julia had laughed at her. Her face suffused with shame at the memory. Long finished that childish infatuation might be, but it still hurt to remember it—just as it hurt to see them together again.

The heat of the great fire stifled her, and quietly she rose and slipped out into the hall. Her dog padded beside her as she fetched a shawl and let herself out into the moonlit garden. None of the others even noticed her departure, she realised with aching heart.

The cool air revived her but could not calm her agitated thoughts. Everything had gone wrong since the moment she had brought Julia that wretched letter! The carefully arranged, passionless future she had planned for herself was shattered. Her relationship with her sister had sadly altered, and that with James had been strained almost beyond repair.

Bess's greying muzzle pushed into her hand as if she sensed her mistress's grief. Even the dog was a reminder of Edmund—his last gift before he left. Passionately Anne wished that Edmund had never returned to confuse all their lives. Yet no sooner was the thought formed than she dismissed it. That was to wish Edmund dead, and she could not bear that. To have him returned safely to them was more than she had ever hoped. She could not wish it undone.

It was only seeing him fall back under Julia's spell that was so disturbing. If her sister really loved him she could learn to bear it but she knew her to be motivated by self interest alone. Still she must live with the situation.

Eyes misted with unshed tears, she stared blindly out across the lake. By her Bess stirred, ears pricked, as heavy footsteps came up behind them. The creak of his corset betrayed James even before she could pick out his form from the shadows.

'What are you doing out here?' Anne demanded ungraciously, resentful at having her solitude invaded. 'I thought you were inside with the others, enjoying the music.'

'I was—at least Julia's part in it—until she decided that she was too worn out for any more tonight. This has all been too much for her. She said she was going to retire early and sent me out with Ashorne. Seemed to fancy that I was as anxious as he was to smoke one of those revolting cigars. Filthy habit! I don't blame poor Julia for not wanting her rooms reeking of tobacco fumes.'

That could be little worse, Anne reflected, than the snuff which James littered everywhere, but she was too weary to argue. Knowing her sister's ways she was not deceived by Julia's sudden tiredness. She might have guessed that Julia would lose little time in making an opportunity to meet Weston. What was there between the two? she fretted. It must be important to make Julia waste her chance to captivate Edmund.

'Poor Julia,' James went on without waiting for any reply. 'I fear she is sadly exhausted by this whole sorry business.'

'I cannot agree that Edmund's return is in any way a cause for sorrow,' retorted Anne. 'I am very thankful to learn that he is alive after all and so, I am sure, is Julia.'

'Perhaps she is at the moment, with the fellow flattering her in such a blatant fashion,' grumbled James. 'You saw how he was making up to her this evening, and she seemed taken in by his pretty speeches. I don't know what she ever saw in him. He's nowhere near good enough for her. I made sure they weren't left alone, but I didn't intend to stay with the fellow once Julia was gone. I left him polluting the shrubbery with his vile smoke and came to find you.'

'While you insist on remaining as a guest in Edmund's house you must endeavour to treat him with more civility,' Anne observed tartly. 'If nothing else, your antagonism creates an impossible situation for me, and as I have already explained, I intend to stay here with Julia until her affairs are properly settled.'

'I cannot see the need. Let the lawyers sort it out between them. We could have a quiet wedding then set off on a tour of the continent as soon as it is safe, as Julia suggested, and take her with us. Poor girl, she needs a change of scene to recover from all this upset. What do you say? You know how delighted she would be to accept such a plan.'

'But I should *not* be delighted to have her accompany me on my honeymoon!' Anne stared hopelessly at his baffled face. James really could not see any objection in arranging their wedding solely to suit Julia, she realised incredulously. He was totally unable to understand how humiliating it would be for a wife to share her honeymoon with the sister whom her groom preferred but who had turned him down. He was just as insensitive as Julia! They would make a fine couple!

She was tempted to tell him so but did not want the inevitable argument yet. As he opened his mouth to reply she cut him off sharply. 'No James! Don't say any more. I too am tired out and should only say things I might regret later.'

James was not stopped that easily, but eventually he went away, still grumbling, leaving Anne to her own uncomfortable thoughts. She knew now that marriage with James was impossible, but it was going to be difficult to get him to accept that decision. He was too thick-skinned to sympathise with anyone else's feelings. She had an uneasy notion that only outright rudeness would force him to accept that she was in earnest.

She shivered as a chill wind blew across the lake. It was too cold to linger outside any longer. Wrapping her shawl tightly around her, she turned back towards the house. If her return interrupted Julia's meeting with Weston then it was unfortunate, but presumably they would have enough caution to

seek a private rendezvous. Julia had plenty of experience of
that sort of problem and so, she was sure, had he.

Without stopping to think, Anne took the shortest route
back to the house—up through the shrubbery. It was not
until the faint scene of tobacco smoke drifted towards her
that she remembered James telling her that he had left
Edmund there.

She hesitated looking at the tall form silhouetted in the
moonlight. It had been an exhausting day and she did not
feel equal to another encounter tonight. Her brain was too
weary to embark on the mental fencing that conversation
with Edmund involved. Better to avoid him even if it meant a
long detour.

Motioning the dog to follow, she turned off on a side path
hugging the shadows. Her soft shoes made little sound on the
grassy path. Glancing back, she was relieved to see Edmund
still facing in the opposite direction. Another few yards and
she would be out of view.

Behind Edmund a roosting bird flew up with a clatter of
alarm. Startled Anne swung round and caught a glimpse of a
dark figure moving in the shadowy trees beyond Edmund.
Was it James returning? She did not think the shape bulky
enough, though it was difficult to make out much in the
darkness. But if it *was* James, why was he moving so stealthily? A shiver of apprehension ran through her as Bess
growled deep in her throat.

Anne put a hand on the dog's collar to restrain her.
Horrified, she saw the glint of metal as the newcomer raised
his arm. He was levelling a pistol at Edmund! She tried to
shout a warning, but her dry mouth produced only a croak.
Desperately she tried again, and this time Edmund heard.
He spun round, and in the same instant the shot rang out
deafeningly.

Sick with horror, Anne watched Edmund clutch at his
side, stagger and fall—oh so slowly—to the ground. His
head struck heavily and he lay dreadfully still.

Bess yelped as her fingers tightened convulsively on the
collar. Anne relaxed her grip and the dog hurtled away into
the darkness, baying furiously. Anne ran to kneel beside
Edmund, feeling frantically for his heart. Thank God, it was

still beating faintly. When she lifted her hand it felt sticky with blood.

As she stared at it, dizzy with shock, she felt a surge of panic bubble up through her. Desperately she fought the impulse to scream. Such cowardly behaviour would not help Edmund. She must stay calm.

Numbly she remembered her fleeting wish that Edmund had not returned to complicate their lives. Had someone else, less scrupulous, determined that their problems should be resolved by Edmund's death?

CHAPTER
FOUR

STRUGGLING painfully back to consciousness, Edmund was aware that something hurt abominably. He was too dazed to be able to pinpoint the source of the discomfort yet. His head throbbed; the ground beneath him was hard and uncomfortable. When he tried to move an intense pain stabbed through his side.

He sank back, staring muzzily around him. What had happened? His flesh prickled with the certainty that danger surrounded him. Something had happened, but what? His blurred vision clearing a little, he was able to make out trees and bushes in the darkness about him, but nothing that stirred a memory in his confused brain. Desperately he tried to remember. Where was he?

The effort of concentration made his head throb more. He let his eyes close, only to jerk them open as the elusive memory flashed of a shot. He remembered the shock of the ball ripping into his side, himself falling—then oblivion. How long ago had that been? more important, what was the marksman doing now? Had his enemy left him for dead as at first after the battle, or were they lurking close by, waiting to finish their work?

The urge to escape overwhelmed him, making him heedless of discomfort. He must be in the woods beyond the château, he decided. Jonas had feigned sickness to give him the chance to overpower the guard, then they had used the keys to free themselves. But compassion had made him too gentle and the fellow had recovered quickly enough to sound the alarm before they won clear.

'We must get well away before daybreak,' he muttered urgently. The noisome torment of his prison cell was vivid in his memory now, and he dreaded to be dragged back there once again. As he strained to lift himself up a gentle hand pushed him back.

'Lie still,' urged an anxious voice that was surely familiar but it could not be. He must be lightheaded, his brain playing another of its foolish tricks. How could Julia be here in France?

No, it was Jonas who had helped him escape; Jonas who shared his peril. With sudden determination he knew he had to make an effort for Jonas's sake. Too much time had been wasted already. If they did not get on their way immediately they would lose their chance of escape yet again. They must reach the coast and find a boat before the French discovered their trail. He had to struggle back to England—to Ashorne and Julia.

Again he tried to push himself up to a sitting position, and groaned as an agonising pain stabbed at his side. He sank back defeated. It was no use. The ball must be lodged in his ribs. He would never make the coast like this. The French would recapture him and throw him back into that damned cell, gloating over his failure. All the same, there was no need for Jonas to be trapped with him.

'Leave me here,' he insisted hoarsely. 'Get clear yourself. I'll be all right.'

But the gentle voice that bade him be still did not belong to his cell-mate. The cool hand checking his pulse was too soft to be Jonas's. He strained to resolve the riddle, and all at once Edmund's head cleared. He remembered everything; knew that the war was over for him, that he was returned to the safety of home. Only home, it seemed, was safe no longer.

'Someone tried to kill me!' he murmured incredulously.

'Yes but he has gone now. Keep still or the bleeding will start again,' the soothing voice told him.

Edmund shifted cautiously, trying to glimpse its owner.

'Julia?' he asked hopefully. He felt the figure beside him stiffen and draw away. There was just the faintest reproach in the reply.

'No, Anne.'

He frowned. Stupid of him to make the same mistake again. The recollection of his foolish behaviour in the library yesterday still filled him with embarrassment. He had not

intended to be so impetuous, had always planned to give
Julia time to recover from the shock of his arrival before
making any demands on her. Then, when he had seen the
slight form in the doorway, so like the miniature over which
he had pored for so many lonely hours, he had lost his head,
forgetting all his sensible plans in the joy of clasping her in his
arms again at last.

It was disturbing to recall how enjoyable a sensation kissing Anne had been before he realised his error. He had not
thought himself so fickle. It had been daunting to discover
that his memory had played him false, that it was Anne who
had received his ardent greeting.

Had it been guilt or disappointment uppermost in his
mind that made him so curt with her when he learned of his
mistake? Had he been trying to punish her for his own folly?
How could he have guessed that Anne would change so
greatly? But if the change in Anne had surprised him, that
had been nothing to the shock, a few minutes later, of
finding Julia so altered. Her lovely face harder, her voice
sharp, shriller than in the memories he had cherished so
long.

That was being unfair, he admonished himself immediately. It was merely agitation at the unexpected shock of his
return that had made Julia appear so different, made her act
so strangely. Tonight she had been her old self. Seated at the
piano in the candlelight the years had dropped away. Then
she had been as exquisite and desirable as he remembered
her. When they sang together he could have fancied himself
transported back six years, to the time before he left for the
Peninsula.

Everything was as it had been then—the piano, the music,
Julia's teasing blue eyes laughing up into his as she sang.
There had even been, just as before, the jealous figure thrusting between them, attempting to mar their pleasure, spoil
their delight in each other.

Six years ago it had been Thomas, envious of the understanding that united them, who had tried to destroy it.
Tonight James had played his role. James, who was supposed to be Anne's future husband, yet gave all his attention
to her sister. Inexplicably, because Anne was equally desir-

able. If his heart were not irrevocably given to Julia he could easily lose it to the younger sister.

All that had been missing was Anne's quiet adoration in the background. She had been in the room this evening, but remote from them—as if she had dispassionately cut herself off from them all. She seemed untroubled by their activities, unaffected even by her fiancé's desertion. Had six years made Anne so insensitive that she felt no jealousy?

He found that hard to credit. She had always lived in the background, outshone by her more lovely sister, but surely she would expect her future husband to put her first. That was not too improbable a wish; Anne had grown into a thoroughly attractive woman.

He could not suppress a selfish pang of regret that time had caused her to outgrow her childhood fondness for him. She seemed now to resent rather than welcome his return. Thomas had mocked at her devotion, but Edmund always valued Anne's affection. Selfishly he missed it now. But, alas, time had wrought its changes in Anne as in so many of the people he had left, he reflected ruefully. Six years had transformed the child he remembered. Obviously, with the calm good sense that had always characterised her, Anne had cast off that early infatuation.

He could scarcely blame her, after his unfortunate error yesterday, if she treated him now with cool reserve. Then to make the same mistake again! All the same, he acknowledged wryly, it was lucky that it had been she who found him here, not Julia. Anne had always been of far more use in an emergency than her sister. Dearly as he had always loved Julia, he had to admit that she had her imperfections. Where Anne had begun to tend his injuries, Julia would have gone into hysterics.

He must have uttered the thought aloud, for smothering a laugh Anne replied, 'I must confess I was tempted myself, but decided this was not the time to indulge in such a luxury. Apart from any other consideration, they would have been completely wasted with you lying unconscious there.'

She grew serious again as she added, 'Are you recovered enough for me to leave you while I go for help to carry you in? I've done the best I can here, but that wound ought to be treated properly. I'd have gone before, but I was afraid to leave you alone in case that man returned ...'

Her words trailed uncomfortably away and Edmund forced his mind back to the incredible fact that here, in peaceful England, someone had tried to kill him.

'You don't believe it could have been an accident? A poacher, perhaps?'

Regretfully Anne shook her head. 'He took too deliberate an aim.'

'Who was it? Could you recognise him?'

'I couldn't see him clearly enough. It was too dark under the trees to make much out—only the pistol.'

'But you called to me?' He frowned with the effort of remembering. He had heard the faint warning cry and turned to see her outlined in the moonlight. With a surge of excitement he had assumed that this was Julia come out to meet him; that the sudden onset of tiredness she had pleaded earlier had been only an excuse to rid them of James's inhibiting presence. She used to do that when Thomas became a nuisance.

He had spun eagerly round to greet her. At the same instant the pistol report deafened him and he felt the ball rip into his side.

'I could see he was aiming at you,' Anne explained. 'I tried to shout a warning, but he fired as I called and you pitched over. For a moment I thought you were dead!' She shivered at the memory, then went on more calmly. 'Perhaps he thought so too, for he ran off. Bess chased after him but I stayed to tend to you. Fortunately the ball seems to have missed any vital spot though it is difficult to be sure in the dark. I think you must have hit your head as you fell and knocked yourself unconscious.'

Edmund put a cautious hand to his head. He could feel no wound, but it certainly felt tender.

'The sooner I can get indoors and send someone to hunt out this fellow, the better.' He tried to push himself up but again the effort of moving made his head reel and he sank back. 'I don't like the idea of you being out here with a madman running loose with a pistol.'

Anne bit her lip as she watched his struggles.

'It is no use, Edmund. We shall have to get someone to carry you. I wish I knew whether it was safe to leave you now! Even Bess has disappeared.' She walked to the end of the path, calling the dog, but there was no response.

With a frown Edmund watched her shiver in the cool breeze and realised that her arms and throat were bare. 'You'll catch cold in that flimsy dress!' he scolded irritably. 'Surely you didn't come out without a shawl. I thought you more sensible.' Then, looking down, he saw that its lacy folds were tucked around him. Dragging it off, he insisted that she took it back.

'I'm as warm as toast,' he lied, 'and you look perished. It's a trifle gory on one side but better than freezing.'

As she wrapped it round her thankfully, they heard James hurrying towards them calling, 'Anne! Where are you, Anne?'

'Here,' she shouted back. Soon he puffed into view demanding peevishly,

'Whatever is going on tonight? I heard that overgrown hound of yours down by the gate baying like a banshee. I tried to pull her away but the damned brute bit me. I couldn't see you anywhere and I got really worried. How am I going to explain it all to Julia?' As he came close enough to take in the scene his voice rose in consternation. 'What the devil has been happening here? Are you all right, Anne? That's *blood* on your shawl!'

'Yes, I'm perfectly safe, but Edmund has been hurt!' Impatiently she shook off his solicitous hand. 'Don't fuss about me, James. Go and fetch some of the servants to carry Edmund back to the house.'

'But oughtn't we to . . .'

'Don't waste time arguing, James!' she snapped. 'Do as I ask, and don't forget to send someone for the doctor. Hurry!'

Deflated, he scuttled away. Edmund chuckled, then winced as the movement sent a red-hot pincer of pain through his ribs.

'Are you always as forthright with the poor fellow?'

'Oh, dear! Was I being a managing female again?' asked Anne repentantly. 'Papa used to say it was my worst fault. I don't mean to be sharp, but I cannot bear to see people dither. What is the point of long discussions when something needs to be done urgently?'

Or of hysterics, he thought, and immediately felt guilty at the criticism that implied of Julia. She could not help her sensitivity. The feminine weakness that made her unable to deal with crises was surely part of her charm. Anne's good sense was admirable, but Julia was infinitely more womanly. She might be different from her sister but, he told himself firmly, Julia was far more to his taste. Once her period of mourning was over he intended to beg her to be his wife.

Within a few minutes James returned with four sturdy footmen. They had had the forethought to bring a hurdle to carry Edmund on and eased him on to it with great care. Even so, he had to grit his teeth to stop himself crying out at the agonising jolt as they lifted the improvised stretcher. Mercifully he felt his senses slip away again, but he lapsed into semi-consciousness confident that Anne would cope whatever happened.

Anne watched the proceedings unhappily, feeling Edmund's agony rack her too. Fighting to control the foolish weakness that made her body shake, her eyes fill with tears, she walked beside them, protecting Edmund all she could from the inevitable jolting as they negotiated the narrow paths.

She was glad to concentrate her thoughts on Edmund and his needs. That left no time for the frightening question of who had tried to kill him. It seemed an eternity before they reached the house, but at last they were there. As the men hesitated in the doorway she forced her numbed brain to work once more.

'Carry him into the library. We'd better make up a bed there rather than try to lift him upstairs.'

As they turned obediently with their burden, Julia hurried downstairs towards them. Anne waited resignedly for the outburst.

'What has happened? I heard James shouting, so I flung on some clothes and ...' Julia stopped aghast as she caught sight of the pale still form on the stretcher. 'He's dead!' she screamed frantically, 'Edmund's dead! Oh my God! What shall we do?'

Edmund's eyes flickered open for a second. Julia gave a shout of relief. Clutching feverishly at him she breathed, 'Thank heaven! You're alive, Edmund! Speak to me!'

Anne thrust her unceremoniously aside. She had neither time nor patience to cope with Julia's folly now. Ignoring her sister's noisy sobbing, she directed the men to lift Edmund on to the couch. Julia fluttered helplessly beside them, getting in everyone's way, until in exasperation Anne sent her to fetch a glass of brandy for the patient.

'Not too much, or it will make him feverish. Just enough to prevent his feeling the pain while I look at his wound. I have to see whether the ball is still in his side.'

Julia's hand shook so much that she could scarcely hold the glass. A great dark splash of the spirit spilt down the front of her gown but she was too agitated to notice it. Watching impatiently, Anne's eyes narrowed in sudden recognition. This was one of the new gowns—the one Julia had been wearing at dinner. She could never have struggled into that unaided without even ruffling her hair. All her jewels were in place too, so she had obviously not retired to bed as she pretended.

Was Anne's guess correct? Was it to engineer a meeting with Weston that Julia had sent Edmund outside—out into danger? She froze as the thought stabbed that Julia had everything to gain from Edmund's death.

She thrust the disturbing idea away. No time for conjecture now. Edmund's needs were paramount. Carefully she lifted the glass to his lips and forced him to gulp down the spirits. He protested weakly, but she made him drain the glass. It soon had its effect, dulling his senses further, driving away the pain.

Julia halted her restless pacing to exclaim, 'It is perfectly dreadful if we cannot walk safely in our own grounds now without being shot at. What are things coming to? Something will have to be done about these wretched poachers.'

'Poachers?' repeated Anne grimly, 'it was no poacher who shot Edmund.'

'What do you mean?' Julia's frightened gaze flew to her sister's face. Shock made her voice shrill as she demanded, 'Did you see the accident, then?'

Anne contemplated her suspiciously. Was there more than horror at the idea in her voice—fear, too, of what else Anne might have seen? It was unbearable to have such doubts of her sister.

'It was not an accident,' she replied flatly. 'What I saw was a deliberate attempt to kill Edmund. It was too dark for me to recognise the attacker, but I could see it was not a poacher.'

'Impossible!' Julia sank down into a chair, overcome by her sister's blunt declaration.

James bent anxiously over her, exclaiming crossly, 'I thought you had more compassion, Anne, than to upset poor Julia in that way! Her delicate nerves will not stand these repeated shocks. Of course it was an accident! Who would wish to harm Ashorne?'

Who indeed, Anne wondered bleakly. Weston? James? Julia herself? Was that why she was so frantic now—for fear of what Anne might have seen, dread that her part in it might be exposed? Anne surveyed her critically. Julia seemed to have aged ten years in the past few minutes. Her face was haggard with anxiety—or guilt? But no! She was being too fanciful. It could not have been Julia. The figure that had levelled the pistol had been unmistakably male.

Even so, a moment's reflection showed Anne that this fact did not entirely absolve her sister. Although she had not fired the shot she might still have been party to its planning. It was horrible to have such suspicions of her sister, but Anne could not shake off the fear that Weston's hold on Julia might be so strong that she had been forced into complicity in his schemes.

In that case, had his been the finger on the trigger? She tried desperately to recall that shadowy form, but it had been too brief a view to allow her to recognise anything familiar about it. Impossible to be sure.

While all these wild conjectures were whirling around in Anne's head, her hands were steadily cutting at Edmund's coat and shirt, easing them away from the ugly patch where blood was now welling strongly. Fighting to overcome her own nausea, Anne glanced across at her sister and told her bluntly,

'I warn you, Julia, that I intend to deal with Edmund's

wound now. If you don't wish to watch the operation you had better leave the room directly.'

'How can you contemplate such a thing?' Julia shuddered. 'I'd sooner die than *look* at all that blood, let alone touch it!'

'Fortunately some of us have less sensibility,' Anne replied flatly, refusing to allow herself to think of what lay ahead. She must stifle her imagination and get on with the task for Edmund's sake. 'It will be Edmund who dies if the bleeding is not staunched soon.'

Not waiting to see her sister go out, she bent to her task. Edmund stirred. 'The doctor ...' he muttered thickly.

'We cannot afford to wait for him. You have lost far too much blood already, and it might be hours before he arrives. Don't worry,' she added with the ghost of a smile, 'I shan't hurt you.'

In spite of the assumed confidence with which she spoke it took a great deal of resolution actually to start, immense effort to keep her hands steady as she probed the mangled flesh. Thankful that Edmund was barely conscious, she still worked with infinite caution, knowing that if he flinched she would be unable to go on. Her hold on self-control was very thin.

Eventually she discovered the small lead ball lodged, as she had expected, in his side. She was very relieved to hear the doctor arrive at this point and to relinquish to him the task of digging it out, although she forced herself to stand beside him to assist where necessary. At last it was over and the side tightly strapped up.

'Best not to move him any more than necessary now,' the doctor ordered, so Edmund was settled for the night on the sofa. Jonas volunteered to sit up with his master.

As Anne ushered the doctor out, they saw Julia hovering anxiously in the hall, James at her side. 'Is—is he going to be all right?' the widow whispered, hollow-eyed with despair.

'Of course he is! Perfectly all right!' The doctor had never had any sympathy for Julia's histrionics. 'Thanks to Miss Wetherly's good sense and prompt action, his lordship will suffer nothing worse than a sore side for a few weeks. I suggest you all go to your beds and let the patient get some rest. That will do him far more good than all this fussing.'

While Anne was giving orders for the doctor's horse to be brought to the door a groom panted up to them. 'If you please, miss, could the doctor come to the estate office as soon as he's done with his lordship? There's been an accident there.'

'Another accident!' shrieked Julia. 'What is it this time?'

'It's Mr Weston, your ladyship, ma'am. He's been knocked unconscious.'

'Good God! He must have encountered the same maniac who shot Edmund!'

Anne, glancing at her sister, was shocked to see an expression almost of satisfaction flit across her face as she spoke, but in a second it was gone. Was Julia so entangled with the steward that she wanted harm to come to him? Or was she merely relieved to find suspicion of being responsible for Edmund's attack lifted from him?

'What has happened to Mr Weston?' Anne asked. 'Is he badly injured?'

'Not really, miss, but he has a nasty cut on his head that needs looking at. The men have the fire nearly out now. Seems someone hit Mr Weston over the head then set light to the place. Terrible mess it's in, but Mr Weston managed to give the alarm before it spread any further.'

'It must be the work of the same madman,' shuddered Julia, clinging to James's hand. 'I shall be too terrified to set foot outside the door until he has been caught and hanged.'

Anne was less sure. There had been such a calm deliberation about the attack she had witnessed that she could not believe the attacker insane. But why else should he fire on Edmund? It would have been logical to do so if Edmund had surprised the intruder or tried to prevent his escape, but he had not even known of the man's presence before he took aim.

It was difficult, on the other hand, to believe that the two incidents were entirely unconnected. But if the man's object had been robbery from the office, then why should he risk discovery and capture by stopping to attack Edmund, who was scarcely likely to be carrying valuables about the garden with him?

After all the strain of the evening's happenings, thinking

made her head throb. Too weary to speculate further, she left Julia and James arguing fruitlessly and went to bed. Sleep came late as she tossed and turned, trying despite all her good intentions to resolve the problem.

She was amazed when she arrived, heavy-eyed, at breakfast next morning, to see Edmund already sitting at the table. He was pale and moved stiffly, but his riding-habit showed that he meant to go out that day.

'Are you mad, Edmund?' Anxiety made Anne's voice sharper than she intended. 'What are you doing here? The doctor said you were to stay in bed for a week at least.'

'Nonsense, a little scratch doesn't warrant all that fuss.'

'It was more than a scratch, and you cannot deny that it still pains you.'

'Not enough to prevent me riding. I've had far worse than this before now. I've made an appointment with the steward this morning and I mean to keep it.'

'But haven't you heard? Weston, too, was injured last night.'

'Not seriously, I understand. In any case, I can sort through the accounts even if he is unable to be there to explain them.'

He refused to discuss the matter further, and Anne lapsed into an angry silence. Let him drive himself into a fever if he wished to be so obstinate! She would not stop him.

James soon joined them but Julia did not appear. To Anne's disgust, Edmund seemed more concerned over Julia's state of health than his own. He nodded sympathetically as James sighed, 'Poor Julia! The dreadful events last night sadly distressed her. She has too mercurial a temperament to withstand such upsets.'

'Mercurial fiddlesticks!' snorted Anne. 'Julia allows her imagination too much rein. She makes herself ill.'

'You are too severe with her. Julia cannot help her nervous nature. You forget that she has not your ability to remain calm in a crisis.'

'And is never likely to gain it while everyone is so foolishly indulgent with her.'

They both stared at her as if she were a murderess. Anne glared in impotent rage at them. They truly believed that

Julia's silliness deserved serious consideration. What was
there about her sister that made even normally sensible men
like Edmund so uncritical of her?

Anne stamped away in a rage, determined to ride over to
Melthorpe Hall to see how the repair work was progressing.
The sooner she could move there the better. Life was too
wearing at Ashorne. She sent a message to the schoolroom
cancelling her lesson with Kit, and rode away. A faint twinge
of guilt troubled her, as she had half-promised to take the
child with her on her next visit to the Hall, but she did not feel
able to cope with his childish prattle today.

A hard gallop shook off the worst of her fury; the warm
spring sunshine gradually soothed her agitated spirits. It was
hard to remain unhappy on a day like this. The place was
busy with the sound of hammers and saws when she arrived
there. It was dispiriting to see how little had been accom-
plished, but at least they had made a start.

Seeking out the chief carpenter, she asked if it were possible to speed up the work.

'Our plans have had to change, Bedford. Now Lord
Ashorne has come home it is my sister and I who must move
in here.'

He shook his head doubtfully.

'I don't see how we can manage any better, miss. There's
more problems than we'd thought at first. The rain has got in
the roof and sent the timbers rotten. To replace them will
take a couple of months. Then there's the floors . . .'

'But surely some of the rooms could be made habitable
fairly soon?'

'Maybe—the south wing is not so badly affected. We
could patch something up there perhaps. But why do you still
need to come? We heard that his lordship was shot dead last
night and Mr Weston left at death's door.'

'Then you have heard a vastly exaggerated account. Lord
Ashorne is only wounded, and Weston not seriously hurt
either.'

'More's the pity,' Bedford growled. 'I don't wish his lordship no harm, but there's many hereabouts would be glad to
see the back of the other one.' Seeing that Anne was
astonished at his vehemence he went on bitterly, 'There's my

own daughter for a start. She was fool enough to listen to his lying tongue, and now she's left with a babe to rear alone and her only sixteen.'

'But surely,' Anne protested, 'something can be done. He should be made to marry her.'

'And what good would a husband like that be to her—a lecher and gamester to boot? She's better off alone.'

'He could still be forced to pay for the child's upkeep,' Anne said indignantly.

'He denies all knowledge of it. Moll tried to get her ladyship to make him help, but she wouldn't listen either. It isn't safe for us to argue too much if we want to keep our jobs. We only hope his wings'll be clipped a bit now his lordship's home.'

He broke off, and following his gaze she was infuriated to see Edmund standing in the doorway.

'What are you doing here?' she demanded truculently, disturbed at that treacherous stab of emotion she still experienced at the sight of him.

Ignoring her discourtesy, he strode across to join them. 'Weston proved too unwell to meet me, and as it turned out that the account books were extensively damaged in the fire I was unable to deal with those either.'

How extraordinarily convenient that must be for Weston, thought Anne. It bore out all her doubts of the attack on him. Or was she being unfair—letting prejudice colour her conclusions? Bedford's story had confirmed her judgment of the steward, but that did not make him capable of attempted murder.

She wondered if Edmund was suspicious too, but no sign of it showed in his face as he went on, 'So when I learned you had come here I decided to follow, and discover for myself the state of the building. Your report of it is so very different from your sister's.'

As Julia had not set foot in the hall for at least twelve months, Anne wondered how she could claim to know so much about it, but with an effort she kept that reflection to herself. Grudgingly she followed Edmund around the echoing rooms as he made his inspection.

All its faults seemed more glaringly obvious as she viewed

them through his eyes. He made no comment, but she grew more and more resentful of his interference as he walked silently beside her, his expression growing blacker as they went on.

'I know it is not perfect,' she was goaded into declaring at last, as he stared forbiddingly at the great patches of damp running down the walls of what had once been Julia's morning-room, 'but it will serve to house us for the time being, with a little more work.'

'You cannot seriously intend to move here while the place is in such a deplorable condition?' he asked incredulously. 'How could you ask Julia to live in such squalor?'

Julia! Always people worried about Julia and Julia's comfort!

'If I am ready to put up with a little discomfort, why should Julia be unable to do so too? At least here we shall be independent.'

'Your sister is content to accept my hospitality. Why are you too proud to do so too, Anne? It is quite impossible that either of you should live here until the house is totally renovated. For a start it needs a completely new roof. As you saw, the rain comes through in a dozen places.'

Anne knew that he was correct but that did not prevent her arguing. 'Bedford says that it can be patched for the present and gradually replaced.'

'False economy. Far better to have the job done properly now, than patch continually and still have to rebuild the whole roof in a few years' time.'

'It is all very fine for you to talk so airily,' objected Anne rebelliously. 'Julia cannot afford to . . .'

'Naturally,' he interrupted, 'I intend to make myself responsible for all the costs of putting the Hall to rights. But for the unfortunate muddle over my capture, the house would not have been allowed to lapse into such disrepair. I feel myself bound to make it good. I will tell all the workmen to send their accounts direct to me.'

Anne's first furious impulse was to refuse his offer, but she knew that Julia would swiftly reverse that decision leaving her looking ridiculous. However delicate Julia's sensibilities might be in face of blood and injury, they were far from tender in financial dealings. She would have no compunction over accepting as much of Edmund's money as he offered—indeed, her abundant new wardrobe showed that she had been making inroads into it unasked.

'I had thought we could make just a few rooms inhabitable at first. Live in those and . . .' she began defensively, unwilling to give in without a struggle.

'Ridiculous! Far more sensible to make a thorough job of it. That will be far less expensive and troublesome in the long run. Could you—or Julia—live in this hubbub?' Seeing her frown still, he demanded in exasperation, 'Why are you so loath to accept my hospitality, Anne? Your sister is more gracious.'

And more grasping, Anne thought grimly. Having to bite back the angry retort did not make her mood any sweeter. How could she tell him that she was desperate to move away because she was frightened—terrified of what Julia might be driven to under Weston's influence? To remove her from Ashorne might not take away all danger but it would lessen her chances of harming Edmund—or of fascinating him, an insistent inner voice whispered, but she thrust that idea away. It was for Edmund's sake she had to leave, not in the selfish hope of parting him from Julia's wiles.

But she could not share those fears. She might be wrong. Julia would never forgive her if she gave Edmund a false impression, though increasingly Anne had come to believe her doubts only too horribly justified.

For her own sake too she must get away from Edmund. Living so close to him it would be all too easy to let that old attraction take root and flourish as strongly as before. She had to face the truth, that she was in danger of falling just as desperately and hopelessly in love with Edmund as ever she tumbled when a silly adolescent. Away from him she might find strength to withstand that potent attraction—here she knew she had little chance of avoiding its insidious growth. The consciousness that sooner or later she might betray her foolish weakness made her stiff and abrupt with him.

'I am not ungrateful,' she replied coldly, 'but obviously I want to see my sister settled into her own home as soon as possible.' Frantically seeking for a valid reason she blundered on, not daring to look at him, 'Then—then I shall be at liberty to—to make plans for my own future. My marriage has already been postponed far too long. It is not fair to James to delay indefinitely, but naturally I prefer to see Julia properly settled before I leave her. Restoring the Hall quickly seemed to be a perfect solution.'

Edmund was not to know that this was only an excuse—that she had no intention of continuing with her engagement—that his coming had finally convinced her that marriage with James was unthinkable. Let him discover that after she was out of harm's way.

'Your marriage . . .' Edmund echoed, hesitated a moment then went on awkwardly, 'Forgive me, Anne, if I speak out of turn, but may I beg the privilege of an old friend to advise you to think very seriously on that subject. Are you sure in your own heart that you are doing the right thing?'

'In what way?' she demanded truculently, though with sinking spirits she guessed what he meant and braced herself to combat the persuasion. She dared not let his kindness weaken her resolution.

'Are you sure that you can be happy with Sir James?' he asked gently. 'For a start, he is so much older than you . . .'

The genuine warmth in his gaze, the compassion in his voice tugged at Anne's feelings unbearably. Yet she dare not respond to it. 'That is true of many couples,' she rejoined lightly, 'but their marriages are perfectly happy.'

'Only those who start with something in common. Forgive me, Anne, but I have not noticed you show more than a very moderate affection for Sir James and your tastes are vastly different from his. Can I not beg you, as one who used to hold a special place in your affections, that you think carefully before embarking on so final a step?'

His perception, echoing her own doubts, was nearly her undoing. Only pride enabled her to stiffen her spirit and prevent him guessing how his words affected her. She took refuge in anger, letting the spark of annoyance his reference to the past evoked, blow into flame. How dare he trade on that childish infatuation! Whatever decision she had secretly arrived at, she would not let him suppose he had influenced her actions.

'How dare you suggest I have not considered the matter?' she cried, rounding on him in fury. 'I don't allow anyone to dictate to me. I am no longer the silly infant who languished after you. I've long since outgrown the stage of being infatuated with a scarlet coat!'

'I am not trying to dictate at all,' Edmund replied, still patient with her. Gently he took her hands in a shamefully disturbing grasp. His touch tingled through her, and trembling, she snatched her hands free. Edmund looked surprised at her action but persevered. 'All I ask is for you to think again, Anne. Your own good sense must do the rest. I am only concerned for your happiness.'

'Then prove it by allowing me to know my own mind,' she retorted. 'I know James far better than you do, so must consider myself the better judge of whether or not we should suit. Why else should I agree to be his wife? What do you expect me to do, throw him over like a common jilt because you consider him unsatisfactory? Do you want James made a laughing stock as ...' She broke off, aghast at where her deliberately stoked fury was leading her.

'As I was by your sister?' icily he finished the sentence for her. 'Don't try to spare my feelings, Anne. But you mistake the matter, that case was entirely different.'

'Yes!' Anne shouted, guilt and rage making her throw caution to the winds in a fervent desire to shake his implacable calm. 'Julia had some justification for her action. I have none. Don't insult me by any further comment on the matter. I am the best judge of my own future happiness.'

But even that could not entirely silence him.

'If that is how you feel I will say no more—except to hope that you will reconsider my words when you are calmer.'

Anne turned her head away, unwilling for him to see the tears that pricked at her eyelids at this generous response to her bad-tempered taunts. Why was it that Edmund could always make her feel so petty when she quarrelled with him?

'Are you ready to leave now?' she demanded ungraciously. 'Or have you any more commands for the workmen?'

He ignored the petulance of that last comment, and Anne had to wait while he sought out Bedford and gave him brief instructions on how the restoration was to proceed. Slowly the anger drained out of her, leaving her bleak and ashamed.

When he returned they mounted their horses silently and set off. It was an uncomfortable ride home, each of them engrossed in their own thoughts. Anne felt worse than ever now. Although she had intended her words to wound him, the suspicion that she had succeeded only made her feel more miserable. This frosty tension crackling between them upset her. In the old days there had never been need to make conversation with Edmund, but then they had shared a comfortable silence, not this bristling antagonism.

What made her so set on quarrelling with Edmund now? Was it the fear that otherwise her love for him might betray itself too plainly? Aghast, she tried to stifle that thought. It was too disturbing, raising ideas she dared not admit to yet.

The knowledge that the fault was hers—that their estrangement was caused by her untruthful insistence that she was happy in her impossible engagement—made her feel utterly wretched. Edmund had not even hinted at the chief obstacle—James's obsession with her sister—and she had repaid his generosity with cruel insults. Was she to lose her long-valued friendship with Edmund because she was afraid that he would read too much into her friendliness? Whatever path she chose, she would be the one to suffer most from her own folly.

She could tell from Edmund's rigid bearing, his grimly set features, that his wound was troubling him, but she dared not offer sympathy lest she break down her own defences. It was his own fault if he felt ill, she tried to convince herself. Let him suffer! There had been no need for him to come poking his nose into her concerns, she was perfectly capable of arranging matters at the Hall. If Edmund had overtaxed his strength going against the doctor's advice, then it was too bad! She would waste no sympathy on him.

All the same, she stole an anxious look at the drawn white face. Edmund stared doggedly ahead, too proud to admit his discomfort. She guessed what an effort it was for him to remain erect in the saddle, but he managed it.

It was a great relief to reach home at last. Thankfully she slid off her horse and handed the reins to the waiting groom.

Then as the animal was led away she could bear the bleak atmosphere no longer. Edmund was so silent and aloof, walking away from her into the stables with his mount, that she had to do something to bridge the gaping rift between them.

'Edmund!' Impulsively she caught at his sleeve. 'I am sorry for my bad temper. I didn't mean to be so rude.'

The warmth that transformed his features was worth every scrap of dented pride.

'Perhaps I was equally to blame. It was presumptuous of me to interfere ...'

'No! You were right to rate me,' she insisted. Suddenly the world seemed bright with sunshine once more. They were at loggerheads no longer. 'Friends ought to be able to advise each other frankly without offence.'

'Then we are friends again?' he asked quizzically, taking her hand in his free one. 'For how long? Till I speak out of turn once more?'

Anne's lips twitched. Edmund had always known how to win a smile from her. 'Probably,' she admitted. 'But don't let me be so unreasonable! ...'

What more she might have added was never to be known. As they stood, hands linked, laughing at each other, a frantic housekeeper ran towards them.

'Thank goodness you're home at last, Miss Anne! Have you seen Master Kit anywhere? He's vanished!'

Julia followed fast on her heels. She flung herself, sobbing, into Edmund's arms, thrusting her sister aside.

'My poor Kit! I know I shall never see him again. What shall I do, now that he has been murdered too?'

CHAPTER
FIVE

ANNE could not suppress a twinge of envy as she saw Edmund's arm close protectively around Julia. It was still hard to see him fall slowly but inevitably back under Julia's spell. She could have borne the pain if Julia truly loved him and regretted her unkind betrayal of him, but Anne knew that his wealth and position were the chief attraction for her sister.

Except perhaps in her dealings with Thomas, Julia had always let her head rule her heart. Self-interest had always been her strongest emotion. Anne had a shrewd suspicion that the pathetic helplessness and distress she was displaying now were all part of her campaign to ensnare Edmund. She doubted whether Julia was half as anxious about her son as she pretended.

The widow raised tear-drenched eyes to gaze forlornly into his. Grasping feverishly at him she cried, 'What shall I do, Edmund?'

Startled by her sudden movement, Edmund's horse whickered nervously and side-stepped, tugging at the rein. Seeing Edmund's wince of pain as the pull of the heavy beast strained his injured side, Anne exclaimed crossly, 'Do be more careful, Julia! You don't want to start Edmund's wound bleeding again.'

Julia drew away from him with a tremulous sob.

'Forgive me, Edmund! I forgot you had been hurt—forgot everything in the relief of having someone to turn to. I have been beside myself with worry! My poor darling Kit!'

Her eyes, swimming with tears, only looked more infuriatingly brilliant and luminous. Patting her awkwardly with his sound arm, Edmund cast a look of anguished entreaty at Anne. Exasperated by the knowledge that, as always, she was expected to deal with Julia's emotionalism, Anne exclaimed, 'For goodness' sake calm down, Julia! There is nothing to be gained from all this fuss. No one has been murdered, and I am sure that Kit will turn up quite safe and sound.'

'No one murdered! How can you say such a thing after Edmund and Phillip have both been savagely attacked and left for dead? What chance would my poor dear Kit have against the brutal ruffian who treated grown men so violently? It is all very fine for you to tell me to be calm,' she went on shrilly, working herself into a frenzy as Anne tried to stem this flow, 'what can you understand of a mother's feelings? Oh my poor lamb! I know I shall never see him again!'

Weeping, she cast herself once more into Edmund's arms. He frowned reproachfully over the golden curls at Anne. Swallowing the angry words that trembled on her tongue, she inquired with commendable calm when Kit had last been seen.

'Not since breakfast time, miss,' the housekeeper told her with gloomy relish. 'He ran off in a tantrum when Nurse told him you'd gone to the Hall without him. She tried to stop him, but he was too quick for her and made off round the lake.'

'The lake! Oh my poor angel! I knew it! He is drowned!'

At this Anne's sorely tried patience gave out. 'Do make up your mind, Julia,' she snapped. 'A moment ago you were convinced that he had been murdered.'

Julia took refuge in tears.

'Your sister does not mean to be heartless,' Edmund tried to soothe her. 'I'm sure the child is safe but to set your mind at rest I'll have the men drag the lake immediately.'

Predictably Julia greeted this offer with a shriek of horror.

'Don't be ridiculous, Edmund!' Anne exclaimed crossly. 'There is no need to do any such thing. Julia knows perfectly well that even if Kit were so foolish as to fall in the lake, it would do him little harm. He learned to swim when he was tiny and is completely at home in the water. All this fuss is quite unnecessary. It is my belief that he has run off somewhere to sulk because he couldn't have his own way. It wouldn't be the first time. He'll come back when his temper cools.'

'That's what Nurse said,' admitted the housekeeper. 'She didn't worry about him at first either, but she got upset when Master Kit didn't come back for his riding lesson. You know how he loves that pony of his.'

Anne had to admit that it was unlike Kit to miss the riding instruction that was usually the high spot of his week.

'All the same,' she added, seeing that Julia was ready to fall into hysterics once more, 'I don't consider that any proof of his being harmed. He may have mistaken the time, or become lost or shut in somewhere. Have you searched for him properly?'

'The maids have been all over the house, Miss Anne, and Charles has been out in the park calling and looking for him, and Nurse is still searching the grounds.'

'One footman and an elderly woman! What good is that to cover so vast an area? Let all the footmen and grooms be sent out immediately,' ordered Edmund. In a short while with military efficiency he had organised a thorough search of the Manor, its outbuildings and grounds. Relays of servants were sent in all directions. Soon one was back with the lodge-keeper's daughter, who admitted to having seen Kit leave the park more than an hour before.

'I thought it odd-like, him being on his own and all, but he said he was going to meet you, miss,' she gulped tearfully. 'So I thought it was all right.'

'We are not blaming you at all,' Anne assured her. 'We are just anxious to find where Master Kit has got to. Are you sure you saw him go along the lane?'

'Yes, miss. Down towards Melthorpe.'

'He cannot have gone to the Hall or we should have seen him on our way back,' objected Edmund.

'Not if he cut across the fields or through Bassett's wood.' Anne, too, was beginning to be worried now. Bassett was reputed to set man-traps. Was Kit foolish enough to risk those?

One of the grooms remembered seeing a gipsy encampment near the wood and was unwise enough to mention the fact.

'Are you trying to tell me that my Kit has been stolen by gipsies?' shrieked Julia.

'Nonsense!' Her own anxiety made Anne sharp. 'That is just an old wives' tale. Gipsies don't steal children. Why should they? Heaven knows they have enough of their own without!'

'All the same, I think I will ride back along that way,' said Edmund. 'The boy may have got himself into some difficulty and need help.'

'No, Edmund! You've ridden much too far already today,' Anne protested. 'Anyone can see you are exhausted.' She had determined not to sympathise with him, but his drawn face and the involuntary wince as he moved, convinced her that Edmund's wound was troubling him. 'You stay here with Julia. I will go with one of the grooms to look for Kit.'

But Edmund obstinately refused to accept this arrangement. He insisted on going himself, although he accepted her company gratefully. A stiff brandy restored some of his colour and he directed a servant to fetch food to make up for the luncheon they had missed. Anne did not want to stop to eat, but he pressed her.

'You will be no use if you are weak from hunger. We may have a long ride.'

She saw the sense of his argument and somehow managed to choke something down.

'What about me?' demanded Julia indignantly as they prepared to leave. 'You are not intending to leave me all on my own, are you? Let my mare be saddled at once. I will come with you.'

Patiently Edmund explained that, as they had no certainty of finding Kit, it would be better for her to wait at home in case he returned another way. He had already sent out search parties in likely directions. Any of those might find the boy, and Kit would want to see his mother when he reached home. Reluctantly, Julia allowed herself to be persuaded to remain in James's care.

'But be as quick as you can or I shan't be responsible for the consequences. The suspense is shattering my poor nerves!'

Anne fidgeted impatiently while all this was being settled. How could Julia be so selfish as to hold them up with her foolish objections? The thought of Kit wandering lost or injured tormented her. She would have spurred away directly Edmund was mounted if his hand on her rein had not checked her.

'Gently, Anne! You will be no help to Kit if you injure yourself dashing off in that neck-or-nothing fashion!'

'But he may be lying hurt somewhere while we delay,' she fretted.

'I very much doubt it. Didn't you admit yourself that this wasn't the first time he had disappeared in this way?'

'Yes,' she admitted with a rueful smile. 'Last year when his papa refused to take him to the prize-fight at Salisbury he started off, quite determined to run away to sea, but by the time he reached the village he had thought better of it and persuaded the carter to bring him back. We were all in a terrible state of alarm when he arrived, as happy as a lark, telling us that he had decided to forgive us after all.'

Although she could smile at the memory, her cheerful words masked a real fear—and a twinge of guilt. She could not help blaming herself, nor avoid the reflection that it was her broken promise that had caused Kit to embark on this escapade. She prayed that he had come to no harm; she would never forgive herself if he were injured— or worse.

At the end of the lane they halted, unsure of which path Kit would have chosen. Anne stared unhappily at the wood. Would Kit have ignored the danger? He was over-confident at times, too trusting in his own ability to cope.

Then to her relief she caught sight of a scrap of brown nankeen dangling from the hedge opposite. Thankfully she pointed it out to her companion. 'I'm sure that is off Kit's jacket.'

'Yes, and see the footprints in the mud on the far side. They are too small to have been made by an adult. He must have squeezed through the gap into the field in order to get to the path to the village that runs down the far side.'

The gap was small, but the horses managed to push their way through without too much difficulty. Soon they picked up the footpath along which an occasional small footmark in the soft ground indicated that Kit had indeed come this way. It was a relief to know that he had at least avoided the dangers of Bassett's wood, but his prolonged absence was still worrying and Anne anxiously spurred her horse on.

They had almost reached the village when they saw a group of extraordinarily dressed people enter the far side of the meadow they had begun to cross themselves. A short plump man in a voluminous black cloak and battered top-hat was assisting two young women over the stile. Both were finding great difficulty in negotiating the obstacle, hampered as they were by the flowing trains of their gaudy dresses. The dazzling scarlet and emerald silk gowns were as inappropriate for a country stroll as the enormous bonnets, trimmed with billowing plumes and tawdry lace.

'Excuse me, have you seen a young boy ...' Edmund began as soon as they were close enough, but broke off as a tousle-headed child in torn nankeen jacket leapt over the stile behind the young women, shouting,

'Anne! Anne! Come and see who I've found. This is Mr Delamare!'

Weak with relief Anne slid off her horse to hug her nephew. 'Thank goodness you are safe! Where have you been?'

'With Mr Delamare, of course!'

Sweeping off his rusty black hat, the portly gentleman made a profound bow. 'I am enchanted to make your acquaintance, ma'am! Allow me to present my daughters, Imogen and Cordelia.'

The outsize feathers quivered and dipped as the two bob-bed curtsies, twittering self-consciously. Close to they were younger than Anne had first supposed, their preposterous gowns loose on their half-formed figures. Before she could do more than nod in acknowledgment of the introduction, their father went on,

'I am Horatio Delamare!' He paused impressively as if this should mean something to them, then, when they made no response, continued with a hint of disappointment in his voice, 'This young gentleman befriended us in the village in our hour of need. We were on our way to restore him to the bosom of his adoring family.'

'That was very kind of you,' murmured Anne, as overcome by Mr Delamare's booming eloquence as by the strong aroma of brandy that wafted towards her with his words. 'I am sorry you were put to so much trouble. Whatever have you been doing, Kit? We were growing really anxious about you.'

'There, young man, what did I tell you? Your sorrowing mamma has been imagining her ewe lamb gone for ever. "*Was ever mother had so dear a loss?*"'

'She isn't my mother,' Kit interrupted. 'That's Anne. She's my aunt.'

'Ah! And now, in the words of the noble Swan of Avon, you may—*Make quick conveyance with your good aunt Anne!*' boomed Mr Delamare, unabashed.

Anne dared not look at Edmund lest his appreciation of the ridiculous situation made her laugh out loud.

'Mr Delamare is an actor, Anne!' Kit told her.

'*A poor player*,' Mr Delamare's gesture of magnificent humility made the impossibly large jewel in his ring glisten richly in the sunlight, '*who struts and frets his hour upon the stage.*'

'Pa specialises in the works of the Immoral Bard,' put in Cordelia helpfully.

'*Immortal*, child. Immortal!—deathless!' snapped her father irritably. 'Immoral is quite another matter, signifying that which is lewd and vile, unfit for the ears of the fair sex.'

'In that case it is quite as fitting for him,' she retorted, with a saucy look in Edmund's direction from under her long lashes. 'Else why did you kick up such a fuss when you found Ginny and me reading that old copy of *Hamlet*, and make us use Mr Bowdler's version instead?'

Imogen clapped her hands together, shrieking her approval of this sally. Their father goggled back in speechless indignation.

'I had not realised, Mr Delamare,' observed Edmund, taking pity on him, 'that there was now a theatre in this neighbourhood.'

'Alas, sir, there is none. We are only stopped here by sad mischance. We are engaged to perform at Bristol tomorrow, but our conveyance has broken down.'

'The wheel came off the cart when Pa hit the milestone,' Imogen explained confidentially. 'Rosy's told him and told him he shouldn't drive when he's bosky, but he don't ever listen! And now we're stuck!'

Glaring at her, Mr Delamare continued, 'So until it can be repaired we are unable to prosecute our calling unless we can find some temporary accommodation to represent *our wooden 0*.'

'I told them they could use our barn,' said Kit eagerly. 'Ferdie said they often do that in country places, but Rosy said we must ask Mamma first. Please say it's all right, Anne!'

'Now, Kit, you must remember that we can no longer make that sort of arrangement. The barn belongs to Lord Ashorne, like everything else. It is for him to decide who uses it.'

'Please!' Kit's huge blue eyes, so like Julia's, were raised in entreaty to Edmund. 'Ferdie told me all about the plays. I'm longing to see him act in one. Ferdie takes all sorts of parts—lords, princes, kings even!'

'He is referring to my youngest offspring—"Ferdinand the Infant Prodigy",' explained Mr Delamare with manifest pride. 'He was born while we were playing *The Tempest* at York. Shall I ever forget that night? His poor mamma, God rest her soul, was a Miranda without peer. Her pains started in the first act, but like a true trouper she soldiered on until the final curtain. She managed one call then collapsed among the scenery, so that my son and heir was born not merely to tread the boards, but actually upon them!'

Anne tried to visualise the scene but failed. She could only reflect incredulously that Mrs Delamare's condition must indeed have presented a new dimension to the rôle.

'And where is Master Ferdinand now?' she asked unsteadily, still not daring to meet Edmund's eye. He had always shared her strong appreciation of the ridiculous in the past, and must surely now be enjoying this ludicrous account as much as she was.

'Ferdinand remained behind in the village to protect his eldest sister.'

'Rosy don't like to walk, so she stayed on the baggage cart,' explained Imogen.

'And won't she be as mad as fire when she finds she's missed meeting a real live lord!' added Cordelia with satisfaction. 'She had a baronet used to send her flowers and suchlike when we was at Bath, but she didn't set much store by him.'

'Well, he was nearly ninety and hadn't a tooth in his head,' her sister pointed out. 'You didn't fancy him neither!'

Kit tugged eagerly at Anne's sleeve to attract her attention.

'Ferdie says that Rosy dresses up as a boy in some of the plays,' he told her, eyes bright with excitement. 'I do so want to see one. Please say you will let me, Anne!'

'Unfortunately, young man, it will be beyond your dear aunt's power to indulge that whim. We have nowhere to present our humble entertainment.'

'I'm sure it will be possible for you to use the barn at Ashorne,' Edmund told him. 'We'd all like to see your performance. The barn is all but empty now, and the little that remains can easily be shifted to another store. I'll have my steward arrange it as soon as possible. Where is your luggage at the moment?'

'Heaven reward you, my lord! *Hourly joys be still upon you.* They are at the Three Crosses with the remainder of our little band.'

'Then if you return there immediately yourself, I will send one of my men with a cart to collect them and take you to look the barn over. I'm sure it will suit your purpose—I remember a troupe of players performing there each year when I was a child. You are welcome to sleep there too if you wish—unless you prefer to return to the inn.'

'You are more than generous, my lord. Come, my loves, let us hasten to deliver these excellent tidings to our companions. Be sure that *We'll hear a play tomorrow!*'

Giggling, his two daughters murmured their farewells before turning to scuttle after their father who was already half a field away in his eagerness to take back the good tidings.

'No, Kit! You stay with us!' commanded Edmund, as the boy made to follow them. 'Up you hop in front of me with no arguments. We must get you home to your mother without further delay. She was dreadfully worried about you.'

'Who? Mamma? I don't believe it,' Kit retorted. 'She don't care what I do as long as I don't tease her. She told me to get out of her sight this morning because my noise was hurting her ears.'

That sounded more like Julia than the display of maternal fondness they had been given earlier, thought Anne, though she refrained from saying so. Let Edmund draw his own conclusions.

'I want to see Ferdie again!' Kit insisted, still hanging back. 'He says ...'

'No arguments!' Edmund repeated in a voice not to be disobeyed. With an ill grace Kit capitulated and let Anne help him scramble up in front of Edmund, before she remounted herself from off the stile. He was not subdued long. He waved enthusiastically after his new friends until they were out of sight, then settled back with an envious sigh.

'Aren't they grand! I wish I could dress so fine. Did you ever see anything like Mr Delamare's diamond, Anne?'

'Never!' Anne admitted with feeling, and was oddly warmed to see Edmund's understanding grin. It was good to be in sympathy with him once more.

'Ferdie says he wears it on stage when he plays kings and such. Wait till you meet Ferdie. He's a great gun! He says he has been acting ever since he could walk. In fact he was born on the stage!'

'So his papa informed us,' said Edmund.

'But not until *after* the final curtain,' Anne reminded him with a chuckle. 'It must have been a revelation to see that performance!'

'You haven't seen Rosy yet,' Kit went on ignoring the hilarity he could not understand. 'She's beautiful! Even prettier than Ginny or 'Delia!'

'Indeed?' Anne observed, not considering this any great recommendation. A brief snort of mirth betrayed Edmund's agreement.

'Yes, she's got long black hair and she laughs all the time. Just like that lady friend of Papa's who used to come and stay in the village such a lot. You know, the one who hurt her back when Papa was killed.'

'Hush,' Anne exclaimed quickly, noting Edmund's shocked reception of this innocent description. 'I told you that you must not speak of her any more.'

'Only when Mamma is by, you said. Because it makes her sad. Edmund don't mind, do you?'

'I *mind*, as you term it, considerably, when you disobey your aunt and are impertinent into the bargain,' Edmund declared icily.

Kit, subdued by the unaccustomed set-down, prudently relapsed into silence. Anne thought the rebuke over-severe for the offence, but dared not say so in front of the child. Clearly Kit's careless words had shocked Edmund into more warmth than the incident warranted.

She stole a quick glance sideways. The face that had been so carefree, lit up with amusement a few moments earlier, was set into stern lines once more, though, as ever, it was hard to guess exactly what Edmund was thinking. She had an insane impulse to lean across and smooth those frown creases from his brow, and clutched her reins tightly to prevent herself. Edmund would think her mad—quite rightly!

Once again silence strained uncomfortably between them. Anne felt forlorn—in need of comfort herself. For a brief space she had been able to forget all the difficulties that divided them but now the gulf gaped wide again. Chilled she remembered all the confused problems that sundered them. Would they ever be resolved?

Hopeless to raise any of them with Kit, a silent but intelligent listener, riding stiffly in front of Edmund. What good would talking do, anyway? Was friendship all she really desired from Edmund? Had that moment of delight when he kissed her not made her long for far more than he was ever likely to offer?

Miserably she rode beside him, horrified to find her eyes brimming with foolish tears, and resolutely kept her face averted lest Edmund guess at her foolish weakness. She was heartily glad to see the Manor gates appear at last.

Kit recovered sufficiently to wriggle down as soon as they reached the stable yard and scurry off in the direction of the house to spread the news of his new friends' arrival.

'Nurse! Nurse! Guess who I've seen! Mamma!' the shrill voice faded into the distance.

Anne started to follow him directly the horses had been led off, but Edmund put out a hand to prevent her.

'Is it—true—what the child says about his father?' he asked hesitantly.

Anne was too conscious of that hand on her arm. His touch roused all those confused emotions she had tried so desperately to suppress. Why had Edmund this ability to make her pulse race, every nerve tingle? However much she despised herself for feeling this way about a man who cared nothing for her, she could do nothing to help it. Despairingly she tugged free from his grasp.

'Well, yes—I thought you guessed that.'

'Thomas was unfaithful to your sister?'

'Of course he was unfaithful. You know what a wandering eye Thomas had. Marriage was not likely to alter that.'

'I don't know how he could look at another woman when he had a wife such as Julia.'

'I'm afraid that I cannot understand male appetites in the least,' Anne snapped. 'But I assure you, Thomas certainly continued to do more than look. He had a string of mistresses.'

'It is incredible!'

'Perhaps, but it is true!' Anne was torn between sympathy for his evident shocked dismay and exasperation at his naïvety. Why did he imagine Julia would alter Thomas's nature—and how? Did he suppose that she had lived like a virtuous wife herself, ignoring all other men to devote herself to her husband?

If so he was very mistaken. Her *affaires* had been more discreetly handled than his, perhaps, but Thomas had been well aware that he was not her sole bedfellow. That was not Anne's idea of a successful marriage, but they had appeared content enough until squabbles over Julia's extravagance produced a more serious breach.

'Poor Julia,' Edmund sighed. 'How she must have suffered!'

This had been a difficult day for Anne. Shocks, misunderstandings and disappointments had combined to leave her tired and dispirited. In spite of all her good resolutions to remain calm, to view dispassionately Edmund's excessive concern for her sister's welfare, those words were the last straw. Why was Edmund so blind to the truth? Her resentment, bottled up for so long, boiled over.

'There are some who would say it served her right for being so stupid as to run off with Thomas in the first place,' she retorted fiercely. 'Julia knew precisely what sort of man he was when she married him.'

She was tempted to go further, to tell him how lightly Julia in her turn had treated her marriage vows, of the flocks of admirers she gathered round her from the very beginning. The shortcomings had not been all on Thomas's side.

But the affection Anne still felt for her sister, faults and all, made her check the angry impulse. That would be too spiteful—and probably unwise, she told herself bleakly. Edmund would not believe it any more than he credited any other criticism of Julia. However clearly he saw everyone else's imperfections he had always possessed the ability to close his eyes to Julia's. Now he shook his head incredulously.

'I did not realise you could be so hard, Anne.'

'Hard! Do you call it hard to be realistic? Julia's treatment of you was scarcely blameless. Why waste your sympathy on her?'

'Oh, Anne! How lucky it is I know you well enough to understand that you don't mean all these cruel words. You are tired and overwrought, but don't let it cloud your judgment. Your sister is a warm impulsive creature. She told me how cunningly Thomas pressured her into that rash elopement—a mistake she regretted almost immediately, but too late. It is unjust to blame her for not possessing your calm good sense.'

'So you grant I am sensible, although I am so unsympathetic. Perhaps it is my good sense which makes me hard,' she countered.

'Don't, Anne! I am too fond of you to enjoy this cynicism you pretend. It is not your true nature. You are not hard! A trifle unsympathetic at times, but that is a fault of youth.'

If only he knew how difficult it was to keep up that show of indifference! It was not she but Julia who, beneath that veneer of tenderheartedness, was hard as nails. Her heart ached for the distress he must feel when the truth finally forced itself upon him. Sooner or later he must be disillusioned with his idol, but Anne did not want to be there when that happened. Till then she must dissemble. Let him think ill of her if he wished. What did it matter? Better he should disapprove than guess at her foolish love for him.

'Youth? I am not young any more, Edmund,' she protested impatiently. 'I am twenty-two now. Many women younger than I are married with families. Perhaps I too should have a child by now, if Julia's bereavement had not upset my wedding plans.'

She could see that idea had startled him. They had spoken of her marriage before but always as a vague future event.

'I forget those lost years,' he said slowly, staring at her as if he suddenly saw her with fresh eyes. 'In my mind I still see you as a child, but I am mistaken. You are almost the age Julia was when we first met. Six years have brought so many changes. We are all vastly altered.'

Was he referring to Julia too, she wondered, or was it too soon for him to glimpse the flaws in the façade Julia presented to the world?

'Older and wiser, I hope,' she said lightly, and hurried away before she was tempted to say more than she ought. Edmund was left behind, staring after her, oddly thoughtful.

Back indoors, she found Kit volubly explaining his adventures to his mother, who reclined weakly on her chaiselongue with James in anxious attendance.

'I'm sure I don't understand what you are about, Anne,' Julia greeted her petulantly, 'encouraging the child to associate with a band of ruffians!'

'They weren't so dreadful. A little eccentric, perhaps, but quite respectable.'

'Not if what Kit is telling me about them is true. They sound totally unsuitable companions for a young boy. Then to persuade Edmund to let them settle so close, too! I cannot imagine what you were thinking of! Don't blame me when we are all found murdered in our beds!'

'I can safely promise not to do so.'

'That's right! Mock at me! I dare say it all seems a joke to you, but I am not amused when my son arrives home in such a tattered condition and expects me to countenance his friendship with a set of vulgar players!'

'But, Mamma, they're not...'

'Oh do be quiet, Kit,' Julia told him peevishly. 'You make my poor head spin with all your noise. Go and tell Nurse all about it if you must bore someone with your chatter.' She sank back into the cushions, one hand pressed dramatically to her brow while the other groped for her vinaigrette.

'Run along, Kit, as your mother bids.' Edmund, who had come in time to hear this, silenced the boy's protest. 'She has had a very distressing time worrying over your disappearance. You should think of other people before you play such foolish pranks.'

Disappointed, Kit ran out, slamming the door behind him. Julia winced at the sound. Edmund frowned and James hastened to proffer her smelling salts to the stricken beauty. While Julia luxuriated in the attentions of her anxious suitors, Anne followed Kit to ensure that excitement did not prevent his making up for the meal he had lost. At his age children needed plenty of nourishment.

Bleakly she wondered why no one else had noticed how soon Julia's maternal fondness had faded once her son was restored to her.

CHAPTER
SIX

IT was always difficult to keep Kit's mind on his lessons, but Anne found it next to impossible the following day. Kit was bubbling over with information about his new friends and questions on the plays they had mentioned. Anne answered the first dozen queries patiently, then pointed out that when he learned to read properly he could discover all these things for himself.

'Even Ferdie had to begin with his A B C. Now no more chatter until you have finished the next page.'

With every ill grace Kit turned his attention to his copy book and consented to toil away at his letters, though Anne could see that his heart was not in the task. His gaze was far oftener directed outside into the park than down to his book.

She could scarcely blame him. Her own enthusiasm for teaching him was very half-hearted this morning. Too many conflicting thoughts coursing through her brain prevented her concentrating on giving Kit the help and encouragement he needed. How could she expect him to be enthusiastic when she was so indifferent?

Perhaps when they finally moved into Melthorpe Hall things would be better. The delay while Edmund's extensive improvements were put into effect would sorely try her nerves. She longed for the time they would move there away from Edmund's disturbing presence, yet dreaded it too. There was a melancholy pleasure in being near him, but pain, too, in watching him fall back under her sister's spell.

Julia had been particularly sweet and attentive to him last evening—perhaps to combat the bad impression her hysterical outburst had given earlier. How long would it be before they married: what would Anne do then? She could not bear to remain at Ashorne with them—perhaps with the additional distress of seeing Edmund grow disenchanted with his bride.

Marriage with James was equally unthinkable. What was the alternative? She could not set up house on her own. Her aunt might take her in, but the prospect of life with Aunt Mattie was not an inviting one. It was almost a relief that her thoughts were interrupted by Kit's excited shout.

'There's Ferdie and Rosy! I knew they'd come. Please may I go down and see them? I'll work twice as hard tomorrow, I promise.'

Following his eager finger, she saw an ill-assorted couple walking across the park towards the Manor. Glad of the excuse to end the unproductive lesson, she allowed Kit to pack up his books. He managed the task in a fraction of the time it had taken to fetch them out and clattered off downstairs to greet his friends. Anne followed at a more sedate pace, curious to meet the remaining members of the Delamare family.

Ferdie was an undersized child. Anne judged him to be around twelve years old, though the contrast between his careworn face and skinny frame made exact calculation difficult. Yet for all his lack of inches there was a distinct resemblance to his father. The occasional dramatic turn of phrase and grand manner, even more ludicrous in one so young, brought Mr Delamare clearly to mind. She wished that Edmund was there to share the joke, then checked the thought—that way lay heartbreak.

Rosy, as she had expected, was a full-blown version of her sisters. The clothes that hung loosely on their adolescent bodies strained over her highly developed form, displaying all her ample charms. She nodded coolly as Kit introduced her to Anne, staring at Anne's simple muslin gown with a hint of contempt in her eyes, and complacently smoothing her own elaborately trimmed creation. But for all its magnificence, noted Anne, it could do with a good wash and press. Rosy's neck, too, showed traces of grime though her face was freshly painted.

'We've brought you an invitation from our father for this

evening's Grand Performance,' began Ferdie impressively, but Rosy shook her head, holding the paper tightly folded.

'Pa said we was to give it to the lord hisself, in person!'

Though Ferdie protested she remained adamant. Fortunately before the argument could grow too violent, Edmund came out of the stable yard with Weston. If he was impressed by the vision before him Edmund gave no sign of it. Weston, less reticent, immediately sized up the newcomer with a calculating gleam in his eye and moved adroitly round till he was standing close beside her.

Exchanging a brief grin with Anne, Edmund declared solemnly, 'I am Lord Ashorne, Madam. How can I assist you?'

Rosy wriggled delightedly and in a refined coo, very different from the strident tones she had employed earlier, she simpered, 'Pa said to tell your lordship how terrible grateful he is to your lordship for your lordship's kindness, and begs that your lordship will honour us by coming to view the performance tonight.'

She handed over the paper with a provocative smile, allowing her hand to brush lingeringly over his in a blatant version of a trick Anne had seen Julia enact more skilfully a dozen times. She wondered whether Edmund would notice the resemblance, but doubted it. Julia's victims rarely seemed to notice her ploys. Only Thomas had seen through them, which was one reason why their marriage had failed so rapidly.

'What is the play to be?' she asked, as Edmund puzzled over the elaborately curled script of the invitation.

'*The Merchant of Venice*. I'm to play Portia.'

'Unless father changes his mind again,' put in Ferdie bitterly. 'You can't imagine the trouble it was to settle on that, miss! Father was all for *Hamlet, Prince of Denmark*, but Rosy wouldn't hear of it.'

'No, I wouldn't! What chance is there for me in *Hamlet*, pray? Pa does very nicely with all those dramatic "*To be or not to be*" s but he always makes me play Orphelia. It's a rotten part. Only one decent speech and a bit of singing then she drowns herself like a ninny before the play is half done.'

'It's not one you can show your legs in, neither. That's why you don't like it.'

Rosy silenced her brother with a shrewdly aimed kick, and continued as if he had not spoken.

'So we finally settled on the *Merchant*. Shylock is one of Pa's most famous rôles, and I flatter myself I make a very passable Portia!' She glared at Ferdie, daring him to disagree, then fluttering long eyelashes at Edmund, confided, 'My gentleman friend at Bath was kind enough to call it a superlative performance. He said I far outclassed Mrs Siddons—and he should know! He remembers her when she was young, before she lost her looks, poor soul. But there, I mustn't brag. As Pa says, "Talent is a Divine gift!"'

Ignoring Ferdie's snort of disgust, she smiled dazzlingly at Edmund and at the same time cast a saucy glance sideways to where Weston's hot gaze was fixed on her in bold approval. 'Shall I tell Pa that both you gentlemen will be honouring us tonight?'

'We must certainly come to judge your performance for ourselves,' replied Edmund, his face solemn. Only the faintest suggestion of a quiver in his voice betrayed his amusement to one who knew him as well as Anne did.

'Father will be overjoyed at the news! It isn't often we get a real nob in the audience—apart from Rosy's baronet, and he only comes to look at her legs.' Ferdie beamed at them. Anne had to bite her lips hard to prevent her mirth escaping.

'Pa asks your lordship to excuse him not being here to present the invite hisself,' put in Rosy hastily. 'Only he is a trifle off-colour this morning.'

'Bosky again, she means,' explained her brother helpfully.

'Well to be honest he is,' admitted Rosy. 'As drunk as a lord!' She broke off with a shriek of laughter. 'Begging your lordship's pardon, I'm sure. Anyone can see your lordship is stone cold sober!'

'Don't mention it,' Edmund told her unsteadily.

'Can I go and see the play, too?' Kit tugged urgently at Anne's sleeve. 'Please say I can!'

As she hesitated, not thinking that Julia would approve of such an outing, Edmund said, 'What do you think, Anne? I'm sure you won't want to miss the chance of enjoying this unique experience. Shall we allow this wholly undeserving young man to join us?'

'*Please!*'

'If his Mamma permits it,' agreed Anne weakly, not proof against the pleading blue eyes. With a shriek of delight Kit raced off to demand permission, dragging Ferdie with him.

'Then thank your father for us, Miss Delamare, and tell him that we shall be delighted to be present at this evening's performance. Till then, *au revoir!*' Edmund bowed gallantly to Rosy, who bobbed a delighted curtsey.

'About the seating, your lordship, sir,' she exclaimed, reluctant to see him escape. 'Pa was wondering if your lordship could see your way clear to letting us use some of the hay. We could ...'

'You had better settle that sort of detail with Weston,' suggested Edmund hastily. 'We have finished our business for the present, so he can walk back to the barn with you and sort out all the problems on the spot.'

Nothing loath, Weston accepted the arm she offered and they went off together, heads very close. Remembering what she had learned of the steward's reputation, Anne had a moment of doubt about giving the girl such an escort, but a second glance at Rosy convinced her that the actress could take care of herself. If Rosy were seduced it would be with her full co-operation. She was no innocent country girl to be taken in by his wiles. Although giggling happily at whatever Weston was whispering into her ear, she still found time to cast back a languishing glance at Edmund. He acknowledged it with a broad smile, murmuring laughingly in Anne's ear, 'I feel confident I have eclipsed the baronet already. Don't you agree?'

'Undoubtedly, but don't let it go to *your lordship*'s head! It is only because you have your own teeth. Weston seems a very dangerous rival—I wonder you risk allowing him such an opportunity to cut you out of the lady's affections.'

'Ah, but you are forgetting that Weston has no title. I rely on that to sway the preference my way!'

When he could read Rosy's motives so clearly why was he not equally suspicious of Julia's, wondered Anne unhappily.

What was there about her sister to inspire so uncritical an admiration in all the men she met?

To everyone's amazement, Julia not only gave permission for Kit to see the play but insisted on making one of the party herself.

'I don't think you'll enjoy it,' Anne warned her. 'They aren't a fashionable company of actors such as you are used to seeing in town.'

'Obviously not, if the female I saw prancing off with Phillip just now was any sample.'

'That was Rosy—Rosalind Delamare, their leading lady. I thought Weston appeared very smitten with her.'

'Rubbish!' Julia exclaimed with unnecessary violence. 'What has Phillip in common with a vulgar hussy like that? I could hardly bear to watch her flaunting herself so shamelessly. She put me in mind of that low creature Thomas used to bring here to vex me. That one was always making eyes at Phillip too, which thoroughly embarrassed the poor man. He didn't want to offend Thomas by being rude to her, yet he was disgusted by her vulgarity. You cannot imagine his taste to be so degraded as to *admire* that blowsy female!'

This sounded remarkably like jealousy on Julia's part but Anne was unwilling to admit that her sister could really be attracted to her steward. She tried to convince herself that Julia's anger was proof only of a reluctance to relinquish any of her admirers, however unfavoured, but the vehemence with which she had spoken left Anne uneasy. The relationship between the two was beginning to look more complicated than she had supposed.

'You'll have to see Rosy again if you come with us this evening,' she warned. 'She is to play Portia.'

'Shakespeare!' exclaimed Julia in disgust. 'I might have guessed!' Then, anticipating Anne's objection, she insisted, 'Even so, I shall come. If you imagine I intend to stay at home moping on my own while the rest of you are off enjoying yourselves, you are very much mistaken. You'd like the chance to get Edmund to yourself, I'm sure. Don't think I haven't seen you playing off your airs on him! But he's mine remember, *mine!*'

Sadly Anne reflected that this confidence was justified. She had seen Edmund's eyes soften as he watched her sister too often not to know that his love for Julia was unchanged. It could only be a matter of time before he acknowledged that love openly. Perhaps only a regard for convention, more scrupulous than Julia had ever felt, prevented his announcing their engagement before the year of mourning for Thomas was over.

Anne must harden herself to accept their eventual marriage. Fiercely she tried to persuade herself that it would not matter to her—that her childhood infatuation for Edmund was over and done with—but that was daily proving more difficult. The rapport that had existed between them years ago, was gradually being re-established—perhaps even more strongly. Automatically her eyes sought for his to savour a joke, and every pleasure felt twice as vivid with Edmund beside her to share it. Over and over she warned herself that she ought not to indulge the bitter-sweet delight, but found it hard to resist although she knew it meant far less to Edmund than to herself.

She hesitated a long while over her dressing that evening, unsure for once of what to wear for the occasion. Full evening dress seemed inappropriate, yet she was unwilling to give offence to the Delamares by making too little effort. They were such showy dressers themselves that anything in her wardrobe must appear dull by comparison.

Eventually she settled on a simple striped tarlatan gown with fine lace trimming and, lest this be thought too plain, swept her hair up into an elaborate coil out of which the golden ringlets cascaded, a style which she knew to be a trifle out-dated but one which was very flattering to her. As an afterthought she added a brightly embroidered silk shawl to the ensemble.

Edmund's warm approval when she came downstairs made all the effort seem worthwhile. Even James, resplendent in skin-tight blue coat and masterly folded white neckcloth, gave her an admiring glance and admitted that she looked 'almost as handsome as your sister in that rigout.'

Kit, who had been ready two hours before the appointed

time, was dancing around the hall in a frenzy of impatience
as they waited for Julia. Even Edmund was frowning over his
pocket watch before she appeared, ablaze with diamonds.
Mourning was completely cast off now. The shimmering
silver gown, cut daringly low, moulded to her slim form.
Sparkling stones glinted at throat, wrist and dainty ears.
Anne felt totally outclassed by this magnificence.

'Exquisite!' breathed James hoarsely in an ecstasy of
appreciation as she posed halfway down the staircase, inviting their compliments. 'You look like a goddess.'

'I am happy that you approve,' she said, but her eyes were
on Edmund. She walked slowly down and stood smiling
expectantly up at him. 'Here I am, Edmund.'

'At last!' Edmund greeted her abruptly. Ignoring the
beautiful outfit, he stared with misgiving at her dainty slip-
pers. 'Surely you don't intend to go out in those flimsy things.
They'll be ruined before we have walked a few yards.'

'*Walked!*' she echoed in shrill horror. 'You cannot expect
me to *walk* in this dress. Why aren't we using the carriage like
civilised human beings?'

'Because the short distance it can take us makes fetching
out the horses ridiculous.'

'Not half as ridiculous as walking in this dress. It would be
spoiled utterly.'

'You should have thought of that before you put it on,'
Edmund told her unsympathetically. 'It is not a court
appearance you are going to!'

'You must not expect the ladies to be as hardy as we are,'
James intervened on Julia's behalf. 'Surely the carriage could
take us across the field if the coachman takes it steadily. The
ground is reasonably firm now.'

Eventually, after much dispute, Julia had her way. Savagely Edmund tugged at the bell and ordered the carriage to
be brought round. Julia relaxed and concentrated on trying
to coax Edmund into a good mood. For once her efforts
failed; he remained coldly disapproving. Impatiently tap-
ping her foot, Julia stared crossly at her sister.

'Good God, Anne, what a frump you look! That gown
must be at least two years old. And why have you done up
your hair in such an old-fashioned manner?'

'I thought it charming,' Edmund observed stiffly. 'I remember that you used to wear yours that way once.'

'Yes, but that was years ago when it was the mode. I wouldn't be seen dead in such a Gothic style now!'

A servant, entering to bring the news that the carriage was waiting, cut off Edmund's angry retort. With difficulty they all crowded into the carriage. It was a tight squeeze, but Edmund flatly refused Julia's suggestion that they should make two journeys. Anne's offer to walk was dismissed equally curtly.

'If we must indulge your sister's foolishness then we will all travel together. Kit can squeeze in beside me, and there is plenty of room for you by your sister if Julia moves across to the far side.'

With loud complaints that she was squashed unmercifully, and her gown ruined, Julia clutched at Edmund, shrieking with terror as they lurched their way slowly down the deeply rutted track. Unsympathetically he pointed out that she had only herself to blame for any discomfort, as everyone else had been prepared to walk. Julia subsided into a sulky silence.

She recovered a little when they arrived, and her appearance caused a rustle of interest among the villagers congregated around the entrance to the barn. Anne suspected that not all the whispered comments were complimentary but Julia felt no such qualms. Smiling graciously to either side, she swept through the crowd, very much the grand lady.

Ferdie, clad in rich purple velvet, met them at the door. Refusing Edmund's proffered entrance money with a grandiloquent gesture that put Anne greatly in mind of his parent, he proudly ushered them inside.

The interior of the barn was transformed. The hay had been swept away or bundled under sacking to form seating for the workpeople who were already in their places at the back. In front of them were rows of wooden benches for the farmers and local tradesmen: amongst them Anne noticed Weston, standing a little apart from the rest. Julia smiled encouragingly at him and he half-moved as if to join their party, then sank back as Edmund acknowledged him with a brusque nod. Anne was appalled at the naked hatred that glinted momentarily in the steward's eyes before he mastered his resentment.

Edmund was walking towards the front row of benches but Ferdie prevented him. 'No, your lordship! You're the guests of honour. We have a box for you!' Proudly he led them to the far side of the barn where a rickety platform supported half a dozen chairs. Kit leapt up with glee, taking the seat closest to the stage. Anne followed gingerly, but her sister eyed the 'box' with horror.

'You can't expect me to climb up there. I wouldn't dare!'

'Of course you can,' Edmund told her curtly as he saw the boy's crestfallen face. 'Thank your papa for all the trouble he has taken to make us so comfortable, Ferdie. Tell him we are eagerly looking forward to the play.'

The boy went away, mollified. Julia turned her back on Edmund and made a great deal of fuss about clambering up with James's anxious assistance. Once up, she waited icily while he dusted off her chair with his handkerchief before seating herself with an air of long-suffering resignation that would have done credit to an early Christian martyr about to be thrown to the lions. It was unfortunate that Edmund, for whose benefit it had been assumed, was not even watching.

A series of bumps, scuffles and squeals from behind the tattered green curtain that cut off the far end of the barn, indicated that the actors were moving into place. An enthusiastic drum roll called the audience to order, and the curtain lurched up to reveal a very bare street in Venice.

Across the front of the stage a dozen tallow candles, pushed into lumps of clay screened by rickety tin reflectors, lit the scene. A pair of actors Anne had not previously seen came on and began discussing the Merchant's business problems.

'There's Ferdie!' Kit exclaimed as a diminutive Bassanio entered, wearing the clothes in which he had greeted them earlier, enhanced by an overlarge scarlet cloak, a sword and whip. In truly professional manner he ignored Kit's excited wave and started to pipe out the tale of his difficulties in a shrill treble that occasionally plunged disconcertingly to a deep bass growl.

'That's my whip he's carrying,' Kit confided in an audible

whisper. 'He liked it so much I said he could borrow it for tonight. Doesn't he look a proper dandy!'

Portia, when she appeared, proved less averse to acknowledging her friends in the audience. She bounced on, winking broadly at Edmund, and addressed her best lines to him rather than to her fellow actors. Weston, in the second row of benches, received similarly flattering attention. Julia sniffed in disgust, giving an ostentatious yawn, but Edmund ignored her pique and grinned back at Rosy.

Anne smiled as she watched Portia bend to fold her pint-sized suitor to her ample bosom. Ferdie, totally obliterated, struggled to the surface like a drowning mariner to gasp out his unconvincing regrets for leaving her. The play was proving enormous fun. She greatly preferred it to the pretentious London theatre performances she had seen. There the ranting of mediocre actors had induced only boredom: the audience had paid scant attention to them, talking loudly to each other throughout. These Delamares were so gloriously bad that their play became hilarious. Her ribs ached with suppressed laughter.

Edmund, she could tell, was equally diverted by the ridiculous accidents that befell the actors, the sheer absurdity of the whole show. Her sister was not. Rigid with disgust, she sat glowering at the antics on the stage.

Still, it was her own fault if she was bored, Anne thought. Knowing her sense of humour to be quite different from theirs, she and Edmund had both warned her she would not enjoy the evening. Anne was surprised that despite this Julia should show so unattractive a side of herself to Edmund when he was already annoyed at the fuss she had made earlier about the carriage. Sitting there like the spectre at the feast was scarcely the way to placate him. Up to now Julia had been more cautious.

Despite the slight confusion the shortage of actors occasioned, the play went smoothly until Shylock's entrance. Clad in a long grey robe he staggered very unsteadily on to the stage.

'The fellow's drunk!' exclaimed James with a censure that Anne felt he was the last to be justified in.

Mr Delamare's tendency to sway gently as he spoke was

disconcerting, but he managed to deliver his lines with thunderous effect and an obvious determination to act everyone else off the stage. They fought back with enthusiasm, especially his eldest daughter. Anne's quick glance at Edmund found him shaking with mirth. How could Julia remain so glum and unamused?

The play moved rapidly forward to the Trial scene. Portia, flaunting her ample limbs in skin-tight breeches, swaggered into the courtroom to a riot of cheering from the rear of the barn. She kissed her hands delightedly to them, and smiled in unmistakable invitation at Edmund.

'What a disgusting exhibition!' muttered Julia. 'The female is shameless.'

'A dashed handsome filly, all the same,' said James incautiously.

'If your taste is for ditch drabs.'

'Nothing like as lovely as you, of course, my dear ...'

'Any comparison can only be insulting. The slut should be whipped at the cart-tail,' Julia hissed viciously.

Edmund paid no heed to her furious comments. Laughing at Rosy's entrance he waved back. Anne smiled too, glad to see on his face an expression of pure enjoyment such as he had not shown since his return home; an expression she remembered well from the old carefree Edmund of six years before.

As if sensing her regard, he turned. Their eyes met in a moment of laughing sympathy that seemed to blot out everything around them and left her cheeks tingling, her heart beating fast. It was in that instant that she knew that her childhood infatuation for Edmund was gone for ever—to be replaced by a far more disturbing emotion. She could no longer deny that she loved him with a deep and abiding passion. If only he had felt the same!

Edmund's rich chuckle showed his amusement as an unidentified wag at the back of the barn offered his aid to Portia to 'sort out the miserable old codger'. Quite unabashed, Rosy waved her appreciation of the offer and launched into her *quality of mercy* speech with gusto. She ploughed remorselessly through it, mispronouncing half the words and altering others with little respect for sense or

scansion, finishing with a hearty slap of her thigh that sent
the flesh quivering.

Mr Delamare clearly resented the shift of interest from
himself to his daughter, and strove valiantly to regain the
audience's attention. It was evident that he had been fortify-
ing himself during his time off-stage. His gait was more
unsteady than ever and his speech faintly slurred. He glared
menacingly around him as he lurched to the centre of the
scene, and waved his knife so threateningly as he demanded
his bond that the actor playing his victim flinched back in
genuine terror. Caught off balance, Shylock stumbled and
drove the weapon deep into his own hand.

The audience gasped as they saw the blood begin to drip
slowly from the wound. Mr Delamare stared unbelievingly at
the reddened blade for a full minute before thundering out,

'*Is this a dagger I see before me, the handle toward my hand?*'

His fellow actors looked even more shocked than the audience as the speech rolled on. Anne remembered hearing that
they were deeply superstitious about *Macbeth*. Even to name
it in a theatre was desperately unlucky; to quote from it
anathema.

When the prompter's frenzied whispers went unheeded
Cordelia slid across from her place beside Rosy.

'No, Pa! Not the Scottish play,' she hissed, tugging at his
sleeve. 'It's the *Merchant* tonight! Shylock!'

Eventually her words pierced his alcoholic haze. He halted
in mid-sentence and switched rapidly back to his former role,
declaiming loftily,

'*We trifle time. I beg thee, pursue sentence.*'

A little shakily, the rest of the cast followed his lead. With a
magnificent effort Mr Delamare completed his scene and
reeled away across the courtroom, making his final '*I am not
well*' totally convincing.

He staggered out, almost falling off the front of the low
stage when his foot caught in one of the candles. It toppled
over and lay unnoticed as Mr Delamare recovered his
balance by a supreme effort and finally disappeared. The
audience tittered nervously, and all attention swung back to
Portia.

Rosy was wholly uninterested in her fellow players. While

Shylock was staggering eloquently off she postured voluptu-
ously for the benefit of her admirers in the audience, filling in
the interval before her next speech with a complete disregard
of what was happening in the play meanwhile. Even when
her cue came and she replied to the thanks Bassanio was
offering, she ignored him and fluttered her eyelashes over his
head in Edmund's direction.

It was not until a cloud of smoke drifted across the stage in
front of her that anyone realised that the candle her father
had dislodged had been knocked into a wisp of hay. Suddenly
it caught, flaring brightly. Before anyone could move to
stamp it out the flames were licking at the curtains. Within
seconds they too had caught fire. The flames spread to the
pile of hay on which the prompter was lounging, and he leapt
up with a shout of alarm which released the audience from its
trance.

With squeals of fright, the men and women at the back of
the barn scrambled to their feet. Fighting to get away, they
pushed each other aside. Those on the benches caught the
infection and jostled their way across to the doors. Shrieks of
terror mingled with cries of pain as people were trampled in
the panic to escape.

Edmund leapt up and shouted for them to be calm but his
words were lost in the hubbub. The epidemic of fear had
taken too strong a hold for his words to penetrate the minds of
the frightened mob. If he had caught their attention before
the rush started he might have prevented it, but it was too
late now. Nothing could halt the wild scramble to get clear.

Wide-eyed with terror, Julia clutched at him, overturning
her chair as she screamed, 'Save me, Edmund, save me!'

The rickety platform on which they stood swayed as the
pressure of the milling throng rocked its precarious founda-
tions. The doors were flung open by the first to reach them,
producing a gust of air that fanned the flames, sweeping them
close to where Anne waited her chance to clamber down from
the shaky platform as soon as the crush in front of her
thinned.

From the corner of her eye she saw Edmund clasp Julia.
Instinctively she turned to shield Kit, but as the press before
them shifted at last he jumped down. With an anxious shout

of, 'My whip! Ferdie's left my whip on the stage!' he ran to
retrieve it from the burning stage, empty now of actors.

'Come back, Kit!' Anne ran desperately after him. She
heard Edmund call for her to stop, but with a pang of
desolation she saw that he was too occupied with Julia to
help. She was foolish, Anne chided herself, to have expected
anything else. The moment of oneness with Edmund that
had so thrilled her had meant nothing to him. His first
thought when danger loomed had, as ever, been of Julia.

She must follow Kit. There was no one else to help the
child. James was too busily hovering beside Julia to bother
about anyone else. In a few strides she had caught up with
the boy. While he hesitated, unsure of how to negotiate the
blazing boards she grabbed at him.

'Leave it, Kit,' she exclaimed, shielding her face from the
heat with her other hand. 'It's too dangerous. You can't risk
your life for that. We can buy another whip any time, but not
a new Kit!'

He was forced to agree and turned obediently back. The
smoke was too dense now for them to see the others. Coughing as it filled her lungs, Anne tried to push Kit across the
scattered benches to the doorway, but he tugged her in the
opposite direction.

'No! This way is quicker, Anne. There's a gap just here
that I climb through when I come to see the ratting.'

Sure enough, close behind them was a small hole in the
wall boarding, and Kit scrambled through with ease. Anne
bent quickly to follow. It was a tight squeeze, but with a loud
rending sound as her hem tore on a protruding nail, she
managed to drag herself through.

'Let us hurry round to the front now, Kit. We must find
your Mamma and the rest. They'll be imagining we've been
roasted!'

They hurried back round the outside of the barn and
through the crowd to where Julia drooped sobbing on
James's broad chest. One arm around her waist, he was
patting her shoulder with the other, his face a mixture of
alarm and delight. 'There, there, Julia! Don't distress yourself so. He'll find them. Don't you fret!'

As Anne drew closer Julia looked up and saw them. 'Anne,

Kit! Wherever have you been? I've been half out of my mind with worry!' she exclaimed peevishly, then searching anxiously past them, she demanded, 'And where is Edmund?'

'I thought he was here with you.'

'No, he left James to look after me. I thought he must be going back for you and Kit. Surely you saw him?'

They all stared aghast at the blazing building. There was an ominous creak, then a thunderous crash as a large roof timber fell into the flames. Julia screamed, and hid her face in James's jacket.

Pale with apprehension, Anne thrust her way through the excited crowd to the barn doorway. A chain of men was passing buckets of water hand to hand to throw on the fire. Sweat running down their faces showed how great the effort was, but their hard toil made little effect on the fire. It burned fiercely on, lighting up the men's tired forms with a hellish glare.

She tried to push past them, calling 'Edmund!', but one of the farm labourers grabbed at her, pulling her back.

'It's no good, miss! You can't go in. It's not safe!'

'But you don't understand,' she cried frantically. 'Lord Ashorne is inside there, looking for me! I must find him.'

'It's no use, miss,' he repeated doggedly. 'You'd only be killed too if you tried to go in now. The roof'll cave in any minute now.'

As if to prove his words there was another hideous rumble and creaking above them. Anne's heart leapt as two smoke-grimed figures staggered through from the murky interior. She started eagerly forward, only to sink back disappointed as she recognised Weston and Rosy. Between them they dragged a huge trunk.

'Did you see Lord Ashorne inside?' she asked anxiously.

Weston shook his head.

'It's too thick to see anything clearly in there. He spoke to us earlier on, but he went on into the blazing part, telling me to help Rosy here. I thought he'd be out before us. There's little chance of escape now.' Was she imagining that triumphant glint in his eye? Weston was a gambler, ready to make the most of any chance. Had he taken advantage of the

confusion inside to harm Edmund? Uneasily she remembered the hatred Weston betrayed for his master earlier. He
could have found a way to give vent to it.

'Edmund!' she called despairingly, staring hopelessly into
the smoke that billowed out, making all efforts to see inside in
vain.

Was Edmund to die there? If he did it would be her fault.
Why had she let Kit persuade her to go out by that wretched
gap? She might have guessed that Edmund would return to
help them. How could she live with the knowledge that he
had died because of her stupidity?

CHAPTER
SEVEN

EDMUND had been astonished at the depths of his dismay as he watched Anne follow Kit into the smouldering confusion while he was powerless to prevent them. That sickening lurch of fear for her safety showed him, as nothing else had, how radically his feelings had altered since he came home. Anne was necessary for his happiness now. The emotion he felt for her was far stronger than the weak sentiment he had cherished so long for her sister. Now Julia's demands caused only annoyance. He tried to break loose from her grasp to go to Anne, cursing his lack of foresight. Laughingly intent on Rosy's coquettish antics he had missed her father's mishap with the candle; it was not until he saw smoke drift across the stage that he had realised what had happened and the danger it threatened.

The fire had taken hold all too swiftly, and fear spread with equal rapidity. He had tried to shout above the clamour, to calm the headlong rush, but it was useless. No one listened. He had to give up and concentrate on getting his own party to safety. Furthest from the exit, theirs was the most hazardous position. He had glanced quickly along the line of chairs. No panic yet. If he kept them calm they might all escape unharmed.

Then a fierce draught of air whipped through the barn as the great doors were flung wide. It fanned the flames into great fury, engulfing the curtain dangerously close to Anne and Kit. Edmund saw Anne flinch, then deliberately calm herself to smile reassuringly down at the child. He must get to them, draw them out of harm's way! Where they stood now there was every chance the curtain might fall and shower them with burning fragments.

His sudden move startled Julia. As he tried to pass her she

clutched frenziedly at him. 'Don't leave me, Edmund!' she sobbed. 'Save me!'

Impatiently he tried to shake her off, but she clung more tightly. Unable to free himself, he saw Kit dart from Anne's side and run towards the blazing stage. What was the foolish child up to? He must stop him! Struggling against the grasping arms that pinioned him he exclaimed, 'Let me go, Julia! You're quite safe. I must get to Kit before he does anything stupid.'

''Don't leave me here!' Julia was beyond reason now. She clung like a limpet. 'Help me, Edmund!'

'Come back, Anne!' he roared as he saw her move forward to follow the child. She took no heed. Held back in Julia's tenacious grip, he could do nothing to prevent Anne going after her nephew into danger. He watched helplessly as the smoke swallowed them up. Try as he might he could not make out where they had got to. How would he ever find them now?

The action was typical of Anne's courage, he thought with a pang of grief. She made no loud fuss about the child; instead she acted. Understanding the danger, she was willing to risk her safety for Kit. That was a far more valuable love than one which showed itself only in hysterical outbursts.

Julia's screams were so wild now that he had to stop her forcibly. The first mild attempt had little effect. Losing patience, he shook her violently and slapped her across her cheek. Between exasperation and concern for Anne, the blow turned out rougher than he intended, but it did the trick. The glazed panic faded from her eyes; her struggles ceased and she drooped weakly in his arms, crying more naturally.

Edmund looked down at her with mingled regret and vexation. Tears were trickling down the lovely face, marred now by the scarlet impression of five fingers; just as her charm was spoiled by selfishness and vanity. It was growing harder to combat his disillusionment with her. He tried to tell himself that this was Julia he held in his arms, the dream of perfection he had worshipped for six empty years, but it meant nothing to him.

There was no rush of tenderness or passion such as her touch had inspired in the past. All that he could think was that, beautiful as she was, the loveliness was flawed. He had fought hard against the knowledge, finding every excuse for her behaviour, but he could deceive himself no longer. He had been mistaken in her. That surface charm was only a thin covering for the conceit and pettiness beneath; in times of stress her true nature showed through. Despite all her loudly proclaimed devotion to her son, it was evident that she was more concerned with preserving her skin than his. And Anne was hazarding her life for the boy.

But however great his sense of let-down, he could not abandon Julia now to help her sister. She drooped helpless in his arms, obviously incapable of getting herself to safety unaided if he left her. He must take her out before he began to search for Anne.

Lifting the exquisite figure up, he followed the last of the crowd, struggling across the overturned benches towards the packed doorway.

'Is she going to be all right?' A distraught voice beside him reminded him of James's presence. Why had the stupid fellow fussed around them instead of trying to help Anne? Could he not see that she was worth ten of her sister?

'Of course. There is nothing wrong with her but panic. I can manage. See if you can reach Anne and the child,' he ordered impatiently, but James was too intent on fondling Julia's limp hand, murmuring broken reassurance, to heed him. If Edmund had had a free hand he would have struck him too. How on earth had Anne contrived to involve herself with such a weak-kneed nincompoop—one so patently devoted to her sister, too?

He was tempted to leave James to deal with Julia, but even if he could free himself he doubted if the portly baronet could manage to get her to safety unaided. Red-faced and shaking, teetering on the edge of panic, he looked scarcely in a condition to help himself let alone her. Frustrating as Edmund found the delay he must go on. Nearly at the doorway now!

He was thankful to find someone clearing the mass of morbid sightseers from the exit so that they could get out relatively easily. Once in the open Julia revived a little, and he tore himself free and thrust her on to James. Ignoring her protests he hurried back to the barn, praying that he would not be too late.

Already a line of men had formed, passing buckets hand to hand to cast on to the burning timbers. Weston was among them, helping, but he was not surprised to see that it was Jonas, standing at the head of the line, who was directing the operation.

'Don't reckon we'll douse this in a hurry, Major,' the groom greeted him dourly. 'It's got too good a hold on that hay, but we should be able to stop it spreading any further.'

'Good man,' Edmund encouraged him briefly, but his main concern was elsewhere. 'Have you seen Miss Wetherly or the boy?'

'No,' Jonas shook his head decidedly. 'They've not come past me, and I was one of the first out.'

'Then they must be still inside. The wretched child panicked and Miss Wetherly went after him. Goodness knows what has happened to them both.'

As they struggled to make out anything in the smoke-filled interior of the building, Mr Delamare's drink-sodden face pressed close to them. All the bombast had been drained from him, leaving him a hunched, pitiful husk. A reek of stale brandy hung about him.

'My properties, all gone!' he whimpered. 'Fifty years' work destroyed. How am I going to be able to support my innocent babes now?'

'Out of my way!' Edmund thrust him ruthlessly aside. 'This is all your fault. If anyone dies as a result of this night's work I'll see you suffer the consequences of your drunken folly.' Wrenching off his neckcloth, he soaked it in water from one of the buckets, then, holding it to his face, he plunged further into the barn. The air was thick with smoke now. Choking, Edmund bent low to escape the worst of it, but still the scorching heat and fumes took his breath away.

'Anne!' he gasped, then more loudly, 'Anne! Where are you? Kit!'

There was no response, and he peered desperately into the swirling gloom. Already his eyes were sore and aching from the acrid smoke. It was impossible to make out anything for certain. The crackle of the flames was so loud now that he doubted whether Anne would make herself heard over it even if she were still capable of speech.

He forced himself to be calm, to think the thing out logically. Dashing about at random would do no good. He must work to a system—it would be all too easy to lose his sense of direction in this darkness. He was in the centre of the barn now. Best to quarter it, searching every part. Anne might be lying injured or unconscious anywhere.

He began on the far side where he had last seen her. Nothing among the chairs and scattered benches that hampered his progress. Then through the swirling smoke he caught a glimpse of movement in the middle of the stage area. It was tantalisingly indistinct, but surely that was a woman's form straining to lift something? Hope flared.

'Anne!' he gasped, struggling towards her. 'Thank God I've found you!'

Relief was short-lived. As he drew closer the woman turned to greet him, and he recognised Rosy's anguished face peering through the smoke haze. All the coyness had gone now; sweat had cut furrows down her painted cheeks. She was panting with the effort of trying to drag a singed wooden trunk from the wreckage of the scenery.

'Give me a hand,' she grunted.

'What the devil do you think you are up to? What's that you are risking your life for?'

'My jewellery's in there,' she wailed. 'All the bits and pieces my gentleman gave me are locked inside, and I can't find the key. Give me a hand to carry it outside!'

'Never mind that rubbish, woman,' he exclaimed, disappointment making his voice harsh. 'Get yourself clear while you can.'

'But I can't leave it all to burn. All my decent clothes are in here. What will I wear if they are all ruined?'

'Don't waste time arguing! This roof can't last much longer. Get yourself outside, or a shroud is all you'll need to wear—if there is enough of you left to put it on.'

With a menacing creak the timbers shifted above them. Reluctantly Rosy dropped the trunk handle and clambered off the stage.

'Have you seen anything of Kit or Anne—Miss

Wetherly—round here?' demanded Edmund urgently as he helped her down. 'They came this way.'

Rosy shook her head. 'I didn't see no one, but I was too busy to notice much.'

'I thought I caught sight of the boy in the far corner there a moment ago, my lord,' a fresh voice from behind them gasped. 'I couldn't be sure, but I suppose Miss Wetherly might be with him.'

'Is that you, Weston?' Thankfully Edmund pushed Rosy towards the sound of the steward's voice. 'Make sure Miss Delamare gets out safely. I'll try to reach the others.'

Not waiting to see his orders obeyed, he moved in the direction Weston had indicated, calling hoarsely, 'Anne! Are you there?' Pray God he would be in time. Unbearable to lose Anne just when he had discovered how much she meant to him.

A great lump of smouldering timber crashed down beside him as he climbed up on to the stage. The barn was old and in ill repair; any minute now the roof must collapse, burying them all inside. Little hope of saving anyone then.

Edmund's skin felt stiff and dry in the fierce heat. His cloth had long since dried out and gave little protection from the smoke. He forced himself on, picking his way carefully across the charred boards, skirting the main heart of the fire. There was a creak behind him. He spun round. 'Who's there?'

No answer. He strained to see through the gloom, but it was impossible to distinguish anything. Edmund shivered. For a moment the dull red world around him had seemed filled with menace. He had felt an irrational shudder of apprehension as a wave of antagonism seemed to reach out of the darkness towards him.

Impatiently he dismissed the fancy. No time for such foolishness now. The hellish atmosphere was causing absurd delusions. He must not let his imagination take charge of him in this ridiculous fashion. He had to find Anne, and quickly before it was too late.

'Are you there, Major?' Jonas's voice came indistinctly. It must have been the groom's approach he had heard, he decided with relief.

'Over here,' he moved towards the sound. 'Have you found them?'

'Not yet.'

The voice was closer now, and Jonas's broad form loomed up out of the red gloom. With a rustling slither the roof timbers shifted and strained. Edmund stared up in alarm. The roof could not last much longer. As he turned back he glimpsed something moving behind Jonas. A hunk of wood crashed down on the groom's head. Had it fallen or had some hand aimed it? His eyes were too sore from the smoke to be sure whether it had been a person he had seen in the darkness, or only a flickering shadow.

Jonas stumbled and pitched forward as the wood struck him. Carefully Edmund picked his way across the debris to kneel beside him. Jonas lay clutching his head. Blood trickled down his face and already a great bruise was forming.

'Somebody hit me!' he groaned.

A huge piece of bloodstained timber by him showed the weapon, but had it fallen by accident or design? Impossible to be sure. If anyone had been there he was gone now. Another heavy lump of wood thudded behind them. Edmund cast a last despairing look round. Too late to find Anne now. He must get Jonas out, unless they too were to perish in the ruins of the barn.

Clasping his arms round the groom's massive chest, he managed to heave him on to his feet. Jonas protested faintly, but he paid no heed. Half dragging, half guiding, he somehow got them both to the doorway. With the last of his ebbing strength Edmund lurched out into the blessedly fresh air.

There willing hands grasped at his burden and laid him on the grass. Edmund crouched by him, drawing in great gasping lungfuls of air. Dully he realised that it had all been in vain. Though he had got out in time, he had failed to find Anne.

As she saw the great timbers of the barn shift, the roof begin to sag in a menacing curve, Anne could bear to watch no longer. It was impossible for Edmund to come out in time; he must be crushed in the inevitable collapse. Choked by tears, she turned away, not wanting to witness the final catastrophe. Slowly she retraced her steps to where she had left her sister.

Before she had gone more than a dozen paces a jubilant shout told her that something unexpected had happened. Scarcely able to breathe for the painful surge of hope, she spun round. The firefighters were running to support two sooty, exhausted men who had just emerged from the blazing interior of the barn.

Anne's eyes blurred with tears, so that for a moment, it was difficult to make out the figures. Then, with mounting emotion, she distinguished Edmund and Jonas. Pale beneath his smoke-grime, Edmund nevertheless seemed in better shape than the groom, who had to lean heavily on his rescuer, a gory wound gaping on his brow.

Relief overwhelmed Anne; her knees suddenly felt too weak to support her. As she swayed, too shocked to move, another great beam crashed down, showering sparks over the excited group. Edmund bent to lift Jonas out of harm's way, but bystanders took the groom from him and bore him to a safer distance. Edmund was left staring stunned into the crackling flames, regardless of his own danger.

Anne forced her jellied limbs forward. A few shaky steps brought her to where he hunched dejectedly, oblivious of his surroundings. Too moved to dissemble, she stretched both hands to grasp his.

'Thank God you are safe, Edmund!' she breathed from an overflowing heart.

For one breathtaking moment he stared incredulously at her. Then his tense face relaxed. The alteration in his expression made her pulses race. 'Am I dreaming?' A tenderness she had never encountered before softened his stern features. 'I thought you buried in that inferno, my love.'

'No, I escaped long before you did. It was you who nearly died!'

Now that her dreadful fears were removed, reaction set in. Anne's breath came raggedly, tears burned her eyelids. Scarcely aware of what she was doing, she tightened her grasp, as if only by touching him could she convince herself that Edmund was truly restored to her. The neck of his shirt, torn wide in his exertions, revealed the firm column of his throat, the broad inviting chest. With an inarticulate cry Anne buried her face in his breast, pressing herself close to draw comfort from his nearness. His arms closed protectively around her, cradling her close.

'Oh, Edmund!' she clasped him frantically, sobbing, 'I—I thought you were dead—I could not bear it—not again—I wanted to die too!'

The warmth from his body flowed into her shivering form, soothing her. His hand stroked her hair in rhythmic comfort.

'Hush, my love,' he murmured. 'It is all over now. Don't distress yourself. No one is harmed, thank God.'

In a daze she felt him draw her closer still. Engrossed in each other, they clung together in the shadows, forgetful of all else but their need of each other.

'I still cannot believe it,' Edmund vowed, his voice husky with emotion. 'I thought I should die when I saw you disappear in that dreadful confusion.'

Gently he lifted her chin till her gaze locked with his. The intensity of his gaze deepened. With a surge of wonder she knew he was about to kiss her. Her pulses leapt, joyfully she reached up towards him. Then as his lips touched hers, an awful thought struck, making her pull sharply away. That expression of passionate longing was too familiar. It reminded her so vividly of the day he had returned—and of the awful mistake he had made then. Was he just as confused now?

Chilled to the core, she remembered her shameful response to that earlier kiss, the bitter regret it had cost her. Foolishly she had let herself be deceived then. This time she must not be so weak, though her whole body ached to respond to the mute invitation in his eyes. If only she could believe that ardour was meant for her!

Alas, the doubts, once admitted, grew alarmingly. When she had given rein to her emotions in this ridiculous way was it any wonder he should mistake her for Julia? It was hard to distinguish anything in this unearthly glare—no wonder he had been fooled yet again. How could she have been so stupid?

Agitatedly she struggled to free herself. Not understanding, Edmund's imprisoning arms tightened their fond embrace. As his lips found hers once more, Anne fought to prevent her feelings taking over, ashamed of the desire that leapt within her. She must not let Edmund guess at it.

'No, Edmund, no!' she moaned despairingly.

'Be still, my love!' Again his warm lips pressed insistently, demanding the response she was all too ready to give.

'You must not—I have to find Julia—she will be frantic—James too ...'

Her broken words had the effect she dreaded. She watched the glow fade from his eyes. Sick with disappointment, she knew that she had been correct. He had supposed that it was her sister whom he held so close. He had lost touch with her too in the confusion and panic.

Jealousy twisted sharp in Anne's breast. It was Julia he loved. However much it hurt, she had to accept that fact. How could she have been so foolish as to have dreamt otherwise? Sinkingly she realised how revealing her impulsive move towards him must have been. Embarrassed, she pulled herself free from his slackened grasp.

'I beg your pardon, Anne. I was carried away by the excitement of the moment,' Edmund declared, his voice stiff with constraint. He kept his face averted. As if he could not bear to look at her, she thought bleakly. 'I had supposed you dead in the fire so the relief of finding you safe made me behave so irresponsibly. I did not mean to upset you.'

A noble pretence. It might have deceived her if she had not already guessed his error.

'Don't apologise, I was equally to blame. It was my foolishness which caused the trouble.' Anne tried to speak lightly to match his calm. 'Kit showed me another way out of the barn. It was just a crack really, but we squeezed through somehow. I should never have let him persuade me if I had realised everyone thought us still inside.' Despite all her efforts, a shudder ran through her and her voice broke. 'You might—you might have been killed in there.'

'But I wasn't—neither of us was!' Unthinkingly Edmund reached out as if to fold her into the comfort of his arms once more. Then, remembering, he checked, contenting himself with clasping her trembling fingers in a reassuring grasp.

'Instead it was poor Jonas who nearly died, searching for me.'

'Then you can guess how I feel at hazarding your lives by my foolishness.' Anne felt the tears well into her eyes again.

'Don't start crying again, Anne!' Edmund groaned, watching the teardrops glisten on her cheeks. 'I've had more than enough weeping from your sister. It isn't like you to give way!'

'I'm sorry!' Somehow she managed a watery smile. 'But when I heard the roof falling I thought you would never get clear in time. When I saw you both staggering out, it seemed like a miracle. I couldn't help crying with relief!'

She swallowed hard, not daring to look at him lest she betray herself further, and so missed the involuntary movement he made towards her, the desperate longing on his face. Another moment and he had mastered the impulse. 'Things looked worse than they really were.' He dismissed the subject curtly.

'You are too modest. But for your help, Jonas must have died. We could all see that he was unable to walk unaided.'

Edmund shrugged.

'Surely I owed him my aid, since it was my fault he was in there at all.'

'What happened to him?' Anne persisted with the safer subject. 'Did a piece of falling debris strike him?'

'No, Miss Anne!' Unseen, Jonas had moved across to join them. 'It's my belief someone hit me deliberate. That blow felt too hard to be just falling wood, and I'll swear there was someone behind me a second earlier. Did you see anyone, Major?'

'No, the smoke was too dense, but to be honest, I had the uneasy feeling that there was someone else in there with us.'

'But who would want to harm Jonas?' Anne asked in bewilderment. 'Surely he hasn't been here long enough to make enemies.'

'I don't know, miss,' the groom admitted. 'Maybe I was mistaken after all. It don't make sense.'

'Unless,' Anne said slowly, 'the blow was meant for you, Edmund. It would be easy to confuse you in the darkness. You are about the same size and build.'

'But who would risk his own life on the slim chance of injuring me? No, Jonas must be wrong. There was enough wood falling to brain anyone. A great lump barely missed me.'

'Someone tried to kill you before . . .' Anne's fingers trembled in Edmund's grasp. He put a comforting arm around her waist, drawing her nearer. Weakly she allowed herself to savour the delight though she knew the action meant little to him.

'That was different, Anne. He ran little risk himself then. I feel sure this was an accident. It would have been easy to imagine anything in the atmosphere inside there. Anyhow, we are both alive still. That's what matters. There is no use upsetting yourself over what might have happened. It takes more than a knock on the head to finish off Jonas!'

'*Edmund!*' a voice thrilled, and Julia bustled towards them. She flung herself upon Edmund with a rustle of expensive silk and a waft of overpowering perfume. 'My poor darling! You look utterly worn out. Whatever made you act so rashly? I thought I should die when I saw you rush back into that inferno. Don't ever do that to me again, I couldn't bear to lose you! Why did you do it?'

'To find Anne. Did you expect me to leave her to burn—and your son too—while I played lady's maid to you?'

'But they weren't even in the barn! The tiresome child claims he discovered some other way out. Says he dragged Anne with him through that draughty crack in the wall. That is why she looks such a wreck, I suppose.'

As Julia's scornful gaze swept over her, Anne was for the first time aware of her grubby face and torn gown, contrasting so greatly with Julia's immaculate grooming. The new silk dress was slightly muddied at the hem, but Julia's face and hair were in perfect order, as ever.

'They were both clear before you ever went in,' Julia went on with a brittle laugh. 'Not that we're not all admiration for your bravery, my dear. James is eternally grateful to you for trying to save his wife-to-be, aren't you, James?'

The baronet nodded obediently.

'Very grateful,' he muttered gruffly. 'Dashed fine thing to

do, Ashorne, even if it turned out not necessary. Indebted to you for the thought!'

Anne felt Edmund's hands drop, releasing her abruptly. In the emotion of discovering that Edmund was unharmed she had forgotten James and the claim he still had on her—not that he appeared eager to press it. She must not allow herself to be deceived by Edmund's kindness. It was friendship he felt for her, not love. That look of naked desire had been intended for Julia, not her. It was Julia he had turned to protect first when the fire threatened them.

'Why are we all standing around here?' Julia demanded irritably. 'Can't we go home?'

There was a clatter of hooves as the carriage approached in response to Edmund's command. The horses shied nervously at the crowd milling round them and the glare of the still burning building. One of the grooms walked at their head, gentling them till they were calm.

'I think Jonas should ride, not us,' Anne suggested.

Julia frowned, but the groom refused the offer.

'I'll be all right, miss, soon as I've had time to get me breath. A walk in the air'll do me more good than that bumpy carriage.'

'I'll stay and see he gets home,' Edmund told them. 'You get the ladies back, Shrivenham.' As James carefully handed Julia in, Anne looked across at the wreckage of the barn. The roof had caved in now. A red glare from the burning mass lit up the sky but, as Jonas had forecast, the blaze had spread no further. A few drops of rain splashed down. With luck rain would help put out the rest of the fire.

'Did everyone get out safely?' she asked.

'Yes, miss. One of the gardeners has a nasty burn, but the doctor is looking after him. His lordship had the luckiest escape—and Weston. Him and that black-headed female got out just in time with a great trunk the stupid girl had gone back to fetch.'

'So Rosy waited for her valuables after all, and persuaded Weston to help. Foolish pair! I told them to go without,' exclaimed Edmund.

Why had Weston helped her—for a share? Anne would not put it past him to demand one. Could it have been

Weston who struck Jonas down, mistaking him for his
master? That would explain his triumphant expression as he
emerged from the barn. Yet the girl had been with him.
Surely Weston would have risked nothing with her as a
witness, however tempted he might have been. Still a talk
with Rosy might prove interesting. That reminded her of the
family's plight.

'Where are the Delamares?' she asked anxiously. 'They
won't be able to sleep in the barn tonight as they did yesterday. What are they going to do?'

'They'll have to find rooms at the inn.'

'But how can they afford it? Everything they have is lost in
the fire, except Rosy's trunk.'

'I'll tell Weston to see to it that they have everything that is
needful,' promised Edmund. 'I cannot spare time myself as I
have to straighten things out here and attend to Jonas, but
they'll be comfortable, never fear.'

Anne still hesitated, unsure whether she ought to volun-
teer her help too.

'It is time you went home yourself, Anne,' Edmund smiled
gently at her. 'You must be exhausted after all this turmoil.'

'Do hurry up, Anne!' Julia called irritably. 'We are all
waiting for you.'

'You see, your sister needs you—Kit, too. We can manage
here.'

The brief glow his understanding generated, died again as
she recognised that once again it was her sister who filled his
thoughts. She was useful for the aid she could supply to Julia.
It was madness to have imagined anything else.

Miserably, Anne let James hand her into her seat. She
must forget the delight of those stolen moments in Edmund's
arms. The memory could only torment her. She must put
Edmund completely out of her thoughts, and to that end, the
less she had to do with him in future the better for her peace of
mind. In her secret heart she had to admit that she loved
Edmund with a passion far deeper than the mawkish infatuation she had cherished six years ago; but she could not bear
anyone else to guess the extent of her folly.

CHAPTER
EIGHT

'GONE?' Anne stared in blank astonishment at the innkeeper. She had risen early that morning, her conscience pricked by the memory of the Delamares' woegone appearance as, stranded in their theatrical costumes, they had watched the rest of their belongings swallowed up in the fire.

Edmund had ensured they had a roof over their heads that night, but, she remembered guiltily, no other provision had been made for them. She had been too weary last night to think of anything but her bed. It was only this morning that she had remembered their predicament and sorted out a few basic clothes to bring down to the village for them.

Still, those would do to tide them over the next few days she had supposed, until she had a chance to make a more thorough turn-out. Thomas's plain country clothes had long ago been given to the poor of the neighbourhood, but somewhere in the house there must be a store of his more elaborate outfits; garments that had seemed too fancy to be of any use to the country labourers would be ideal for the actors.

She could just imagine Mr Delamare strutting across the stage in the spangled jacket she had discovered in the back of one cupboard while she was sorting the linen. Thomas had worn it to a masquerade years ago, then discarded it as too extreme for even his flamboyant taste, but it was exactly Mr Delamare's style. There must be other, similar garments tidied away somewhere. This would be an excellent opportunity to be rid of them to a good cause. Anne hated waste.

Julia's wardrobe, too, was crammed with gowns barely worn but condemned as unwearable because they were out of date. She had taken a selection of them, but there were plenty more to choose from. She did not suppose the younger Delamare girls' adherence to fashion was as strict as Julia's. Rosy might turn up her nose at Julia's cast-offs, but after all she

had salvaged her trunk and so could afford to be fussy. Her
sisters, left with only the masculine attire they had been
wearing for the Trial scene, would be less choosy. Julia's
clothes were more their size anyway, and far more flattering
than the bedraggled finery she had first seen them in.

The details could be settled later, she had supposed. In the
meantime she had brought the first fruits of her search for
their immediate use yet already, it seemed, she was too late.

'It is the actors I want to see,' she repeated, thinking the
man must have misunderstood her. 'The ones who gave the
play at Ashorne last night. Mr Delamare and his family.
They came to stay the night here after the fire, didn't they?
Surely they cannot have left already.'

'That they have, miss! Sneaked up before dawn and done a
flit,' the innkeeper told her indignantly. 'Real quiet they went
off. Never even woke the dog, and he's usually the best watch
you'd want to meet. I reckon this'll not be the first time
they've crept away without paying their shot, the cunning
vagabonds! Last time I takes in any play-actors!'

'But did Mr Weston not explain when he brought them to
you that Lord Ashorne intended to settle their bill for them?'

'Not him,' a contemptuous sniff showed his opinion of the
steward.

'But he must have told them so,' she persisted. 'Lord
Ashorne asked Weston to take responsibility for their welfare—I heard him myself. He knew that they had lost everything in the fire, so was anxious they should be properly
cared for. Surely Weston explained!'

'I don't know nothing about that, miss. That Weston
brought them into the snug but he never stopped for no word
with me. Just went off with the dark wench when there wasn't
room for her. Very busy we was last night with the fire and
all, and that one was too pernickity to share with her sisters,
or so she made out.'

'But the rest of the family lodged here?'

'Yes, they made themselves comfortable enough, drat 'em,
though I remember thinking the old fellow sounded powerful
scared of his lordship—seemed to think he blamed him for
the barn burning down and all. Took half a bottle of brandy
to take the shakes out of him. My best French brandy too! I'd

not have given it him without I saw the colour of his money first, but he was crafty enough to deal with the pot-boy instead. That one's been a mooncalf since birth. He was fooled by the ruffian's grand words into thinking him a real gentleman—not that that's always a guarantee of payment neither!

'Anyways, the brandy calmed him down a trifle and they all went off to bed as soon as the rooms was made ready. We thought they was lying in late after all the fuss when they didn't appear at breakfast. Then when at last the maid went in to rouse them there they was—gone!'

'But you must have some idea of the direction they went,' exclaimed Anne, concerned at the thought of the family wandering the countryside destitute.

'No, miss, they covered their tracks too well for that. As I told you before, I'll lay odds that wasn't the first time they've played that trick, not by a long chalk. They'd know well enough that I'd have sent after them for my money if I had any notion where they was off to, and they had the means to pay the bill all right! The old fellow may have been too drunk to know what he was at, but I saw the young shaver had the takings-box safe under his cloak right enough when they came in. Now I have to whistle for my money.'

'Don't worry. I'm sure that his lordship will settle the reckoning,' Anne assured him. 'He fully intended to do so last night, and I am sure this will not alter his mind. He will not want you to lose by it. I would give you the money myself if I had it on me, but I left in a rush thinking that the Delamares would need clothes more than anything else.'

'Thank you, miss. That's a relief.' The man looked a little more cheerful. 'Though it's more than those rascals deserve.'

'And you really have no notion which way they could have gone? Perhaps they merely wanted cheaper accommodation. Have you made enquiries?'

'It'd do no good, miss. Like I said, that old devil was too downy a bird to leave any traces behind him. He'll be twenty mile and more away by now, and a good riddance too.'

'Nevertheless, I'll have a word around the village. I don't want to have to carry all these things back home with me if it isn't necessary. May I leave them here, and my horse, for the present?'

'If you like, miss,' he shrugged unconcernedly. 'But you'll not find anyone who's seen hair nor hide of them, I'll warrant.'

Anne's subsequent enquiries showed the truth of this prediction. No one she spoke to had seen or heard anything of the players' departure. The cart, with its wheel repaired, had been removed stealthily from beside the forge during the night and the horse spirited from its stall to draw it away.

'With not a penny piece left in payment,' pointed out the aggrieved blacksmith. 'I'm out of pocket for all the wood, not to mention shoeing that broken-down nag that has been eating its head off in my stable.'

'And you saw nothing of any of them?'

'No, miss. Except ...' he hesitated, then went on doubtfully, 'I did think I saw the young woman this morning—the shameless hussy who wore those—those *breeches*, if you'll forgive the word, miss, in that play-acting last night.'

'Rosy? Where was she?'

'Along by the mill. They takes in lodgers sometimes when the inn is full. I only got a glimpse, for she whisked out of sight when she saw me coming but I couldn't miss that hair, She'd been talking to that fancy Mr Weston—leastways I thought it was him, but I didn't get a good look at him neither, so I might have been mistook.'

Anne did not think so. She hurried along the village street in the direction he indicated. It seemed impossible that the whole family could disappear so completely without trace. Also, Rosy might be able to throw some light on Weston's movements in the barn last night.

The miller's cottage, a ramshackle building, lay beyond the rest of the houses, masked from them by a line of willows. No Rosy was to be seen but Weston stood at the door, deep in conversation with the miller, a shifty-looking individual whom she remembered as a one-time crony of Thomas's, whose lady-friends often used the miller's spare room. Presumably Weston was following his late master's example in billeting Rosy there.

'Where is Miss Delamare?' Anne greeted them abruptly.

'I fear that I have not the faintest notion, ma'am.' As ever the steward's slightly derisory tone infuriated Anne. 'I understand that she departed this hamlet in the early hours.'

'And I was told that she had been seen here with you this morning!'

'Impossible!' Was it her imagination or did he dart a warning frown at his companion? 'I have it on the best authority that the whole family ran off in a panic before anyone else woke this morning.'

'And why did they leave in that way?' demanded Anne. 'Surely you explained that Lord Ashorne wished to help them, not punish them for an accident that harmed themselves more than anyone else.'

'I tried to tell them so,' he replied with an uncaring shrug, 'but that poor fool Delamare must have been too drunk to take it in. I had supposed he understood me, so was as surprised as anyone to find him gone.'

The words did not ring true, but Anne had no way of disproving them. She glared in frustration at his bland expression. Was he lying, or did her dislike of the man so colour her reaction to whatever he said that she automatically doubted him? Curbing her indignation, she asked coldly, 'And you are positive that Rosy went with him?'

'As far as I know, or care, she did. You'll find no trace of her or any of the others in the village now. She had come along here to spend the night at the mill because there were only two rooms free at the inn, but Luton has seen nothing of her since she went up to bed last night. Have you, Ned?'

His companion smirked confirmation of this statement. He grinned smugly at Anne as he disappeared into the mill. She felt his word was as little to be trusted as the steward's.

'I thought she might have stayed behind to express her gratitude to you for helping to save her valuables yesterday,' she persisted. 'Without your aid they would have been lost.'

'True, but then she hadn't as nice a sense of gratitude as you. Perhaps it is just as well. She wasn't my type at all.' He flicked an audacious glance over her. 'As you know, Miss Anne, I've always preferred blondes myself.'

His tone, falling barely short of insolence, grated on Anne, but somehow she managed to bite back the angry retort. It would do little good to antagonise the steward. As she tried to move away Weston stood his ground, blocking her path. 'Why so desperate to run off, Miss Anne? Aren't you going to thank me for the compliment?'

Disturbed at the aura of menace he managed to project, she still refused to be intimidated. 'Your preferences do not interest me,' she told him coldly.

'No, it is his top-lofty lordship who takes your fancy, isn't it? I've watched you making sheep's eyes at him when you thought no one was looking.' He cut off her furious protest with a careless laugh. 'Don't pretend I'm wrong. I see as much as the next man. But you'll need to work a lot harder if you want to cut out your sister. She has him besotted like all the men. Poor fools!'

'How dare you ...'

'You'd be surprised at what I dare! But I don't understand why you let Julia outshine you as you do. You could easily rival her if you made some effort—if you didn't copy her so slavishly—wear her colours, her hairstyle. Can't you see that puts you at a disadvantage? No wonder no one gives you a second glance.'

'I've heard enough of your impertinence!' Anne's eyes flashed in fury; her voice shook. 'Move aside immediately, or Lord Ashorne shall hear of your insolence. I've often been tempted to complain of your behaviour to my sister and refrained as I thought it her business, but I will not endure such rudeness myself.'

'I don't advise you to mention it,' he said softly, 'unless you want your sister's guilty secrets made public. Or would it serve your purpose, perhaps, to have her exposed and leave the field clear?'

'I am not so contemptible.'

'More fool you. Your sister won't play fair. She'll take any chance to play a dirty trick on you—or anyone else.'

'She won't be very happy when I tell her your opinion of her.'

He shrugged indifferently. 'I don't imagine you will tell her, but it doesn't matter if you do. Julia won't dare to cross me.'

The familiarity was unendurable.

'*Lady Ashorne*,' Anne began, stressing the title furiously, then stopped as she remembered that Julia had no real claim to it. 'My sister,' she corrected herself crossly, 'does not . . .'

'Difficult, isn't it?' he smiled in triumph at her frustration. 'Poor Julia so resents the loss of her dignities, doesn't she? One feels so sorry for her.'

'Then you have a strange way of showing it. I've seen you try to browbeat her. What are these precious "secrets" you hold over her?'

'You must ask Julia that question,' he responded provokingly, and regarded her angry flush with interest. 'That colour suits you—you should lose your temper more often. Looking like that, it wouldn't be difficult for you to cut out dear Julia. Her charms are fading fast now, that's what makes her so desperate. Just stop being a doormat to her.'

Anne tapped her whip furiously against her boot. She was tempted to strike his insolent sneer off his face, but retained enough self-control to resist the impulse. Weston would retaliate for sure, and he was bound to come off best in any contest of that sort.

'If you have quite finished, I would like to leave,' she told him, taut with suppressed rage.

'Of course! But don't forget what I say,' he moved aside with exaggerated politeness.

'Please let me know if you discover any more about the Delamares,' she said stiffly, determined not to let him see that he had upset her. 'I am very concerned about them.'

She walked swiftly away, trying to dispel her fury in action. It was useless to hope that she would really learn anything from the steward. As ever, he was too much on his guard. Fetching her horse from the inn-yard she rode home. All the way Weston's words rang uncomfortably around her brain. However unwillingly, she had to admit that he was correct. All her life she had admired and copied Julia. Was that as great a mistake as he suggested? Would she have been wiser to develop her own style? Would Edmund prefer that to a slavish imitation of Julia?

Angrily she dismissed the thought. Why should she take any heed of the steward's opinion? Weston was arrogant enough to believe that any female must be grateful for his admiration, and had spoken just to arouse her interest. Well, he would not succeed with her!

Back at Ashorne Manor, Edmund was surprised by the story of her fruitless search for the Delamare family. 'Whatever could have made them leave in such a secretive manner?'

'No one seems to know.'

'And no one had any clue as to where they were going?'

'None. They might have vanished off the face of the earth.'

'I don't understand why you are worrying about the tiresome wretches,' Julia exclaimed. 'After all the trouble they caused us yesterday, you should be thankful to see the last of them.'

'I suppose I am,' Edmund replied, 'but at the same time I can't help feeling responsible for their flight. In the stress of the moment I was more brusque with Delamare than events justified. I fear it was that severity that drove them away.'

'You cannot blame yourself,' Anne exclaimed. 'You tried to help them, after all.'

'But not very successfully, if this happens. I should have been less thoughtless. Delamare was so terrified that he ran off not daring to face me. I'm sorry my harshness has cast the family out into the world penniless.'

'Not entirely penniless,' Anne reassured him. 'Ferdie was prudent enough to rescue the money from last night's performance, and they don't appear to have wasted any of it on settling their debts in the village.'

'And that blowsy female has the trinkets she risked Phillip's life to save,' Julia pointed out acidly.

'I can't see Rosy sharing her nest-egg with her family,' Anne commented. 'Even if she is with them, which seems in doubt.'

'What do you mean by that?' demanded Julia. 'Where else should she be?'

'I suspect that whatever the rest of the family have done,

she has stayed nearby here to be with Weston, although he denies it, of course.'

'Then I believe him,' Julia declared shrilly. 'You are letting your imagination run away with you again, Anne. He can have no interest in that sort of girl!'

'He is interested in any type of girl,' Anne told her curtly. 'It is time you faced up to the truth. Weston has a thoroughly bad reputation in the village for his carryings-on. I am only sorry that we put Rosy in his way, so that she was tempted to split away from her family.'

'Don't torture yourself over it,' Edmund put an impulsive hand over hers. 'Rosy is capable of looking after herself. In fact the whole family seems pretty resourceful. They appear well able to fend for themselves. Look at the way they whisked themselves away so successfully. I don't approve of their method of leaving, but have to admire the efficient way they carried out the manoeuvre.'

'I suppose you are right.' Anne relaxed a little to smile back at him. 'I don't suppose this is the first setback in their career.'

She coloured as Julia's eyes glared down at her hand, still clasped in Edmund's. She pulled it away sharply then felt annoyed a second later that she should be ashamed of accepting the friendly gesture. Even if Julia had misinterpreted her attitude she knew Edmund would not.

'They'll soon bounce back.' He continued to smile at her, ignoring Julia's disapproving scowl. 'It is kind of you to fret over Rosy, but she's a far tougher character than you give her credit for being.'

'Well, I cannot see why she is so concerned about the wretches!' Julia burst out. 'That ridiculous old mountebank nearly killed us all because he was too drunk to see where his feet were. It was criminal carelessness! If I had my way they'd all have been flung into jail, and so I told that stupid child who had been hanging round Kit all day yesterday. That took the grin off his face, precocious little brat!'

'Ferdie!' Anne exclaimed. 'You shouldn't have upset him, Julia. He must have told his father what you said. No wonder they were scared enough to run away.'

'What if they were? Why are you making such a fuss over

them? Good riddance, I say! I'm sure Edmund is as glad to
see the last of them as I am. My poor gown was utterly ruined
in the fire they caused. Fifty guineas it cost me, and I have to
throw it out after one wearing. That material never washes
properly. I don't know where I'll find the money to replace
it.' She paused hopefully, but Edmund failed to take the
hint.

'I'm sorry to think of them wandering friendless and afraid
that we are hounding them still, but they are resilient enough
to overcome that. It's done now and can't be mended. I
suppose I must go and see what can be done about the barn.'

As soon as he was out of earshot Julia rounded on her
sister. 'What do you think you are up to now? Holding hands
with Edmund again! That's the second time in two days I've
caught you at it!'

'I wasn't . . .'

'Don't try your lies on me!' Julia cut her off ruthlessly. 'I'm
not blind! Don't imagine I can't see you are doing your best
to cut me out with Edmund. Buttering him up and finding
fault with everything I do!'

Anne opened her mouth to apologise, then stopped. Why
should she always be the one to give way? Julia was in the
wrong, after all, totally misinterpreting the situation. That
wretched steward was right. She spent too much time placat-
ing her sister. It did not help matters really. Julia just grew
more unreasonable.

'I warn you your tricks won't work,' Julia continued
shrilly, working herself into a passion. 'Edmund is in love
with *me*. He means to marry me as soon as my year of
mourning is up—and that's not long now!'

'In that case,' Anne was stung into retorting, 'you can have
no cause for alarm whatever I do.'

Was it true? she wondered bleakly. Edmund had seemed
impatient with her sister lately, but when the fire threatened
it had been Julia he saved. Surely that indicated his real
feelings.

'I'm not concerned for my own sake,' Julia hastened to
explain mendaciously. 'It is you I am thinking about—I
don't want to see you hurt. I know how gallant Edmund is,
but he means nothing by it, so don't let yourself be misled. He

still thinks of you as a child, and doesn't realise how seriously you take his friendly overtures.'

Dejectedly, Anne reflected that this was all too credible. Edmund's behaviour towards her had changed subtly in the past few days, but it was an easy comradeship they shared—nothing like the passion he bore for Julia six years ago. To read anything stronger into his manner was only to indulge in wishful thinking and court greater disappointment. Perhaps Julia took her silence for dissent, because she went on more aggressively.

'What I say is true, Anne, whether you want to believe it or not. Oh, I admit he hasn't said anything officially yet, but that's because he is always so correct. But he'll marry me—just you wait and see! He has made it clear in all sorts of little ways that he is still of the same mind as when he left six years ago—and it is very natural that he should be. After all, it is only right that we should marry for the child's sake.'

'The child's sake?' echoed Anne in surprise.

'Kit, of course! He needs a father, and who more appropriate than Edmund?' As Anne stared blankly at her, Julia looked away, unwilling to meet her sister's eye. Twisting her fingers in the trimming of her gown, she hurried on disjointedly, 'I've never spoken of this before—it is all very awkward—I'm sure we need never mention the matter again, but surely you agree that in the peculiar circumstances Edmund and I must marry for Kit's sake. With the—the special relationship it is only fitting that we should.'

'What special relationship do you mean? They are only cousins—second cousins at that.'

'That is what I have always allowed everyone to believe,' Julia frowned in exasperation at her obtuseness, 'but it isn't the truth. Do I have to spell it out to you? Edmund is Kit's father!'

'*Father!*' For one awful moment, cold to the heart, Anne believed her. Then commonsense reasserted itself. 'Don't be foolish, Julia! How could he be?'

'It's true, alas!' Julia hung her head still lower. 'Have you never suspected why it was I married Thomas so hastily? I was forced to run off with him, much as I regretted it, because I was expecting a child—Edmund's child!'

'I cannot pretend I have never had such a suspicion,' admitted Anne. 'Much as I tried to suppress my doubts, I couldn't help noticing that Kit was remarkably large and strapping for the seven-month baby you claimed him to be, but it was Thomas I cast as villain then—and still must. No one can make me credit an eleven-month pregnancy. You aren't an elephant, my love!'

'Well!' gasped Julia in outrage. 'Of all the vulgar remarks! I don't know how you can speak of such things! It's disgusting!'

'You introduced the subject,' Anne pointed out drily. 'You really cannot expect me to swallow such a farrago of nonsense, Julia. Or did you imagine I could not add up to nine?'

'I am astounded you should be so well-informed on such matters,' Julia directed a sulky frown at her sister, 'let alone speak of them in so brass-faced a way. I am sure I was properly ignorant of anything of that nature before I was married!' She glowered as Anne burst into laughter, demanding furiously, 'Now what have I said that is so amusing?'

'Don't be so hen-witted, Julia!' Anne spluttered, diverted in spite of her indignation. 'How can you lay claim to snow-white maiden modesty when a second ago you were insisting that your knowledge had passed from theory to practice? It is too ridiculous!' Her laughter dying away, she stared narrowly at her sister's baffled scowl. 'You haven't been trying to pass this tale off on Edmund, have you?'

'Of course I have not! And I forbid you to breathe a word of it to him. I should not dream of mentioning so indelicate a subject to a gentleman!'

'No! Because he would know there wasn't a grain of truth in it,' Anne commented shrewdly. Julia's crestfallen expression betrayed the accuracy of this guess. 'I can picture Thomas in the role of seducer, but not Edmund. He put you on a pedestal—worshipped you like a goddess. It was Thomas who was the earthy one!'

Despite her exasperation at the tissue of lies Julia had spun, Anne could not help an unwilling sympathy for her. 'Whatever made you so foolish as to land yourself in such a scrape? Thomas wasn't worth it!'

'I don't know,' Julia shrugged hopelessly. 'It just seemed to happen. Edmund had gone off to the war, all patriotic fervour, and I was furious with him—and miserable at the same time. Thomas was all sympathy then—seemed to know just how I felt. I suppose he just swept me off balance. I wasn't the first to fall for his wiles—nor the last! I hadn't meant to marry him, but things turned out differently from what I intended.'

'Different from what he planned too, I'll warrant. I am only surprised that he agreed to marry you—child or no child.'

'Oh, he was still wild for me then and eager to spite Edmund. It wasn't hard to persuade him.' Julia hesitated before adding diffidently, 'You won't tell him, will you—Edmund I mean?—it's bad enough now. I wouldn't want him to know how foolish I had been.'

Anne could believe that. Incredibly, Julia seemed to see nothing wrong in her conduct—only being found out struck her as being a disgrace. How was it that their standards were so different? Still, Anne was not so petty as to betray her sister to Edmund.

'It is scarcely a subject I am liable to raise with him, is it? Whatever you may think, I am not that brazen. Your guilty secret is safe with me, though it might be more sensible—and more honest—if you told Edmund about it yourself.' With sudden inspiration she demanded, 'Is this silly business the secret which Weston is holding over your head? Is he threatening to tell Edmund of it?'

'Good lord, no! How could he have found out?'

'But there is something?' Anne persisted.

'No! No! No! I don't know why you are always harping on about Phillip Weston. He is an old friend of mine, that's all! Sometimes we have our differences, but I'm not in the least bothered about that. I've told you already that I can handle him!'

'Can you? Are you sure he is as harmless as you pretend? He seemed remarkably confident of his hold on you when I spoke to him last. And apart from whatever he is trying to do with you, I mistrust him. Don't you ever suspect that it is he who is trying to kill Edmund?'

'Of course he is not!' Was she mistaken, or was there a touch of desperation in Julia's vehement denial, as if she were trying to convince herself too? 'How can you suggest such a thing? You know Phillip was injured by the same intruder who shot Edmund.'

'He could have rigged up that incident to deceive us. What about last night? He was in the barn and had the opportunity to stun Jonas—mistaking him for Edmund.'

'With the Delamare creature hanging on his arm the whole while? Talk sense, Anne. I heard the girl say she had never lost sight of him in the smoke. No, Edmund is making a fuss over nothing. The stupid groom hit his head in the confusion and has seized the chance to appear interesting by making a great song and dance about it. All those years cooped up in prison have turned Edmund's brain—made him suppose everyone is against him. Don't you be taken in by his delusions!'

Anne was shocked by her callous tone. She had noticed how Edmund avoided the subject of his captivity. His uneasiness at being confined, for even a short period, had given her some inkling of the torment those six years must have been to one of his temperament. But to say that it had turned his brain was totally unjust—how could Julia be so unfeeling when she claimed to feel affection for him?

'Do you love Edmund?' she demanded bluntly.

'What has that to do with anything? He loves me!'

Which was probably true enough, Anne had to admit. Though at times she suspected that he was less blind to Julia's faults than he used to be, his action in saving her first when the fire threatened them proved where his preference lay.

'And I mean to marry him!' Julia added sharply, 'no matter how you scheme!'

'Don't worry, I can see that it is you he wants. There is no need for you to invent any more fantastic tales to scare me off.'

'I'm sorry about that,' Julia had the grace to look abashed. 'It wasn't one of my brighter ideas. It was just that I was worried, and somehow the story seemed so right—you know how it happens.'

Anne did. She had seen Julia in action too many times to feel great indignation over the incident. Julia never meant to lie, but somehow the facts became twisted to a version that suited her best.

'I didn't want you breaking your heart over Edmund again, love. And I don't want James hurt either. He worships you!'

Anne doubted whether even Julia could believe that. James hung so devotedly on Julia's every word that she must realise his love was concentrated on herself. However, she let the remark pass without comment. She had decided days ago that nothing would induce her to marry James now; she must have been mad ever to have considered the idea. Even before Edmund's return reminded her how high her standards had once been, she had begun to realise how unlikely the match was.

James and she were totally unsuited. Now that she realised that his love was given to Julia and her own to Edmund, it was impossible. However, she knew better than to announce that decision yet. Julia would never follow her reasoning. She would be bound to leap to the conclusion that this was confirmation of her fears that Anne was hoping to win Edmund from her. Heaven knew what commotion that would cause!

The faint doubt that putting off the evil moment was unfair to James, was easily stifled. Anne suspected that he would be more relieved than anything by her decision. He too was having second thoughts, and once he got over the shock of being rejected, he would be happy in the knowledge that nothing now stood in the way of his devotion to Julia.

With sudden clarity Anne realised that Julia would be better off with James than with Edmund. With the baronet's totally uncritical admiration she would be free to act as she pleased for the rest of her life. Nothing she did seemed to shake his faith in her: Edmund would prove a far more demanding husband. All the same she doubted whether Julia was ready to accept the idea—James might be rich and doting, but Edmund's rank was a greater attraction in Julia's eyes.

Anne made a noncommittal reply and her sister flounced

away, trailing her gauze scarf petulantly behind her. But however much she resented Anne's earlier words, they clearly bore some fruit. Anne was not surprised, a little later on, to see Julia deep in conversation with Weston. They were too far off to be overheard but from the expression on Julia's face and her angry gestures, Anne guessed she was taxing the steward with the rumours about Rosy.

He appeared, as ever, coolly unconcerned, pooh-poohing her furious reproaches. Julia's claims of dominion over him seemed scarcely borne out by this encounter. Fiery, abrupt movements betrayed her fury. At last she jerked away, sharp-faced with rage, while he looked after her, an amused half-smile, half-sneer on his face.

With sinking heart Anne saw her fears confirmed. Whatever hold Weston had over Julia must be very strong if he was ready to risk her anger in so careless a fashion. What might it not drive her sister to do? Anne wished she could believe that Julia would stop short of active participation in his schemes, but she could not rely even on that.

CHAPTER
NINE

IN the following days an uneasy atmosphere filled the Manor. Julia was jumpy and fretful; she watched Anne's every move yet seemed unable to meet her sister's gaze. Anne kept out of her way whenever possible. Edmund's temper was equally frayed; he snubbed James and snapped at Julia. Was the memory of those unsuccessful attempts to kill him bothering him too? Anne found herself starting at any sound, hourly expecting some new disaster to overtake them.

Nothing more had been heard of the players. Odd reports had come of Rosy being seen, but Anne was unable to get any firm details. If Weston had her secreted away somewhere he was keeping her well hidden. That uncertainty did not help.

Things could not go on this way, Anne decided at last. It must be easier for them all when she and Julia were able to move to Melthorpe. Living on top of each other like this was trying all their nerves. After the disquieting episode of the fire and its aftermath, the move could not come soon enough for Anne. The fear of betraying her true feelings for Edmund made her manner curt and unfriendly towards him.

No news had come yet of the renovations at Melthorpe Hall, so Anne decided to ride over and see for herself what progress had been made. At least that would get her away from everything here for an hour or so! She had always loved Ashorne, but now its echoing corridors filled her with trepidation.

After a brief hesitation she invited Kit to join her, mindful of the disastrous results of her broken promise last time. He accepted with glee and rode beside her, chattering excitedly all the way. Fortunately he appeared to expect little response from her, so Anne was free to concentrate on her own uncomfortable thoughts until they reached the hall.

Looking round her she could see little change since her

previous visit. Confusion still reigned throughout the building. There were odd piles of materials everywhere, but no signs of fresh work, except where more plasterwork and timbers had been torn out. Dust hung chokingly in the air where another inner wall had been demolished.

Kit, with a whoop of delight, plunged into a heap of shavings. Anne left him rolling happily like a puppy while she sought out the carpenter, demanding to be told why there was so little to show for a week's work. He listened to all her reproaches with studious calm.

'That's all very fine what you say, miss,' he replied stolidly when she had finished, 'but his lordship says we're not to rush things. "Take your time, Bedford, and make a good job of it" was his very words to me, and that's what I means to do.'

'But he didn't tell you to spend days and days doing absolutely nothing!'

'Nor we haven't, miss. While I've been waiting for the materials to come I've been measuring and drawing up plans for his lordship's approval.' As she snorted in disgust, he added, unruffled, 'It makes sense, miss. Once you've calmed down you'll admit it. The job may take longer this road, but if it's done properly it'll last a sight longer too.'

'What is the use of that if we are all dead and buried before it is even begun! There must be something you could be getting on with!'

'Not without timber, miss.'

'Then re-use what you have taken out!' She poked impatiently at the rubble by her feet. 'See, this piece is sound—and this. Use them!'

'His lordship says not, miss. We're to wait for some decent stuff to be brought over from Ashorne.'

No amount of argument would shake him, and the other workmen proved equally adamant. Anger, pleading, cajolement were all met with the same infuriating response; all her suggestions for short cuts countered with an impassive, 'His lordship says not.'

Eventually she gave up the struggle, convinced that if she heard those words once more she would scream. She gathered Kit up, shavings clinging to every inch of him, and ignoring his protests rode furiously home to have it out with Edmund. His orders ran too contrary to hers to be borne.

Was he being deliberately obstructive? Trying to delay their removal to Melthorpe in order to keep Julia beside him? Surely not! To ensure that she remained he had only to propose marriage. Julia had made it abundantly clear that she would accept him, and once the marriage was arranged there would be no need for the expensive repairs at Melthorpe. Anne had no desire to live there alone. Why else should he put every obstacle in the way of their leaving Ashorne?

Whatever his motives, he had no right to interfere: the Hall was Julia's not his, and as Julia's representative it was her place to negotiate with the workmen. After all, she and Julia would be living there, not Edmund. Why was she not able to arrange matters as she wished? It was intolerable. She would insist on being given a free rein!

Anger feeding her determination, Anne resolved on prompt action. Once back at the manor, she flung herself off the horse and stalked indoors to settle the matter with Edmund at once. If the workmen would not listen to her then Edmund must.

In the hall she halted. A faint chink of glass came from the library—the room Edmund had used as a retreat since he returned. He must be there now. Her resolution wavered a little. For a moment she hesitated, unsure whether it was better to confront him now while her anger was at fever pitch, or wait for it to cool when she might reason more carefully. One needed a clear head to deal with Edmund. Anger won, pushing her on.

She reached for the doorknob, determined to act now while she was buoyed up by her fury, but before she could grasp it the door opened. Weston walked out, nearly colliding with her. Anne stepped back out of his way, amazed to see him there at that hour. He glared back. Later she was to remember how startled he had seemed in that first second, but just now she was too keyed up to confront Edmund to pay heed to anything else.

'Is Lord Ashorne there?' she demanded trying to see past

the steward. 'I wish to speak with him on an important matter.'

'Unfortunately you are unable to do so,' Weston told her, his composure soon regained. 'He is not here.'

She stared narrowly at the sneering face. Was it Julia then who had been entertaining him? The sound that had attracted her attention had undoubtedly been the chink of the glass decanter-top fitting back into place. She had heard that particular note too often in Thomas's lifetime to be mistaken in it. Had Weston been drinking with Julia? What fresh devilment had they been toasting?

'Then I will speak with my sister instead,' she declared icily, determined not to waste the opportunity.

'Unhappily, that too is impossible.' Weston surveyed her boldly from head to toe before adding, 'I see you are taking my advice. That green is far more flattering to you than the pastel colours your sister affects.'

She coloured angrily, knowing that he was right. She had found out this old habit in the colour she knew to be a favourite of Edmund's. Her hands tightened on her whip, tempted once more to lash out at him. He laughed.

'That angry colour is most fetching as I told you before.'

With an effort Anne swallowed her rage. She had a strange suspicion that he was deliberately provoking her. But why?

'Let me pass!' she demanded acidly. 'My sister shall hear of your impudence.'

'If you must,' he shrugged, 'but she is not here.'

As if to prove him correct, Julia came through the garden door into the hall. She stopped, frowning in annoyance, but whether at the sight of the steward or Anne, it was impossible to decide.

'Whatever are you doing here, Phillip?'

'Enjoying a chat with your young sister, but I came hoping for a word with you, your ladyship!' Was it her imagination, wondered Anne, or was there the faintest hint of menace underlying his words?

'I was on the point of leaving,' he went on harshly, 'thinking you must have forgotten!'

Julia frowned, jerking her head in an almost imperceptible warning towards Anne. What was there between them? He must feel very confident of his position to speak so boldly to Julia. None of the other servants would dare. And he must have been whiling away the interval by sampling Edmund's port, she thought contemptuously. That was the sort of petty dishonesty she might have expected from the fellow.

'I can't talk to you now,' Julia exclaimed quickly, with another sidelong glance at her sister. 'There's barely time to dress for dinner as it is. Another time!'

Turning tail, she hurried upstairs. Anne watched the steward curiously. Weston bowed his acceptance of the dismissal, but the tightness of his lips betrayed his anger as he stalked away. It tokened ill for Julia at their next meeting. The widow was courting trouble there, Anne feared, but let her deal with it herself. Anne had wasted too many years sorting out her sister's problems. If Julia did not want help then she would not force it upon her.

Frustrated in her wish to see Edmund, and knowing better than to tackle Julia in her present mood, Anne too went upstairs to change her gown. The militancy had faded now.

As she had anticipated, dinner was an uncomfortable meal. Julia had clearly still not forgotten their disagreement when her bluff had been called. She hated to be put in the wrong and, as ever, vented her resentment on the person who had disconcerted her. That the fault was her own only increased her pique. She turned her exquisitely gowned back on her sister, totally ignoring her, making the snub more pointed by the warmth with which she concentrated on charming their male companions.

Perhaps to prove the validity of her claims to Edmund's affection, she mounted a determined attempt to demonstrate her mastery over him. Gazing soulfully into his unresponsive eyes, she embarked on a campaign of eye-fluttering and breathy sighs that reminded Anne forcibly of Rosy's performance in the play. It proved an unusually bad error of judgment on Julia's part.

However susceptible Edmund might have been to such tactics six years ago, they had little effect now except to render him more withdrawn and silent. When all her wiles proved vain, Julia pouted and gave up. With sudden volte-face she switched her attention to James instead, presumably in the hope of compelling Edmund's interest by jealousy as coquetry was unavailing.

Predictably, James was an easier conquest. A fatuous grin spread over his features as he responded in an ecstasy of delight to her advances. Julia blossomed under his admiration, but if her aim was to rouse Edmund it failed. He shrank back into his chair, more grimly taciturn than ever.

A discreet study of his expression convinced Anne that it was disapproval, not jealousy, that darkened his frown. She felt his eyes on herself as much as her sister, as if to judge her reaction to James's blatant shift of affection. Colour heightened, she tried to pretend an ignorance of the tension in the room that she was far from feeling, as Julia's attention swung back to Edmund.

Another long screed had come today from Fanny, full of the festivities planned in London to fête the French king and reinspiring Julia with a longing to join again in the social whirl there. 'Surely you don't mean to bury yourself here all year long,' she fretted.

'There is still a great deal to be settled here before I can think of leaving it. I am perfectly content, but you may move to London if you prefer it. I'll put the house there at your disposal for as long as you wish.'

'It is too late to put that morgue to rights.' Julia looked furious at the reminder that it was no longer hers. 'By the time I had got it anywhere near right there would be nothing but a mob of Cits left in town. Why can't we hire a house in Brighton instead? Fanny has one on the Steyne for the season, close by the Pavilion. Wouldn't that be near enough for you to ride over to deal with any tiresome business that cropped up? The estates have managed to survive six years without your aid. Why are you so concerned about them now?'

'I prefer to remain here. Prinney's set are not my choice.'

'My Brighton house is at your disposal,' James assured Julia. 'It is in the best part of town. I can soon fix myself up with something else.'

'Dear James! You are too generous.' Julia favoured him with a taut smile, unwilling to give up all hope of influencing Edmund yet. 'But how can we dream of leaving poor

Edmund here alone? It is noble of him to offer, but we must not be selfish.'

None of her hearers looked particularly happy with this decision, but only James attempted a protest. It was speedily dismissed.

With most of her mind on her sister's antics, Anne failed to notice how white and strained the butler looked until Julia's angry shriek called her attention to him. His hand had trembled as he poured the wine, spilling a little on Julia's bodice.

'Clumsy oaf! Look what you are doing!' she screamed, rubbing furiously at the crimson stain spreading across the delicate silver-threaded fabric.

'I beg your pardon, my lady!' The words came thickly. His face green, he swayed and clutched at the table to steady himself.

'It is too late to be sorry now. You should be sorry *before* you did it!' shrieked Julia with fine lack of logic. 'Look at my dress. Ruined!'

'Put down the wine, Stone,' Edmund's calm voice interrupted her tirade. 'You are obviously too unwell to continue. John may serve in your place this evening. Get yourself off to bed, man.'

'Unwell! The wretched creature is intoxicated!' Julia snapped, still intent on her stained gown. 'Just look at this! Wine stains are hopeless to remove. Nothing will hide the mark. Dismiss the wretch at once! Two gowns ruined in a week. It is beyond enduring!'

Stone mumbled a further apology before he staggered away, but she refused to listen. Regarding the man carefully, Anne was convinced that he was genuinely ill this time, not suffering the results of secret tippling as in the past. Julia's slipshod control of the household had encouraged laxity in her staff. Anne had found difficulty when she first arrived in bringing them to some kind of order; Stone's drinking had been one of the thorniest problems to overcome.

She doubted whether he would ever completely lose his habit of dipping into the port, but he was generally more careful now, restricting his drinking to his off-duty hours. Moreover, his imbibing had always produced a red face and

over-deliberate movement, not this quivering sweaty pallor.
She hoped he was not suffering from any serious ailment.

Stone staggered away and John hurried to take his place.
The difficult meal dragged on. Julia's animated mood had
vanished, leaving her in a gloomy sulk. Frantic to coax her
from it, James went to ridiculous lengths to placate her. For
once he spent little time over his port before hastening to join
them in the drawing-room. Edmund followed, drank his tea
swiftly, and left before Anne had summoned enough resolution to broach the subject of Melthorpe Hall.

'Gone off to smoke another of his filthy cigars, I suppose,'
Julia hunched a fretful shoulder. 'At least that is one vice
Thomas did not have!'

James, brushing the snuff he had spilt over his sleeve on to
the tea tray, was equally loud in disapproval. Anne buried
her head in a book, trying to concentrate on that and ignore
James's pathetic attempts to coax Julia into a good humour,
but it was no use. Though her eyes scanned the page her
brain would not take in the words. Eventually she gave up
and went early to bed, only to lie restlessly fretting over the
events of the past weeks.

If only the Hall were ready for them to move into! She
doubted whether Julia would agree to go to Brighton leaving
Edmund behind, but once her home was ready she could not
refuse to move into it. Things must be easier then. Anne
resolved to tackle Edmund on the subject first thing in the
morning.

At last she dropped off into fitful sleep. It seemed only a
short while later before she was woken by a scratching at the
door. Mrs Norwich hurried into the room in response to her
sleepy invitation, her plump face taut with concern.

'It's Stone, Miss Anne!' she burst out. 'Terrible ill he is.
I've never seen no one so sick. We've been up half the night
with him, but he don't seem to get no better, only weaker.'

'Sick?' Anne struggled up. 'What does the doctor say is
wrong with him?'

'He wouldn't let us send for one, Miss. His lordship offered
last night, but Stone wouldn't hear of it. Said he was better
after the stuff his lordship gave him, but he was took bad
again in the night and he looks like death now. I'm sorry to

disturb you so early, miss, only his lordship was called out to deal with some poachers. I daren't rouse her ladyship but something has to be done or Stone will die!' She ended on a smothered sob.

'You did quite right. Have John ride for the doctor at once. I'll come and see what can be done in the meantime.'

Quickly Anne dragged on her clothes and followed the housekeeper to Stone's room. One glance told her that Norwich had not exaggerated; Stone was desperately ill. Slumped in the rumpled bed, his portly form seemed oddly shrunken. He moaned feebly as great shudders racked him. Anne put a hand to his forehead. It was clammy with sweat, yet deathly cold.

'Fetch a warming-pan immediately, and more blankets,' she directed, ashamed that her own problems had made her forget the butler's needs last night. 'We must keep him warm. Pray God the doctor comes soon. I've never dealt with anything like this before.'

It seemed an eternity before he bustled in. Thankfully, Anne handed over her patient and waited outside while he made his examination.

'He has been poisoned!' the doctor said bluntly when eventually he emerged from the sickroom. 'He's lucky to be alive. He can thank Lord Ashorne's prompt action for that. But for the emetics he gave the man last night, your butler would be dead. I've bled him to be on the safe side, but there's not much else I can do. With care he'll pull through now.'

'Are you saying that someone has tried to kill Stone?'

'Good gracious, no! I wouldn't think it was anything so melodramatic. Shellfish, bad meat—anything could have caused it. It's common enough, unfortunately, but I advise you to find out what was the cause or you are liable to have a run of it. The next victim might not be so lucky.'

Norwich, when questioned, was adamant that Stone had eaten nothing that the rest of the servants had not shared.

'In which case we'd have been took bad too, miss. That Ned eats like a horse. If anyone ought to be ill it's him, but he's as hale and hearty as ever and tucking into bacon and eggs in the kitchen this minute.'

'Undoubtedly anyone who shared the contaminated food would be ill by now,' the doctor confirmed. 'There must be something you have overlooked. Send for me if there is any change for the worse but I anticipate he'll slowly improve now.'

Anne saw him out to his horse. She was just returning to her own room to wash properly and tidy her hair when from above Norwich called sharply, 'Miss Anne!'

Anxiously Anne ran up to the sickroom. 'What is it? Is he worse?'

'No, miss, but I was asking what he'd been eating yesterday like the doctor told me and...'

'The wine!' Stone struggled feebly up. 'It was the wine!'

'Which wine?'

A faint colour stained the pallid cheek. 'His lordship's port wine in the library. I took half a glass before dinner. I remember thinking it tasted a bit queer, but I've a cold and put it down to that.'

'It's a judgment on him; that's what it is!' Norwich declared sententiously. 'God's punishment for thieving!'

'Never mind that now,' Anne hushed her impatiently, a cold dread at her heart. 'Is the rest of the wine still there, Stone?'

'Yes, miss. The decanter was nearly full—I thought a little drop wouldn't be missed—Do you think His Lordship put something in it to teach me a lesson?'

'No, I am sure he would not do anything so cruel. I fear it must have been yet another attempt to kill Lord Ashorne. I must hurry and remove the decanter before he gets home.'

'He's back already, miss,' Norwich told her. 'I saw him come in the back way while you was seeing the doctor out the front. He's in the library now!'

Heart thudding, Anne ran headlong down the stairs and burst into the library. Edmund looked up in astonishment.

'Whatever is the matter, Anne? Wasn't that the doctor I saw as I came in? Is Stone worse?'

Anne was too out of breath to do more than point at the decanter and gasp, 'The port!'

'You want a glass?'

'*No!* Have you drunk any?'

'At this hour of the morning? What do you take me for!'
Edmund looked pained at the suggestion. Then, seeing the
strain in her face, he demanded urgently, 'What is all this
about, Anne? I can see something has upset you.'

'Nor last night?—no, you could not or you would be ill by
now.'

'Calmly now!' He took her hand in a comforting grasp
and forced her to sit down before he would let her continue.
'Now, are you saying there is something wrong with the
stuff?'

'So Stone insists. He is sure it was the wine that made him
so ill. The doctor said he could have died!'

Edmund listened gravely to her disjointed account of the
butler's story.

'It certainly sounds possible!' He took the stopper out of
the decanter and sniffed at the contents. 'It doesn't smell any
different but we can have tests made. Fortunately I rarely
touch the port—a much overrated beverage in my opinion. I
had noticed the level went down, but suspected Sir James of
sinking it, not Stone. Poor fellow! This should teach him to
keep his hands off if nothing else does!'

'But don't you understand, Edmund? It was meant to kill
you!' Anne said despairingly.

'What nonsense you do talk, Anne dear,' observed a cool
voice from the doorway. Julia swept in, calm and fresh in an
attractive sprigged muslin, a lacy parasol in her hand. 'You
are becoming quite hysterical over these imaginary attacks
on Edmund. I could hear your voice from above-stairs. Such
a commotion this morning with all the noisy comings and
goings, I had to give up any hope of further rest! Why are you
trying to upset Edmund with your ridiculous accusations?
No one wishes him any harm!'

'Someone put poison in that decanter there. Providentially
Edmund did not drink any, but Stone did and nearly died as
a result.'

'Which is just what the dishonest wretch deserves!'

'That is a matter of opinion. But the important point
is—who put the poison in the port?' Memory flooded back of
the odd chink of the decanter-stopper fitting into place as she
stood outside the library door yesterday, and of the startled

panic that flashed momentarily in the steward's eyes as he emerged to find her confronting him.

'*Weston!*' she breathed. 'I heard him in here. I thought he must have been helping himself to a drink, but in that case he'd be ill too.'

'And he certainly is not,' Edmund put in. 'I was speaking to him this morning.'

'So he was putting something into the decanter, not taking it out!'

'Poppycock!' Julia snorted. 'Just because you dislike the poor man you accuse him of everything that goes wrong. Why should he have touched that wretched decanter?' She made a disdainful gesture with the parasol, which caught the decanter, tipping it on to the floor where it shattered into fragments. 'A good riddance!' Julia exclaimed with angry satisfaction. 'I've never liked that ugly thing!'

Anne stared horrified as the wine spread over the floor like a huge bloodstain. Was it an accident, or had Julia deliberately destroyed the evidence? Was that why she had come? Despairingly, she tried not to believe that, but the niggling doubt lingered.

'What about all the other incidents, then?' she asked unsteadily. 'He was involved in them all. No one else saw the intruder he claimed had injured him and set fire to the records. Who did that profit but Weston? He would have had plenty of time to get back to the office after shooting Edmund and fake the attack. And he was in the barn when Jonas was knocked unconscious and left to burn. That blow could easily have been intended for Edmund.'

'But why should Phillip want to harm Edmund?'

'Because he knows that I suspect him of cheating you for years,' Edmund answered her sternly. 'Destroying the records made it more difficult to prove, but I am slowly gathering evidence from other sources. He has been milking the estates for years—no doubt to cover the debts he has incurred all around the district with his gambling and petticoat adventures. He must have realised I would soon have enough evidence to prove his villainy and made these desperate attempts to silence me. The reckoning has come a little quicker this way, but it had to come eventually. I'll send

Jonas to his lodgings to pick him up, and we'll have him in front of a magistrate before he can do any more harm.'

'But he's not . . .' began Julia, then broke off. Great hollow eyes stared out of her shocked white face at them, then, shaking off Anne's sympathetic hand, Julia hurried away.

Anne felt little like work this morning but Kit's lessons had been far too often neglected lately, so she forced herself to seek him out. She toiled with him throughout the period, desperate to forget that awful moment when Julia stared so complacently as the poisoned wine flooded out over the library floor. She did not want time to think, to wonder whether her sister was really a party to murder.

At eleven she had to let him go for his riding lesson. Kit rushed off in relief and Anne spent the remainder of the morning in the stillroom, sorting the accumulated pickles and preserves of ten years and more. With disgust at the sad lack of organisation in the household to exercise her mind, she was able to keep disturbing speculation at bay.

She had some of the jars taken down for lunch. James tucked into the pickled walnuts with relish while Anne voiced her complaints over the state of the stillroom, and Julia listened to them absent-mindedly.

'I'm sure it is very remiss of Norwich, but I cannot be bothered with such petty details. Speak to her yourself.'

'Quite right,' James exclaimed warmly. 'Can't you settle it, Anne, without worrying poor Julia? She has enough problems already. These walnuts are really fine! You must give me the receipt for my housekeeper before I leave.'

Julia absently smiled her acknowledgment of his sympathy but it was evident that her thoughts were elsewhere. 'Is that you, Edmund?' she called tensely as a door banged.

It was. When he came in, face grim with fury, she faltered, 'Have you got him? Weston, I mean.'

'No, we have not! Jonas missed him at the lodgings. We tried the office, only to find that cleared out. He must have had warning we were after him. He's sneaked off, heaven knows where; left only minutes before Jonas got there, but he has covered his tracks as craftily as those actors.'

Relief flooded through Julia's face, only to drain away as

he added grimly, 'And to ensure a safe getaway he has taken Kit with him.'

'No!' she shrieked, 'He could not be so cruel!'

'But why should he do that?' asked Anne.

'To make certain that we don't follow him. Somehow he must have learned of our suspicions and made his plans accordingly. He's left clear warning that any pursuit will mean danger to the boy.'

'You'll let him go free now, won't you?' pleaded Julia, her hands twisting frantically. 'For Kit's sake. It's all a mistake! Phillip is not a murderer, but panic might make him injure Kit if he is driven to it. Let him go free!'

'And have him kill the child when he has served his purpose?' protested James unwisely.

Edmund glared at him as Julia fell into hysterics. 'We cannot be certain what is the best course, but it is out of my control now. The warrant is issued for his arrest—we cannot easily recall it.'

'But Kit...' moaned Julia.

'Is in equal danger whatever we do. How can Weston set him free without betraying himself?'

'How could Phillip be so cruel!' Julia sobbed frantically. 'I never dreamed he would do such a thing. Oh, what have I done?'

'What are you trying to say, Julia?' demanded Edmund with dangerous calm. 'Was it you who warned Weston?'

Blue eyes, misty with tears, gazed pitifully up at him. 'I had to!'

'Why, for God's sake?' Only sobs answered him. He questioned more sternly, 'Why, Julia? Why should you warn him?'

'Leave her alone!' James exclaimed fiercely as Julia's tears redoubled. 'Hasn't she enough to bear already without all these questions? Her child is missing—in danger! I'll not let you bully her!'

'Don't waste your sympathy,' Edmund told him bitterly. 'She thinks only of herself. This is of a piece with all her behaviour. It was the same at the play—I could not credit her selfishness when I tried to prevent Anne and Kit going into danger and Julia grabbed me back, concerned only with her own skin. They could have died then for all she cared.'

Anne's heart thudded unbearably as she listened. So it had been Julia's action that forced him to remain with her, not his own choice. How different that made things look! But there was no time to consider the implications now. Brusquely she thrust James aside. Half measures were useless. Grabbing her sister's shoulders, she shook her violently.

'She sent him warning because he was blackmailing her. Wasn't he, Julia? Wasn't he?'

'Yes!' Julia sobbed. 'Yes, yes, yes! Oh it all started innocently enough. You cannot imagine how mean Thomas was. He'd never give me money for clothes or anything. Phillip could see how miserable that made me. He offered to arrange things so that I got a share of the rents. After all, it was my due! Thomas was supposed to support me, wasn't he? I don't know how Phillip managed it, but he seemed to get it past old Stoneleigh easily enough. The money came and that was all I cared. I just had to borrow Thomas's seal and a few papers. He never suspected a thing, so I suppose Phillip was tempted to take a little extra for himself too.'

'More than a little, and it carried on after Thomas died,' Edmund commented. 'He got greedier and greedier. Why didn't you try to stop him? Or had he some other hold over you?'

'It was the letters,' Julia admitted at last. 'Phillip was so kind and sympathetic after Thomas got mixed up with those dreadful women that I was indiscreet. I wrote some foolish letters. . . . He threatened to publish them if I tried to stop his borrowings from the estate. So I said nothing, and all the time he needed more and more—for gambling and women too—like that slut of an actress,' she added viciously.

'And what happened when Edmund came home and he saw his source of income drying up?' prompted Anne.

'He was terrified that Edmund would find out. I begged him to confess. I promised I would not let Edmund prosecute him. But he said that if I breathed a word he would show Edmund the letters, and I was too ashamed.'

And afraid that it would wreck her plans to marry Edmund, thought Anne but kept the reflection to herself. She contented herself with observing, 'So you let him try to kill Edmund without saying a word?'

'I didn't know that it was Phillip,' Julia insisted. 'All those things could have been accidents. I kept hoping that you were mistaken. I pleaded with Phillip—promised that whatever Edmund did I would keep him on at Melthorpe—but that didn't satisfy him.'

'The pickings are richer at Ashorne,' Anne pointed out tartly.

'It wasn't only that.' Julia hesitated then went on jerkily, 'He'd become very—very ambitious—wanted to marry me—I kept putting him off but it was getting harder...'

Anne stared in amazement at her sister. She knew Julia was foolish, but had never dreamed she had got herself into such an entanglement with the steward. Edmund seemed equally dumbfounded. Only James was unshocked. Putting his arms around the stricken beauty, he tried to shield her from their interrogation. She clung to him, sobbing.

'Don't worry, Julia dear,' he comforted her. 'I won't let them torment you any more.' Turning on the others he said fiercely, 'Can't you see she is overwrought?'

'Not too upset to try to wind another poor fool in her toils,' Edmund told him bluntly. 'Her own sister's fiancé at that! I've come to realise over the past weeks that she is vain, shallow and selfish, but I had never supposed her so unfeeling as to ignore her son's peril in her eagerness to charm another victim. I am ashamed that I ever believed myself in love with her!'

'Anne understands my affection for her sister,' James replied stiffly. 'Our relationship is no concern of yours. I have never made a secret of my deep regard for Julia.'

'Never mind that now,' Anne interrupted impatiently. 'It is Kit who matters, not our quarrels! How can we rescue him? I hold little hope for his safety if he remains with Weston.'

'Phillip won't harm a child,' said Julia without much conviction.

'Don't fool yourself,' Anne urged. 'He has already shown himself ruthless in his dealings with Edmund.'

'But Kit is only a baby...'

'And so more easily silenced,' said Edmund. 'Live in Cloudcuckooland if you wish, Julia, but I am not so naïve. I know how it feels to be a captive, and I don't want that poor child to suffer it too long. We've only returned to fetch more men and fresh horses. I can see them ready outside now.'

He hurried out, flinging his last words over his shoulder. 'I mean to do my best to rescue the boy and bring that rogue to justice. I think when you come to your senses you'll thank me for it!'

Anne looked coldly at her sister who had relapsed into tears on James's shoulder. For once she had no sympathy at all for Julia. 'You deserved every word of that. I hope you realise that you've dished yourself properly with Edmund now! If you are wise you will make the best of a bad job and settle for James instead!'

Drenched blue eyes widened in amazement. 'But—but James is going to marry you.'

'Not if there is any chance of your having him. Surely you know that he has been crazy over you for years? He doesn't care a fig for me.' James began to protest, but she cut him off with, 'Don't try to be polite, James. You know our engagement was a ghastly mistake—one I have intended to put right for some time now.'

'You are still hoping to catch Edmund, I suppose,' Julia commented waspishly. 'I don't give much for your chances.'

'Nor I,' Anne agreed. 'I doubt if he will ever want to see any of us again when all this is over. Fortunately that was not my aim.'

'No?' Recovering a little now, Julia raised disbelieving eyes.

'No! I just discovered that I could not face the prospect of a lifetime of watching James drool over you. I've too much pride. But don't let us quarrel over that. It is Kit *I* am concerned about, if you are not! Edmund has little idea where to start searching, but I suspect that you have. Where would Weston have taken him?'

'Phillip won't hurt Kit if we leave him alone,' Julia said defensively.

'Your faith in him is touching, but I'd rather not run the risk of your being wrong. Oh granted he'll keep him alive for a while yet. Kit is his safe-conduct at present, but once that rôle is played the child becomes a liability. Can Weston afford to let his hostage go free to betray where he has disappeared to?' As she saw indecision waver in the delicate features, Anne pressed more urgently, 'You know where he might be, don't you? Somewhere he is likely to have Rosy Delamare concealed, waiting for him. Tell me before it is too late.'

As she had hoped, the reference to the girl tipped the balance.

'There is a cottage,' Julia said slowly, 'where I sometimes used to meet Phillip . . .' She peered from under long lashes to gauge James's reaction to the admission. 'I know it was foolish of me, but what could I do when he had such a hold over me? I had to agree . . .'

'Was this before or after Thomas died?' Anne asked tartly, then repented. 'I'm sorry, Julia, that was uncalled for. Where exactly is this place?'

'Just off the London Road—along the track about a mile before the toll gate.'

'I know it. A derelict building surrounded by trees. Just the spot to hide Rosy. I'll warrant he calls back for the jewellery if not the girl. Pray heaven it is not too late to catch him there!'

'You cannot mean to go careering off round the countryside?' exclaimed James, catching at her arm. 'Not when poor Julia needs your support.'

'I shall not need to if you let me go. If I hurry I may catch Edmund, otherwise I shall have to follow him.'

'But poor Julia is too distressed to be left,' bleated James.

'Not half as distressed as Kit must be. He needs me more than Julia does. Or were you offering to go in my place?'

'No, James!' shrieked Julia. 'Don't leave me. You are such a comfort. Let her go if she must, but I need you!'

Anne was forgotten as he clasped the sobbing widow to his chest. Almost she felt sorry for James, but not quite. He deserved all he got, though probably he would be content however badly Julia treated him. Anne felt only relief that she was rid of him.

She sped to the stables, but Edmund was already gone, taking all but one elderly groom with him. The best horses were gone too, only three badly winded mounts and one slow mare were left. Anne wavered in an agony of indecision. What was her best course? Was there time to follow and enlist Edmund's aid, or must she act alone?

It was useless to appeal to James. He was too slow and ponderous to be any help, even if he could be induced to leave Julia. From the look in his eyes as she left, he had been about to chance all on an immediate declaration. Neither he nor Julia would forgive an interruption. She would risk their anger if it served any useful purpose, but she could not believe it would.

Grimly, Anne recognised that time was running away fast. Weston would lose none in leaving the area and she doubted whether he would burden himself with either of his encumbrances for long in his flight. If she wasted precious minutes seeking Edmund they might be too late.

Reluctantly she accepted that there was no real choice. She might not be able to tackle Weston unaided, but she could watch to see which way he went, if nothing else, and tell Edmund when he caught up. She ordered the groom to saddle the least weary of the horses for her and the mare himself. As he worked she gave him detailed instructions.

'Go alone, miss?' He stared in horror at her. 'I can't let you do that. His lordship would never forgive me. Anyway, you can't ride like that—you'll ruin your dress.'

'What does that matter?' she snapped. 'There is no time to change into riding clothes. I must find Master Kit before any harm comes to him. No more arguments, they only waste time. Take the mare—she is at least fresh—and deliver my message to Lord Ashorne. Hurry now!'

As he spurred away to find Edmund she set off alone, with sinking heart, towards the cottage.

CHAPTER
TEN

HURRY! *Hurry! Hurry!* The rhythm of her horse's hooves drummed the words into Anne's head as she thundered along the lanes, too anxious to have any fear for herself. All her energy was concentrated in urging the tired horse to go on.

A picture of Kit—small, bewildered and frightened—filled her mind unbearably. What trick had Weston used to persuade the child to go with him, she wondered. Kit would not have accompanied him willingly. He had always disliked and mistrusted the steward as instinctively as had Bess. Should she have brought the dog or would she have proved more hindrance than help? Anyway, to have fetched her from her kennel would have wasted time Anne could not afford. She had to hurry. Pray heaven no harm had come to Kit yet!

At this time of day the roads were deserted. There was no one likely to be about to whom she could appeal for help, except perhaps at the toll-gate. That was constantly manned but riding on there would lose valuable minutes and there was no certainty that the elderly gate-keeper would believe her tale or agree to leave his post.

She had to make her way to the cottage alone and trust that Edmund would not be too long. The groom must soon overtake him with her message, then Edmund would lose no time in coming to her aid. Still, however long help took to arrive, she must not falter in her resolve. Kit might need her now. If only she was not already too late!

At long last the track she sought opened out beside her. Hand trembling on the reins, she turned her foam-flecked horse down it, reluctantly checking his headlong pace. The ground here was too uneven to risk a full gallop. Even at a canter the branches snatched at her clothing as if to drag her forcibly back. She tried to calm her racing heart, clear her brain, force herself to think coolly and constructively.

What could she hope to achieve alone against a ruthless opponent? Little enough! She had no weapon and no skill to use one if she could procure it. No, she must rely on her wits. All she could try was to delay Weston until Edmund arrived. How long that might be she had no power of knowing, but until then all depended on her.

She could just make out the chimneys of the cottage now, rising among the trees in front of her. A faint wisp of smoke drifting from one showed that the place had been used recently. Cautiously now! She reined the horse to a halt. The first essential was to discover whether Weston was still inside, and that was best done on foot. There was no point in rushing into danger. That would only mean delivering herself into the steward's hands as another hostage.

The flimsy muslin of her gown tore as Anne slid off her mount, but she paid no heed. There were more important things to worry about than her appearance. Leading him well off the track she tethered the bay out of sight among the trees. Immediately he lowered his head to crop at the grass. No one was likely to spot him here. Then, knees weak with nervousness, she moved closer to the cottage.

It was impossible to see anything through the overgrown hedge that encircled it. Cautiously she eased open the gate and froze as its rusty hinges creaked loudly. No reaction from the cottage. She slipped into the garden, where huge unpruned shrubs shielded her from any watcher. Crouching in their cover, she crept along the weed-encrusted path till she reached the front of the cottage. Then, with infinite caution, she risked a look through the grimy windows. The room beyond the dusty panes was bare and deserted. No sign that anyone had entered it for years.

A stab of doubt pierced her. Was it all a mistake? Had Weston gone elsewhere? Was she leading Edmund here on a wild-goose chase away from the proper trail? But someone had lit the fire whose smoke she could still smell eddying down from above. They must be in the back rooms.

Noiselessly she edged around to the rear of the cottage. There, close to the door, stood two horses—Kit's pony and

Weston's showy chestnut, already loaded for a journey. Anne breathed a sigh—half fear, half relief. So Weston was here and ready to depart. What now?

She could stay where she was and watch, but if he did make his move she had no way of preventing him. He might be miles away before Edmund arrived, and what might he not do to Kit in the interval?

If only she could remove both mounts that would slow Weston sufficiently to allow Edmund to catch up. But could she do it without being detected? To fail would be fatal; would drive him away more rapidly. If only she knew how long it would be before he made his move she could wait here in safety, but that was too risky. Edmund might be ages yet and Weston could leave at any time. She would have to risk capture to be sure of detaining him here.

Keeping a wary eye on the cottage, she inched closer to the horses. Calmly now, or her panic would infect them! Animals were quick to sense nervousness. Her heart thudded unbearably but she managed to still her trembling limbs, murmuring soothingly to the horses as she approached. Kit's pony, recognising her, took little notice, but the stallion fidgeted apprehensively as she came up to him.

Scarcely daring to breathe, she unfastened first the pony them the stallion. So far, so good! Too risky to try to mount here. She doubted whether she could seat herself astride either of them easily in this wretched muslin gown. Then even if she managed it, there was the narrow gateway to be negotiated. It would be safer to lead them until she reached open ground.

Whispering reassurance, she coaxed them across the untidy garden. Kit's pony followed peacefully but the stallion jibbed at the strange hand on his bridle; he strained away, neighing in shrill protest. She struggled to calm him but he tugged backwards, rattling his hooves against the gate with a resounding clatter.

There was a startled shout from inside the cottage. Desperately Anne pulled at the chestnut's head but his strength was greater than hers and she could not budge him.

'Who's there?' Weston appeared swiftly in the doorway.

Anne knew it was hopeless to try to mount the prancing stallion now. The pony had caught some of his panic and refused to stay still enough for her to clamber up one-handed. To loose the more powerful mount now would defeat her purpose.

There was only one chance. Abandoning all hope of escape for herself, Anne slapped both animals hard on their rump to drive them off. At least that way she could spoil Weston's intention to leave on horseback. Both hurtled away, squealing in fright. She chased behind, urging them on with whoops and yells, praying that they would not catch their hooves in the trailing reins. Behind her Weston pounded, cursing in fury.

Anne's breath came in great gasps now. She knew she could not go much further. He hesitated for a second as he caught up with her, uncertain whether to pursue the fleeing horses or make sure of her. With a last despairing spurt Anne darted sideways, but it was no use. He easily outran her.

Twisting her arm savagely behind her he marched her into the cottage.

'Anne!' Hope flared briefly in Kit's wan face as he saw her, but faded as Weston flung her on to a chair.

'Sit there, you interfering jade!'

Swallowing the tears of pain that threatened to engulf her, Anne stared around the room. Kit was bound to a chair beside the hearth, Rosy sprawled on a rumpled bed, her hands tied to the bedpost.

'Make him let us go, Anne!' Kit's trembling plea wrung her heart.

'There now, sweetheart,' Rosy's throaty reassurance filled the pause as Anne sought for words of comfort. 'Don't fret. You'll be right as a trivet in a bit. 'Tis only a silly game the naughty man's playing with us.'

'I don't like it!' There was a sob in his voice now. 'Take me home, Anne.'

'Quiet, brat!' Weston ordered, 'or I'll give you something to cry for.'

Kit sniffed, choking back his tears, and Anne moved instinctively to comfort him. With an oath Weston hauled her back, wrenched her arms behind the chair and tied them to the bars. When she kicked out in retaliation , her legs were fastened with equal savagery to the rungs.

'Now!' Her captor loomed menacingly over her. 'Perhaps you'll explain how you came to discover us here.'

'Don't tell him anything, Anne!' Kit urged fiercely. She managed a reassuring smile and remained silent.

'Sullen, eh?' Weston sneered unpleasantly. 'I haven't time to be patient. Does this help your memory?' Her slapped her hard across her face, and she felt a trickle of blood run down her cheek where his ring caught her. Grimly she set her teeth, refusing to answer.

'No, of course, those tactics cut no ice with you, do they? You're shaped in the heroic mould.' He stared down at her with a mirthless smile that did not reach his cold blue eyes. 'It might be good sport to discover how much pain you could stand before you cracked, but I haven't the time. Luckily there's a simpler way.' With great deliberation he moved across the room to stand over Kit, his knife at the boy's throat. 'The truth now, or I slit his windpipe!'

'No!' The protest was wrung from her. He smiled mockingly, and she knew that this was the true Weston she was seeing now—the ruthless bully she had sometimes glimpsed under the façade of humility. He was thoroughly enjoying her terror.

'Do you suppose that I would hesitate to kill him? Try me.'

She believed him. Now that he need no longer dissemble, malice rang through every word. She must not let him guess how frightened she was. 'I thought you needed him as a hostage.' She forced unconcern into her voice.

'Not any longer. You will do equally well for that purpose. Better, perhaps!' She shuddered as his eyes lingered considering over her figure. He laughed callously, then prompted her, 'Hurry now. I've little time to waste. How did you get here?'

'I came on my own,' she admitted reluctantly as she saw the knife press into Kit's neck.

'Obviously, or we'd have seen your companion by now. But how did you know where to find me?'

'Don't tell him!' Kit exclaimed, then broke off with a gasp as the knife pressed closer.

'Quiet!' Weston's eyes blazed with fury. Anne dared to prevaricate no longer.

'I—I was out riding. I saw the cottage and recognised Kit's pony.'

'Do you generally go riding in that garb?' Stony blue eyes surveyed her grimly. 'Think again!' As she glanced down at the tattered muslin, he continued with icy menace, 'And make it the truth this time or . . .' He did not need to specify the alternative. She saw red stain the knife-tip as it pricked Kit's flesh.

'Julia told me I might find you here,' grimly she fought down her nausea, 'so I came straight over.'

'That sounds more like the truth.'

'Julia? How would she know about this place?' demanded Rosy. 'Is that prissy madam another of your conquests, then? Another poor fool you've inveigled here to share your favours?'

Weston ignored her taunts, concentrating his attention on Anne. 'But why should Julia tell you now? She's always been too concerned for her precious reputation to blab. Are you hiding something?'

Anne trembled under his searching gaze, but determined not to let him guess her panic. Putting up her chin, she stared him out.

'Because of Kit, of course! You made a big mistake in abducting him after she had so generously warned you. Yes, she told me all about that too! Perhaps that was self-interest as much as thought for you, but that is all over now. She thinks more of her son than of her good name.' As she saw him hesitate, not quite convinced, she hurried on, 'I'll admit that even so it wasn't easy to get the full details out of her, but once she'd betrayed her part in warning you I guessed she'd know where you might have Rosy hidden, and forced her to tell me.'

'I don't suppose that was too difficult for you. The silly bitch has always been as weak as water. I don't know why I ever bothered with her.'

'For her money?' suggested Anne contemptuously, then

wished she had resisted the temptation as his grip on the child tightened and Kit cried out in pain. Weston smiled in cruel satisfaction.

'You were forgetting, weren't you? Watch your tongue, or the brat will suffer. Now the truth! Why did you come alone?'

'I told you. I came on impulse.'

'Why? What did you imagine you could do?'

'Nothing. I don't know! I didn't think of anything but Kit and helping him.'

'Who else knows you are here?'

She watched the hovering knife, her mind numb with dread. It was hard to think of anything but that reddened point. She had no doubt that Weston would carry out his threat if she forced him. Then all her effort would be in vain. Yet he could not know what was truth and what not. As long as she made her story credible he must accept it, and every moment she delayed him brought Edmund nearer.

'Only Julia,' she admitted with feigned reluctance. 'She wouldn't tell me about the cottage until I promised to keep the information from Lord Ashorne. By the time I'd wrung it out of her he had gone off searching for you. He was convinced you'd leave by the London Road—oh!' She broke off with a dismayed gasp as if alarmed at letting this fact slip.

'So I shall be safe in taking the other? Can I trust you, I wonder? There's more sense in your head than in your pretty sister's. I've watched you trying to turn her against me, but luckily she was in too deep by then to listen. You've never liked me, have you? Always looked down your genteel nose at me. I've often longed to get you in this position and teach you a lesson.'

She shivered as his lascivious eyes surveyed her boldly from head to toe. Then to her relief he turned away. 'No time to pay off old scores now, more's the pity. I'd enjoy taming you, my lady, but it isn't worth putting my neck in a noose for a few minutes' satisfaction. I can't waste any more time here. There's my horse to be caught, thanks to your meddling. Unless—you must have ridden here even if you did not wait to change into your habit. Where is your mount?'

'I set him loose and sent him home,' Anne lied without a

qualm. Weston was not likely to find the bay hidden in the trees. 'He'll be halfway home by now.'

'Are you sure?' he asked silkily. The knife moved again. Grimly she fought down her panic. To tell the truth would only add to their danger. Weston could not afford to harm them until his means of escape was sure. If she kept calm and faced him out, he had to believe her.

'Why should I lie to you? He is gone.'

'I suppose I must believe you.' To her relief he lowered the knife, and Kit's taut muscles relaxed. 'Let's hope for your sake and the brat's that my horse has not strayed far.'

'What are you going to do with us when you leave?' Rosy asked, her voice shrill with fear.

'What do you imagine, my dear?' he responded with a chilling laugh.

'Take me with you, Phillip,' she begged reaching out the bound hands towards him. 'I've money in my box. You can have it all, and my jewellery too, if you let me come with you.'

'I fully intend to take it, but without burdening myself with you,' he sneered. 'What use have I for an idle strumpet?'

Bending down, he smashed the lock with a poker. Tossing the gaudy clothes aside, he drew out a wash-leather bag and tipped its contents on to his palms. They glittered faintly in the firelight.

'The miserly old goat can't think much of you if this is all he can manage. A paltry collection, but it'll raise a few shillings. Enough for a bed for the night and a wench to share it with me. I'll think of you when I lie there snug and warm. Now where's the cash? Only six guineas? Not much of a nest-egg, but you'll have no need of it, will you, Rosy dear?'

'You thieving bastard ...' Rosy bit off the curse and whimpered in a poor attempt at her old coquettish manner, 'I thought you enjoyed being with me, Phillip. You seemed satisfied enough with my company this past week.'

'You flatter yourself. Your eagerness bores me. I'm not likely to want for female companionship, but if I felt the lack I'd sooner take that supercilious madam there than you.'

'Her!' Rosy exclaimed shrilly. 'What would you want with her?'

'Now Rosy, my sweet, what a question!' he taunted her. 'Isn't there one of your drunken father's quotations to fit the bill?'

'How about *The devil damn thee black, thou cream-faced loon*?' Rosy spat out.

He laughed at her fury.

'Poor drab! Can't you manage better than that?'

'Let Kit go free and I will come with you,' Anne offered desperately.

'I believe you mean it!' He smiled unpleasantly. 'Perhaps there is more of your sister in you than I guessed. What a pity I did not discover it sooner! It might have been fun to set one against the other. But no, willingness spoils the prospect. I think I'll forgo the pleasure tempting though your offer is. The child may be a safer bargaining object after all, and less likely to cause me problems. I don't trust you.'

'But Phillip,' Rosy wailed, 'you can't mean to abandon me here.'

He rounded viciously on her.

'Shut your mouth or I'll close it for good.' As she subsided into noisy sobs he turned back to Anne. 'Now to find my horse. Woe betide you and the brat if it has gone too far. I'll take every setback out of him!'

He strode out. Immediately he was gone Anne began to struggle against her bonds, but it was hopeless. They had been tied too efficiently to give. Movement only cut them more painfully into her cramped limbs.

'I'm frightened, Anne,' Kit quavered. 'What is he going to do with us?'

'Nothing, love!' She tried to put more confidence into her voice than she felt. Edmund must be here soon! She longed to tell Kit that rescue was on the way, but hesitated to mention it in front of Rosy. The girl might try to buy her own freedom by betraying them. She must avoid that at all costs. Edmund's best weapon would be surprise.

'Be brave, Kit,' she urged. 'You may have to go with Weston for a little while, but he won't do anything to hurt you if you do as he bids.' She prayed that she was right. The alternative was too dreadful to contemplate.

'I don't want to leave you ...'

'It won't be for long,' she lied with feigned cheerfulness. 'Don't let him see you are afraid of him. That's the best way with bullies.' Her heart ached for him but she was powerless to help. Too much sympathy might make him break, and Weston would not want to be burdened with a hysterical child. That would tempt him to dispose of Kit sooner.

All too quickly Weston returned, and an air of smug triumph showed that his quest had been successful.

'A clever try, my fine lady,' he gloated, 'but not good enough. I found the stupid brute not a hundred yards from the gate. He knows where his best interests lie, if you don't.' Slicing through Kit's bonds he dragged the boy roughly to his feet. 'Come along now, brat. No fuss, or it'll be the worse for you.'

Kit rubbed his cramped limbs and cast a look of piteous entreaty at Anne. She tried to smile encouragement.

'Phillip!' Rosy shrieked, straining towards him. 'Don't leave us here like this. We could die before anyone found us. Untie us!'

'And have you run off for help before my back is turned?'

'I vow I wouldn't, and I'd make sure she didn't either. Untie my hands at least. Please!' Rosy was sobbing uncontrollably now. 'You know you can trust me!'

'I'm not such a fool as that. Stay here and rot for all I care! I have the money. That's all I am interested in.'

He pushed her contemptuously back, and with a scream of fury she lashed out with her feet. He evaded the wild movement easily but unable to stop her feet kicked over the bedside table. It crashed down throwing the heavy brass candlestick on it on to the floor. Weston watched it roll to rest, a calculating gleam in his eyes.

'That was very rash of you, my dear. That fit of temper could have been dangerous for us all if the candle had been lit. How careless the members of your family are, to be sure! Only a few days since your father burned a whole barn down with one candle, and here you are carelessly knocking another flying. What a tragic accident! Two young women burned to death.' He bent to pick a taper from the hearth.

'No!' screamed Rosy, struggling frantically as she realised what he intended.

'That's right. Thrash around a bit. Make it look more natural.'

'Convenient accidents are your stock in trade, aren't they?' Anne said bitingly, determined not to let him see her fear.

'Well, they make so much less trouble all round. Effective results, yet no difficult consequences. For example, who has ever suspected that your brother-in-law's death was anything but an accident?'

'You killed Thomas?' gasped Anne. 'But how?'

'By a minor adjustment to his carriage. One simple little sawcut in a vital place was enough to get rid of him and that little tramp with him without anyone guessing—except perhaps that flighty sister of yours—and her suspicions only gave me a stronger hold on her. She dared not cross me if she wanted to. Then, but for your damned interference, everyone would have thought that other idiot shot by a chance-met intruder. Only you had to rush up to save him. I was tempted to let you die with him, but the dog was too close for comfort.'

'Bess never liked you.'

'I can't help her bad taste.'

'And you did poison the wine in the library?' Anything to keep him talking. Every minute gave Edmund more time.

'Naturally, but I didn't allow for that drunken oaf's meddling. I hope the old fool dies,' he spat viciously.

'But surely that was dangerous. I had seen you coming out of the library.'

'That wouldn't have mattered if all had gone to plan. No one would have known the poison had been in the port. If I hadn't been able to remove the decanter myself then Julia would have done it for me.'

'You're lying,' Anne said uncertainly.

'Are you sure? She'd do anything except give the actual dose. You know she would have been too relieved to see the end of the usurper to suffer any qualms of conscience.'

Uncomfortably, Anne had to admit it. 'Then you meant to marry her, and after a while there would have been another unfortunate accident?'

'You are too shrewd, my dear. But we are wasting time. Is that deliberate, I wonder, or are you so reluctant to see me go?'

Anne watched in fearful fascination as he stooped to light the taper from the fire. Was he going to kill them first or let them slowly burn to death? That he was willing to admit to murder proved that he had no intention of letting any of them live. Numbly she watched him light the wick on the fallen candle. It burned steadily, licking at the threadbare blankets.

Rosy screamed and struggled more violently, but to no effect. Her arms stayed firmly bound to the bed. Pride forced Anne to remain silent, but she could not prevent her limbs quivering with fear. Weston stood for a moment savouring their terror. Then as the blankets began to smoulder he turned and dragged the squirming, protesting Kit away. A few seconds later they heard the clatter of horses' hooves fade into the distance.

'Can you get free, Rosy?' Anne called sharply, struggling vainly against her own bonds.

'No! Do something!' Rosy shrieked, coughing in the suffocating cloud of smoke that rose from the damp blankets. 'I can't breathe.'

'Get as low as you can. The air is clearer there.'

'It's no good,' Rosy wailed. 'Why didn't you bring that fancy lordship of yours instead of trying to be so clever on your own?'

'I've sent word to him. He'll be here soon.'

'He'll be too late to save me,' Rosy gasped. 'I can't hold out much longer. Oh, why wasn't I satisfied with my gentleman friend! Pa was right. He told me I'd regret playing fast and loose with him. What if Gussy *is* old and bald! I could get him some china teeth. If we ever get out of here I'll go straight to Bath to beg his forgiveness. But we won't get out! I know it!'

'Don't give up hope. There must be something we can do!'

Anne rocked her chair, trying to bring herself up to the burning mass that now threatened to engulf the bed. If she could only reach the blankets she might be able to roll on them and smother the flames. They were so old and musty that they were burning with more smoke than flame—not that that was not equally lethal. Anything was worth a try, was better than letting the smoke overcome her without a struggle, sitting here helplessly waiting to die!

The chair moved a little. She tried again but her efforts only succeeded in overturning it. She crashed down, unable to break her fall. The air was fresher on the floor, and she gulped in a few clear breaths, but soon even here the smoke drifted, slowly filling her lungs. Rosy's sobs cut off as the smoke overcame her.

Ironic, Anne thought light-headedly, that they had escaped from the barn only to be burned to death here instead. Her lungs felt as if they would burst from the effort to breathe. If only Edmund would hurry! What was holding him up? Soon it would be too late for her, but he might be in time to rescue Kit. The boy had seen and heard too much for Weston to risk setting him free if he had any choice in the matter.

'Edmund!' she muttered hoarsely as she drifted into unconsciousness. 'Hurry!'

CHAPTER
ELEVEN

'ALONE!' Edmund exclaimed so harshly that the groom
flinched away, fearing his master would strike him. 'Are you
mad? How could you let a young girl ride after that murder-
ous villain on her own?'

The man had a fleeting regret that he had managed to
intercept his master. He had expected to be blamed, but not
so violently as this. It had taken him far longer than Anne
supposed to catch up with the search-party. Edmund's
urgency infecting them all, spurring them on, they had
moved swiftly through the countryside.

The groom had needed to push his mare to her limits,
uncomfortably aware that their mounts were far better than
his. The mare had been left because her wind was suspect
and her pace far slower than the rest. With their head start
he had begun to doubt whether he could ever overhaul
them.

Anne had told him the general direction the searchers had
intended taking, but a few miles north of the village they had
moved off the main road, after a chance-met farm worker had
reported seeing a man and child whose description matched
that of their quarry. So he had had to waste more time tracing
their route. The mare had begun to flag badly and he was
rapidly giving up all hope of catching them up and delivering
his message when, to his relief, he saw them riding dis-
piritedly back towards him, having discovered that they had
been following the wrong couple for miles.

He had urged his weary mare forward to meet them and,
somewhat apprehensively, delivered Anne's message.
Edmund listened grim-faced until the groom's explanation
trailed off into silence, then lashed out with sharp condemna-
tion.

'She would not listen to me, my Lord,' the man tried

to justify himself. 'I tried to stop her, but she wouldn't listen.'

'You should have forced her to listen! God help you if anything has happened to her, I'll ...' Edmund broke off knowing it was unfair to vent his anxiety and frustration on the servant. A man who had been trained all his life to obey without question was no match for Anne's determination. He had to admire her courage, foolhardy though her conduct was. Anne was no weak, shrinking female! 'We are wasting time in argument,' he went on more mildly. 'You did what you thought best, I suppose. What is most important now is to hurry to Miss Wetherly's aid before any harm comes to her—or Master Kit. You'll have to follow as quickly as you are able. I can see that animal is too blown to keep up, and we cannot afford to delay for you.'

Thankfully the groom dropped behind as the party reformed and set off with renewed enthusiasm for the cottage. They were all fond of Kit, and liked and respected Anne. No one relished the idea of either being at the mercy of Weston, whose vindictiveness most had cause to remember.

Edmund, in the lead, tried to forget all the perils that could have overtaken Anne. Such speculation served no useful purpose. He forced himself to concentrate only on riding, to channel all his wrath into action. He was furious that so much energy had already been expended on this wild-goose chase. It was exasperating that Anne's clear-headedness had found out the steward's destination when he had failed to discover it.

Convinced that Weston would make straight for London to lose himself in its crowded streets, he had wasted little time in inquiries before he sped away. How had Anne learned that Weston was at the cottage instead? The groom had hinted that the information came from Julia, though why, in that case, the stupid female had not disclosed the fact sooner he could not imagine. Still, he admitted resignedly, Julia's thought processes had always been a mystery to him.

How could he ever have imagined himself in love with her? True she was beautiful—though the peevish frown she wore so often now marred her looks—but what was beauty without the character to support it? Anne's courage and dependability were worth all her sister's beauty to him. Not that Anne was ugly! Far from it! The lively sparkle of her smile was far more to his taste than Julia's empty perfection.

Pray heaven he would see that smile again! How had he ever been so blind as to prefer Julia? Even at fifteen Anne's qualities had been clear to see, but in his infatuation he had discounted their value. Julia's beautiful face had filled his brain to the exclusion of all else.

He had come home from France prepared to dote on Julia as before. Though the news of her marriage had been a shock, he had been willing to forgive that. But gradually his love had faded. Now Julia filled him only with irritation at her artificial manner and selfish disregard of any interest but her own.

Why had he not recognised those faults before? Julia could not have changed so radically while he was away. In his prison cell he had brooded over her portrait, over the sweet smile he now looked for in vain in the original, and in his daydreams had endowed her with all the qualities she had never possessed—loyalty, courage, unselfishness. It was a shock to find them absent when he returned—only to recognise them in her sister instead. Too late, he feared! If that fiend had harmed Anne he would track him down and kill him, however long it took.

Why had he wasted so much time? Since that disastrous mistake when he first arrived home, Anne had treated him with cool reserve, keeping him carefully at a distance. Although at times he had dared to hope that her affection for him was unchanged, he had shrunk from betraying that his own feelings had altered so completely.

Even when anxiety over Anne's danger on the night of the fire had convinced him where his love lay, he had hesitated, fearing that she would be suspicious of his sudden change of heart; concerned, too, that her engagement to James would make her refuse to listen. Undeserving though James was, she remained fiercely loyal to him. So Edmund had forced himself to go slowly, feel his way. Now he was dreadfully afraid that Anne might be lost to them both.

He was riding automatically, urging his men on, while the

appalling doubts raced around his head. What was happening to Anne? Weston was too deep in trouble to have any qualms about killing anyone who hindered his escape. If only he had taken more care to find out the steward's destination before he left Ashorne! But it was useless to torment himself with might-have-beens. He must concentrate on following Anne to ensure her safety—or to revenge her if the worst had happened.

He spurred his horse on, mercilessly. Jonas pressed close at his heels, the rest strung out behind. Their journey seemed endless but eventually they reached the track leading to the cottage. Edmund halted briefly to let the stragglers catch up. They would be more effective as a unit.

About to give them the signal to move on, he motioned them to silence as the muffled drum of hooves sounded from along the leafy track. Weston? Who else on this little-used path?

Swiftly he sized up their position. The ground dropped sharply from the road and the trees grew thick on either side. If this was indeed their quarry approaching, then here was the ideal spot to ambush him. Any rider must slow to negotiate the steep slope and corner, and the undergrowth was dense enough to screen them from his view until the last moment.

Quickly Edmund stationed his men in the shelter of the gorse bushes on either side of the track, whispering a few essential commands. This was like going into battle once more, but with the outcome more vital. War was less personal, always holding the possibility that a fresh day could bring a swing of fortune. Here there would be no second chance. If they failed then everything was lost. Weston would not give them another opportunity.

Edmund cast an anxious look round to see if he had missed any detail that might betray their presence. The tracks! The dusty path was criss-crossed with hoofprints. Following his glance, Jonas swung down and with a leafy branch swept the ground, obliterating all trace of their passage. The old soldier had served in the American wars too, and learned some useful tricks from the savages.

Tense and silent, they waited until the single horse came

into sight, moving swiftly despite its double burden. With relief Edmund recognised Kit, seated, pale but unharmed, in front of the steward. At least the boy was still alive! What of Anne?

But he must not think of her now. This was no time for emotion; that only clouded the issue. He must keep his head clear and concentrate on the immediate task of capturing Weston and freeing Kit. Carefully now! Unless they moved skilfully the child might suffer.

As Weston slowed to negotiate the rise into the turnpike road, Edmund rode out to block his path. Weston cursed, wrenching at the stallion's mouth to turn him back, only to find that way barred too, as Jonas and another groom closed in behind him. His eyes darted fearfully all round; estimating his chance of escape.

Then, swiftly, he recovered his poise. The momentary panic vanished and light shone on bright steel as he drew his knife. Pale with hatred he glared at Edmund.

'Out of my way or the child will die!'

The knife held steady over Kit's heart showed the threat was no idle one. Edmund's hopes plummeted, but he remained where he was, blocking the path.

'I mean it,' Weston snarled. 'What have I to lose if I kill him?'

'Your liberty,' Edmund told him calmly. 'Kill him and we have you. Give me the boy and you may go free.'

Sensing his reluctance, Weston laughed mirthlessly. 'Even if I did trust you, how far do you think I should get without my safe-conduct? No deal! The brat goes with me. Let me pass and I'll loose him when I reach town—but no tricks, mind!'

'How can we tell that *we* can trust *you*?'

'You can't, but I vow I'll kill him if you don't move away this minute!'

With heavy heart, Edmund saw that he meant it. He did not trust the steward's promise, but there was little choice. A certain death for Kit had to be weighed against a probable one if they let Weston go free. A slim chance, but one they could not ignore.

'Very well!' he said grudgingly. 'But keep your part of the

bargain, or I'll hunt you down if it takes a lifetime!' Slowly he began to move aside. Weston smiled in triumph—prematurely.

'I won't go with him!' Kit panted, struggling desperately in the cruel grip. 'You can't make me!'

With a shriek of fury he kicked the stallion's flank. As it reared up, he flung himself sideways, away from the knife. Taken by surprise, Weston lost his grip on both and clung to the reins in a frantic effort to retain his seat. The knife clattered down on to the ground. As Kit tumbled down beneath the horse's feet, Jonas seized the animal's bridle, forcing the terrified beast down clear of the boy. It stood quivering with nervousness.

Edmund levelled a pistol at the steward and motioned him to dismount. Sullenly he obeyed. 'Now, where is Miss Wetherly?' Edmund demanded.

'That damned jade! Curse her! I've had nothing but ill luck since I met her. I might have known the bitch was lying to me!'

'What have you done with her?' Weston spat, but refused to answer. 'Answer me, damn you!' Edmund thrust the barrel into his chest.

But Weston was confident that he would not shoot an unarmed man. 'Find her!' he sneered. 'Pretty piece, isn't she? Worth two of that drab of a sister. I wish I'd had more time to enjoy her company.'

'What the devil have you done with her?'

Weston flinched back from the naked fury in Edmund's face, but whether from terror or spite he stayed silent.

'Tell me, or I'll choke it from you!'

From the ground where he lay gasping, all the breath knocked out of him by his fall, Kit wheezed, 'The cottage!' pointing down the track.

Turning, Edmund froze in horror. A cloud of black smoke was billowing up above the trees.

'It's on fire! You devil, Weston! God help you if she is harmed.'

Tossing his pistol to one of the grooms with a terse 'Shoot him if he moves an inch!', Edmund spurred forward, wheeling at perilous speed along the winding track. The gate loomed before him. His horse checked but he gathered it up firmly, forcing it to leap. The rear hooves rapped the bar, but they were over.

Edmund pulled the horse to a standstill by the door and tumbled off. The door would not budge. He put his shoulder to it and heaved. With a grinding crash the lock gave. A dense cloud of smoke surged out. One hand across his face to shield his smarting eyes, Edmund plunged through the gloom to the back room.

'Anne!' he called urgently. 'Where are you? Anne!' He must not fail now. Fear, far greater than any he had felt in battle, spread an icy chill within him.

The smoke was even thicker here, and he could barely see his way. He despaired of finding her alive in the choking blackness, yet a last glimmer of desperation drove him on.

A faint moan made his pulses race with expectation. The eagerness drained away as he discovered that the sound came from Rosy, sprawled unconscious on the bed. Yet that must be a hopeful sign. If Rosy was still alive, perhaps Anne had survived. But where?

Jonas had followed him in. Edmund indicated the limp form, then felt his way across the smoke-filled floor seeking Anne. She must be here! Fate could not be so cruel as to defeat him now.

At last he stumbled upon her, slumped on the floor bound to her overturned chair. Was he in time? With trembling fingers he fumbled at her bodice, feeling for her heart. At first the pounding of his own pulse drowned everything, then relief flooded through him as a shallow flutter of her breast showed she was still alive. Thankfully he drew her limp body closer, burying his face in her fragrant hair, suddenly aware of how weary he was. He had driven himself on desperately, but he dare not relax yet. Anne's hold on life was very weak.

If he did not get her out of this suffocating smoke very soon she might not revive. Already Edmund could feel it tearing at his own lungs, its acrid fumes making his eyes stream. Frantically he hacked through the ropes that bound her then carried her into the garden, thankfully gulping in the fresh air to clear his lungs.

Resourceful as ever, Jonas had managed to find some

water. Wrenching off his neckcloth, Edmund dipped it in the
cool liquid and tenderly bathed Anne's well-loved features.
In an agony of suspense he cradled her in his arms, watching
the colour creep back, so very slowly.

Even now he hardly dared hope he had been in time. He
ignored everything around them to concentrate all his ener-
gies upon her, as if the very intensity of his determination
must bring her back to consciousness. After what seemed an
eternity, her eyes flickered open, focused wonderingly on his
anxious features, then widened in delighted recognition.

'Edmund!' she murmured, her eyes fixed upon him in such
glowing trust that his whole body pulsed in gratified
response.

'Thank God!' The fervent words were husky with emotion.
'I was so afraid I would be too late, my love.' Too moved to
go on, he clasped her tightly to his chest as if he would never
let her go.

'I knew you would come,' Anne whispered, her arms
closing trustfully around him.

Edmund groaned, remembering how nearly he had failed
her. A few more minutes and rescue would have been impossible. Bending his head down, he pressed his lips passionately
into the hollow of her throat, vibrantly aware of the tiny pulse
that fluttered there.

'Oh Anne! Anne!' he murmured thickly. 'Don't ever be so
foolhardy again, my love. I thought all that I cared for in the
world was gone for ever. I wanted to die myself when I saw
the dreadful fire and knew you were in it.'

'You got the name right that time,' Anne whispered wonderingly. Her brain felt hazy still. Was this really happening?
It seemed like a dream to have Edmund gazing so lovingly
down upon her, his eyes filled with such tender concern. A
dream she had no wish to awaken from.

She twined her arms around his neck drawing his head
closer. As his eager warm lips took possession of hers she
knew it was real—no dream had ever moved her like this.
With a low, inarticulate moan of pleasure she strained closer,
twining her fingers through the springy curls at his neck, a
tingling response searing through her whole body. Every
sense clamoured surrender. Blissfully she abandoned herself

to the rapture thrilling through her, everything forgotten but the instinctive need to respond to the urgency of his kiss.

Almost everything ... The memory of a wan frightened face swam reluctantly into Anne's consciousness. Kit! How could she have forgotten!'

Anxiously she strained to free herself. Edmund, not understanding, gathered her closer, murmuring in husky protest. As desire threatened to overwhelm her she struggled more desperately, knowing she must fight the so-seductive temptation.

'*Kit!*' she gasped. 'Weston has taken Kit with him. You must go after them before it is too late. Weston will kill him if...'

'Hush, my darling,' his arms formed a loving prison holding her still. 'Don't fret over that young imp. We have him safe already.'

'And Rosy? She was tied to the bed when he set it alight!' Shuddering, Anne hid her face in Edmund's broad chest to blot out the awful memory. 'He meant to burn us alive.'

'Don't think about it, love!' She felt the shiver of remembered terror run through Edmund too as he cradled her close. Anne clung to him, grateful for the comfort his nearness gave her. The warmth of his body drove the chill of fear from hers, the strong beat of his heart gave her new courage.

'Rosy is safe too,' he went on consolingly. 'Jonas carried her out. She is burned and badly shaken, but recovering fast.' A ripple of amusement ran through him as he remembered the scene he had barely registered earlier in his anxiety over Anne.' Perhaps it is as well you were unconscious and didn't hear the names she called Weston. She set about him like a wild cat. Jonas pulled her off him, but not before she'd drawn blood. Now be still, my love, and think of yourself for once.'

He settled her more comfortably in his arms before demanding, 'Whatever made you rush here in such an impetuous manner? You might have died. Damned near did!'

Feeling the shudder that ran through him at the thought, Anne clasped his muscular body tightly, anxious to return a little of the comfort his nearness afforded her. The fervour of his response was enormously gratifying.

'I had to get to Kit,' she explained when she had the breath to do so. 'There wasn't time to wait for you. I didn't mean Weston to catch me, but I was forced to risk it to slow him enough for you to get here.'

'Don't ever be so rash again, my love!' His arms tightened in a possessive grasp that Anne found immensely satisfying. 'I could not bear to lose you!' Edmund loosened his hold a little, and looking remorsefully down at her admitted reluctantly, 'I promised myself that if only I found you safe I would willingly surrender you to that idiot, Shrivenham, if he was the one you truly wanted. But I find I am very loath to do so!'

'You feared I wanted to marry James still?'

'Yes, damn him! You are not serious about meaning to have him, are you, Anne?' His eyes rested beseechingly on her, dark with a passion that made her catch her breath in wonder. She had never dared hope his need for her was so violent.

'I—I am afraid I have lost my chance now if I do,' Anne's mournful voice was belied by the dancing mischief in her sparkling eyes. The temptation to tease him a little was irresistible.

She could not mistake the glowing intensity with which he gazed so longingly upon her. This was the expression she had first seen when he arrived home and mistook her for her sister. But it was vastly more powerful now, and far more disturbing. Amazingly, Edmund loved her as deeply as she adored him. Her entire being ached with desire for his caress. Suddenly shy of him, she lowered her gaze and hurried on to explain, 'James is no longer interested in me. He was all set to propose to Julia when I saw them last.'

'Poor fool! Still, it is his own fault if he chooses to let her make his life a misery. The fellow must be out of his wits to prefer Julia to you.'

'You did so once!' she pointed out laughingly, delighted at the violence of his scorn.

'But I have realised my error now, although only just in time! It terrifies me to think how nearly I left it too late!'

Impatiently he drew her close, his mouth seeking hers with an urgent pressure which grew more demanding as her lips parted in eager response. Everything faded into insignificance but their passionate need for each other, their seemingly insatiable longing.

'How could I have been so blind!' he groaned at last, shaking his head in self-disgust. 'She has beauty, yes, but nothing more. I let myself be deceived by an empty shell. I suppose I mooned over that wretched portrait so long while I was a prisoner that I imagined Julia perfect to match it. It has taken far too long for me to recognise that the picture and the reality were so different.'

'Do you mean the miniature Julia gave you the Easter you left?' Anne asked in an oddly uneven voice. 'The one in that dreadful gold frame with diamonds all round?'

'Yes—though the frame was lost long ago. Fool that I was, I supposed the picture more valuable.' He smiled ruefully as Anne choked back a gurgle of mirth. 'You may well laugh at my foolishness! I languished after your sister when it was you who really had all the qualities I supposed her to possess, but I was too moonstruck to see the truth.'

'I was not laughing at you, my love!' Contritely Anne leant forward to brush her lips lightly to his cheek, only to find herself seized to be kissed with ruthless thoroughness once more. When she could speak again she hastened to share the joke. 'Truly I was not mocking you, Edmund, but the whole thing is too absurd. That portrait was really of me—or partly so, at least.'

'Whatever do you mean?' Edmund stared uncomprehendingly.

'Papa commissioned an artist to paint Julia, but she could not bear the sittings—she could never stay still for two minutes at a time. The poor man grew so distracted at her fidgeting that when she threw a tantrum and told him I was sufficiently like her to take her place, he was too relieved to argue. He painted me then tried to alter the features to seem older, more mature, hoping that way to make it resemble Julia. Of course it didn't answer. For a start she is far more beautiful than I am . . .'

'Never!' Edmund interrupted firmly. Lovingly he traced

each feature with gentle fingers, and the featherlight touch set Anne a-quiver. Suddenly breathless, she laughed up at him with the teasing smile that was all her own. She knew he exaggerated, but it made very satisfying hearing.

'Flatterer! But you will admit we are different? Whatever the reason, Papa was, not unnaturally, dissatisfied with the result. He refused to buy the portrait. Julia did not dare let him know the truth, so she paid for it secretly and gave it you. I really believe she could not see how unlike her it was.'

'So it was you whom I have been worshipping all these years!' Edmund shook his head wryly. 'I ought to have guessed, but I have been so confused since I returned home that I haven't had the heart to look at that picture. Now you have told me, I can see the smile is yours entirely—quite unlike your sister's self-satisfied smirk. I was too blindly infatuated to be critical of the likeness when she gave it me. Then over the years my memory of her faded—it was the face in the picture I clung to.'

He laughed ruefully. 'No wonder I mistook you for her when I returned. How furious you were when I kissed you that day!'

'Only because you thought I was Julia,' Anne admitted, blushing rosily at the memory. 'At first it seemed as if all my dearest wishes were coming true, then such a rude awakening! I was so ashamed of having betrayed my feelings that I lashed out to protect my pride.'

'There was little danger of my noticing anything amiss. I was too confused myself to think of your reaction till long after. Then I supposed I had been mistaken. You froze me utterly for days!'

'I was terrified that otherwise you would guess how desperately I still loved you. I was too scared to admit that even to myself. I had kissed you back without thinking, and was furious with myself. Not that I should be at all sorry,' she added, glancing provocatively from under long lashes, 'if you were to repeat the error now.'

'No error!' he murmured thickly, jerking her into a crushing embrace. 'But I will repeat it with pleasure till you beg for mercy!'

Edmund's warm lips took possession of hers gently at first,

then more urgently till they floated high on a wave of desire and longing that would surely take the rest of their lives to satisfy. No need for dissembling now. Rapturously Anne felt her senses reel in the joy of responding with all her being to a lovemaking which was meant for her alone. Pressing ever closer to the firm masculine body that moulded to hers, she felt the echo of the need thrilling within her ripple through him.

'That first kiss ought to have shown me the truth,' Edmund declared shakily at last. 'Kissing you was so much more exciting than anything I had ever experienced before, but I was too bewildered to admit it. Gradually I realised it was you I loved, but I feared it was hopeless. When my impulses got the better of me on the night of the fire, you struggled so fiercely to escape!'

'Because I thought you had confused me with Julia yet again,' Anne admitted. This was heady stuff, she thought, affecting her like wine.

'How could you imagine such a thing!' he exclaimed with gratifying amazement. 'I knew my heart well enough then to be sure you were the only woman for me. I did not know your feelings had changed too.'

'Changed? Never! My love for you has only deepened over the years.'

'And I never guessed it. What a fool I have been—I supposed that my ardour had frightened you.'

'No, only my own urge to respond to it did that,' Anne told him truthfully. 'That was why I was so brusque with you.'

'How much time we have wasted,' he groaned. 'I can still scarcely credit all this! You will marry me, Anne? Very soon?'

She nodded, too overcome with happiness for speech. Everything was forgotten but the intensity of their need for each other.

'Anne! Anne!'

A persistent hand tugged at her sleeve, and reluctantly Anne became aware of the shrill voice that sought to break through their absorption in each other. She turned a bemused face upon Kit, who was dancing up and down with impatience.